"But as for you, ye thought evil against me; but God meant it unto good, to bring to pass, as it is this day, to save much people alive."

—GENESIS 50:20 (KJV)

Savannah Secrets

Savannah Secrets

Meant
for Good

DeAnna Julie Dodson

Guideposts

Danbury, Connecticut

Meant
for Good

Chapter One

MEREDITH BELLEFONTAINE HURRIED UP TO the offices of Magnolia Investigations, already sweating in Savannah's July heat. She never knew whether having a Monday holiday was a blessing or a curse. The Fourth had been on Sunday, making yesterday "Independence Day Observed," and she'd enjoyed two days of grilling and fireworks and spending time with friends and family.

Now, though, she was running behind, finding as always that the more she hurried the further behind she fell. She was supposed to meet a new client at nine. It was 8:57. Carmen Lopez, the agency's receptionist, would already be there, of course, but Meredith hated to rush in when a client was waiting.

Her phone rang just as she got to the door. She noticed it was her partner, Julia Foley, so she stopped where she was to answer it.

"Mere!" Julia said breathlessly before Meredith could even say hello. "I'm sorry, but my car overheated and I had to drop it off at the garage. Now I'm driving Beau's. I should be at the office soon. If the client's already there, go ahead without me. You can fill me in when I get there."

"Okay," Meredith said when Julia finally took a breath. "I'll take care of it. You be careful. See you in a little while."

"Thanks for seeing to everything." Julia sighed. "I hate to be late."

"Not a problem. See you soon."

Meredith ended the call and took a deep breath before she opened the door and stepped into the cool hallway. She hated to have to be "on" the minute she stepped into the office. A few minutes to get settled, to get her humidity-frizzled blond hair back into some kind of order, would be nice, but it was 8:59 now. Maybe the client was late.

"Good morning," Carmen said as Meredith peeped into the reception area. Carmen had on a flattering navy skirt and a white blouse, and there was a red headband in her glossy black hair. Her earrings were a spray of red, white, and blue sparkles. "Mrs. Cooper is here."

"Mrs. Cooper," Meredith said, smiling and extending her hand, "I'm sorry to have kept you waiting."

"Oh, no." The woman shifted her purse to her left arm so she could shake hands with Meredith. "You're right on time."

"I'm Meredith Bellefontaine. My office is across the hall. We can talk there."

"Thank you. And, please, call me Lydia."

"All right. Would you like some coffee, Lydia?"

"Thank you, but I've had a cup already this morning. More than that doesn't agree with me. But, please, you go ahead."

Meredith led her across the hall and settled her in the chair in front of her desk. "Give me just a minute. Thanks."

She walked back into the reception area. "Julia called. She's running a little late, but she'll be here soon."

Carmen nodded. "Okay. You don't have any messages yet."

"Good. Thanks."

Meredith got herself some coffee and then went back into her office and shut the door. She didn't know much about this case yet, and over the long weekend, she had forgotten most of what she had read. But thanks to Carmen's awesome efficiency, the file for it was already on her desk. Meredith flipped it open as she sat down.

"I understand you want us to investigate a theft," she said, smiling at Lydia.

Lydia was still clutching her large black purse, looking as if she didn't quite know what to do in a private investigator's office. Probably in her late fifties, she was bright-eyed in her preppy, black-rimmed glasses. There was determination in her firm mouth, a determination that had obviously overcome her shyness.

"Yes. Since it's not a recent theft, it might be a little bit hard for you to find out anything at this point, but I'm hoping you can find out more than I've been able to."

"That's our specialty," Meredith said.

"That's what I was told." Lydia opened her purse and took out a newspaper article. "Your assistant said you and your partner saw this last week. As it says, I was trying to get some information about what happened when my great-grandfather was sent to prison for theft. The online group I was talking to said you might be able to help me."

Meredith took the article from her, skimmed it, and handed it back. "And how did this end up in the newspaper?"

"One of the members of the group writes human interest and local history articles. She's always on the lookout for something she thinks will make a good story." Lydia smiled shyly. "She says she wants to write a follow-up article about it when I find out what really happened."

"I hope we can do that. Do you know when this theft took place? The article isn't very clear."

"I'm not sure of an exact date, but it was in 1918, maybe September or October."

"That was certainly a while back."

Lydia nodded. "Is it too long ago for you to look into?"

"No, of course not. We've done several historical investigations. Please, tell me what you know about this theft."

"I'm sorry to say it's not a whole lot. Dale, he's my husband, says it's way too late to find out anything, but I figured a real private detective agency would have ways to find out things that regular people don't, right?"

Meredith couldn't help smiling at her eagerness. "We've learned a thing or two since we've opened."

"Well, anyway, my mother, Sheila Bryleigh, is in a memory care home."

"Oh, I'm sorry," Meredith murmured.

"It's a nice place, it really is, but it's so awful for her to be losing her memory like that. But here's what made me come to you. A few weeks ago, she started saying that Matt Van Orden wrote her a letter."

"I saw that in the article about you and your mother. But I don't know enough yet about the Van Ordens to know how that figures into anything."

Lydia winced apologetically. "I'd better start at the very beginning. My great-grandfather, Mother's grandfather, was named

James Brandon. He worked for Van Orden Munitions & Manufacturing during World War I and before then."

"And Matt Van Orden was the owner of the company?" Meredith asked, taking notes.

"No, that was his father, Thomas. From what I've found out, the company did a lot of work for the government, mostly in supplying things for the army. My great-grandfather worked for Thomas Van Orden from when he started as an errand boy in 1903 until 1918. He was basically Mr. Van Orden's right-hand man by then. I had always been told by my mother and grandmother that even though he didn't have any official title in the company, he took care of Mr. Van Orden and handled pretty much anything he needed done."

"I see. And 1918 was when he was sent to prison for theft."

"Mr. Van Orden had a very valuable jewel collection. He had inherited several expensive pieces that he gave to his wife at the time of their marriage and afterward, and he bought several more too. And after she died when their son was born, he kept the jewels locked in his safe."

"And he blamed your great-grandfather for the theft."

"Yes. My grandmother, his daughter, was eleven at the time, but I remember her telling me what it was like when the police came and arrested him. Her mother had died the year before, and she had to be taken to a neighbor's house until one of her aunts could come get her."

"Had Mr. Van Orden seen the jewels before that night?" Meredith asked, continuing to write as fast as she was able.

"That's the problem. He said he hadn't looked in the safe for some time before then, so my great-grandfather's being home that particular night didn't mean anything. The jewels could have been taken anytime."

"So why did he think your great-grandfather was guilty? Did he have the combination to the safe?"

Lydia shook her head. "Not according to my grandmother. She told me her father always said that Mr. Van Orden was very secretive about that safe combination. He didn't think anybody could get into the safe but Mr. Van Orden himself, but the prosecutor convinced the jury that since my great-grandfather had access to Mr. Van Orden's private office and knew where the safe was, he could have figured out the combination over time by getting a glimpse of his boss opening the safe over the years and piecing together what he saw."

"That seems like it would be very hard to do."

"I think it would be almost impossible," Lydia said, "but I guess it could be done if someone was patient and observant enough. That wasn't what really hurt him at the trial though."

"What did?" Meredith flipped to a new page in her notepad and kept writing.

"Evidently he was sort of lost after his wife died. Grandma was still a little girl, like I said, and she really wasn't in a position to help him get through it. She said he drank a lot then, and he got himself into trouble with gambling debts. The prosecutor found out about that and brought it out at the trial. Back then, that was about enough to convict a man of nearly anything."

"So he was sent to prison."

Lydia nodded. "He was sentenced to twenty years. He served nineteen, and then he died there."

"I'm sorry."

"He died nearly twenty-five years before I was born, so I really don't know that much about him. Just what my grandmother said about him. My mother was six when he died and never met him, but she still felt the shame of what happened to him. Of what happened to her mother because of him. My grandmother was passed from relative to relative until she was old enough to get work to support herself, but even after she married and had a new name, people would find out that her father was in prison and distance themselves from her."

"That must have been so hard for her," Meredith said, writing as quickly as she could.

"My mother never even met her grandfather, but some parents wouldn't let her play with their children. I don't know if they thought she was going to steal their toys or what."

There was hurt in Lydia's eyes, bitterness in her words, pain for the mother and grandmother she obviously loved.

"Are you sure you wouldn't like some coffee?" Meredith asked her after a moment. Sometimes it helped to take a little break when a client was having a hard time.

Lydia took a deep breath. "No. Really, it's all right. I didn't expect to get all emotional about this. My great-grandfather died a long time ago. My grandmother passed away when I was in my teens, but she lived with us after Grandpa died. I heard all the stories about her father and about how hard it was for her and Mom because of what happened to him. I've always felt bad for Mom because I can tell she still feels like she's somehow less than everybody else. And now—" She blinked hard, obviously fighting tears. "Now she's telling me that Matt Van Orden wrote her a letter."

"Could he have?" Meredith asked. "How old would he be now?"

Lydia sniffled and blinked again. "I looked it up not long ago. He was born in 1898."

"So he'd be over 120."

"Yes. But that doesn't matter anyway, because he died in 1918. When he was in the navy during World War I."

"Your mother wasn't even born by then, right?"

"Right. He couldn't have sent her a letter. I asked Mom's doctor about it, and he said it's possible that she's imagined that he sent her a letter because in her mind she needed to have some closure about everything that happened to her family once her grandfather was sent to prison."

"Does she say when Matt sent her this letter?"

"No," Lydia said with a sigh. "She says she doesn't remember but that she knows he did and that she kept it because it was important."

"But you haven't found anything like that?"

"No. And I have looked. I thought maybe it could have been from someone in the Van Orden family or something, and Mom was only confused about it, but I haven't found anything at all from anybody about the case. Certainly nothing from anyone named Van Orden."

Meredith tapped her pencil on her notepad, thinking. "Could she tell you anything about what was in the letter? What did she say about it?"

"All she's told me is that it says her grandfather was innocent and shouldn't have gone to jail. She also said that the Van Ordens knew all along what was going on."

"What was going on about what?"

"I don't know. If I ask her, she gets confused." Lydia grimaced. "I know that's no help, but I guess that kind of backs up what the doctor said about her wanting some closure about what happened to her and her mother."

"Is your mother aware of what's going on around her?" Meredith asked as gently as she was able. "Does she recognize you?"

"She has her lucid times. They seem to be further and further apart lately. She does still recognize me, but she asked me the other day who the man was that I had with me. I could have cried. Dale and I have been married for nearly thirty years. I told Mom he was my husband, and she was upset because nobody had told her I was married."

Meredith reached across the desk and patted Lydia's hand. It was so hard to deal with this kind of situation. No wonder Lydia wanted to exonerate her great-grandfather while her mother could still be comforted by it.

"Anyway," Lydia said more cheerfully, "it really doesn't matter whether or not there's actually a letter. I want to find out about the theft, if it isn't too late."

Meredith got the pertinent information about Lydia's great-grandfather, including his full name, his date of birth and date of death, the date of his conviction, and which prison he'd been sent to. Then she got more information about the family in general.

"What about the Van Ordens?" she asked finally. "Does the family still run the company?"

Lydia nodded. "There's only one left, as far as I've ever heard. Thomas Van Orden's daughter-in-law, Vanessa."

"Matt's widow?"

"No. I believe she was married to Thomas Van Orden's younger son, but I'm not sure what his name was. David, maybe?"

"I can look it up," Meredith said, thinking as she jotted down the information that the woman must be very old by this time. "I'll see if I can find out more about her too. Now, if you have it, I'd like to get the address where your great-grandfather lived while he worked for the Van Ordens."

"I'll have to look up the addresses," Lydia said. "There were two or three different places they lived during that time, according to my mother and grandmother. I'm sure I have something that would show the addresses. I'll get them to you."

"Thanks."

Meredith took down the other information along with the full names of Lydia's mother and father and her maternal grandparents. She also got Lydia's current address and the name and the address of the insurance office where she worked.

"What else can I tell you?" Lydia asked. "I don't know what kind of information you need."

"This will get us started. My partner and I can find out a lot from this much, and if we have questions, we'll give you a call. Oh, we also have a friend of ours who knows a lot about the history of Savannah. She's been very helpful in past cases. Is it all right if we talk to her about your case?"

"That would be wonderful. You're welcome to share this information with whoever you think can help."

"Great. Is there anything more we ought to know at this point?"

"I can't think of anything, but I'll keep looking for whatever letter Mom might be talking about. There's not all that much in her room. I don't know where it could be."

"It's possible, of course, that there never was a letter. Then again, sometimes people in your mother's condition hide things for safekeeping and then can't remember where those things are hidden. If you don't have any luck, maybe my partner and I could come by and have a look too. That is, if you think it wouldn't upset your mother."

"That would be a big help." Lydia stood up, looking relieved. "Thank you so much. I'll be praying that you'll be able to find something soon. I really want Mom to know for sure about her grandfather. This has weighed on her for so long."

Meredith stood too and opened the office door.

"We'll do our very best," she said as she led the woman out. "If anything comes up, if your mother remembers anything or if you think of something we could check out, let us know."

Lydia thanked her profusely as she went out the front door.

"*Pobrecita*, poor thing." Carmen clicked her tongue sympathetically as she handed Meredith the messages that had come for her since she came in. "She was telling me about her mother while she was waiting."

"I know. I hope we can help her with this, but it's a very old case. Julia and I are going to have our work cut out for us."

Meredith heard the back door open and a moment later Julia came into the foyer, elegantly dressed and with every strand of her silver hair in place despite the heat.

"Sorry I'm running late. I must look a mess."

"Oh, stop," Meredith said with a grin. "How's the car?"

"Mine or Beau's?"

"Either."

"Mine's in the shop. They have no idea what's wrong with it yet. Beau's is always hard for me to get used to, but it's fine. And he's okay with staying home for the day as long as he has Bunny to hang out with."

"That cat," Meredith said. "I don't know if you rescued her or if she took the two of you hostage."

Julia laughed. "I hope you both had a good Fourth."

"Harmony and I went to the beach," Carmen said.

Harmony was the little seven-year-old girl Carmen mentored through the Boys & Girls Club.

"That sounds like fun," Julia said.

"Yeah, she's teaching me to swim."

"She is?" Meredith asked. "But you can already—"

Carmen gave her a knowing grin. "Sometimes it's easier to teach them if you let them think they have to help you."

"That's adorable. So true," Julia said and then looked at Meredith. "Looks like I missed our new client."

"Let's get some coffee," Meredith said, "and I'll tell you about it. Do you know anything about Van Orden Munitions?"

"Not much. I've seen a few things about them in the paper, about contracts with the government and that kind of thing. Why?"

"I was wondering about whoever owns it now."

"That would be Vanessa Van Orden," Julia told her.

"Really?"

Julia nodded. "Does she have something to do with this case?"

"I don't know, but I was wondering how hard it might be to get to talk to her."

"Might not be easy," Julia said as they walked into the hall to the coffee maker.

"I was afraid of that. I was actually surprised to know that she was still alive, but I'd imagine she doesn't get out much anymore."

Julia frowned. "Why would you think that?"

"Maybe our client has her information wrong, but she told me Vanessa is the wife of Thomas Van Orden's younger son. He was running the company and had an older son go into the service in World War I. That was 1918. His daughter-in-law would have to be pushing a hundred at least."

"Well, I've seen her on TV a couple of times," Julia said, following Meredith into her office. "Either she has some great genes, or she found the fountain of youth. Vanessa Van Orden doesn't look a day over forty-five."

Chapter Two

"You're kidding me, right?" Meredith asked. "Forty-five?"

"That's about what she looked like to me," Julia said. "It's hard to say exactly. She's very pretty. Tall and slim, blond hair, big eyes, stylishly dressed. I wouldn't be surprised if she was a Miss-something when she was younger. You know, Miss Southern Empire or Miss All-Star or something local."

"Now I have to find a picture."

Meredith woke up her computer and did a quick internet search. She found a picture of Vanessa Van Orden, Owner and CEO, on the Van Orden Munitions website. Meredith had no way of knowing how old the photograph was, but the woman in it fit Julia's description perfectly. Beautiful, stylish, and in her midforties. She was sitting behind a massive desk with her hands folded in front of her, and she was looking a little to one side. She wasn't smiling, but there was a serene confidence about her that said quite clearly that she knew what she was doing.

"Pictures posed like that always make me think the subject is looking into the future," Julia observed, looking over Meredith's shoulder.

"She hits it just right, don't you think? Completely in charge and looking good doing it." Meredith shook her head, went back to the search results, and found another photo. "Well, well."

"The wedding day," Julia said. "And that's Thomas Van Orden's son?"

The man in the tuxedo was tall, and what little hair he had was completely white.

"That's what the caption says. He's sixty-seven, she's twenty-six. That's wild."

"That would make her about forty-eight now, right?"

"I suppose," Meredith said. "She still looks very good."

"Her husband must have been thirty-something years younger than his brother, guessing by the date of that picture, if Matt was old enough to go into the service in 1918. Really wild."

"It's kind of amazing that Vanessa is Matt's sister-in-law and she's got to be about eighty years younger than he would have been if he were still alive."

"But did she and the brother, uh, David?"

"David," Meredith said.

"Did she and David have any children?"

"I don't know. We'll have to check that out. Either way, I would imagine she inherited everything when David died. She must be pretty well off."

"Looks like it." Julia sat down on the other side of the desk and drank more of her coffee. "She's been smart enough to run the business and not squander everything she inherited. I'd like to know more about her."

"Let me see if she really was in any pageants." Meredith did another search, this time for VANESSA VAN ORDEN BEAUTY PAGEANT. "Aha."

"What?" Julia leaned across the desk to see.

"She did win a pageant twenty-seven years ago. Her name was Vanessa Carroll then."

"I want to know what people were saying about their marriage when it was announced. It might not have been as much of a scandal as his father's marriage to a really young woman back in the twenties or thirties, but I bet people talked."

Meredith gave her a sly grin. "We're supposed to have lunch with Maggie Lu tomorrow, right?"

Julia's gray eyes lit. "Oh yeah."

"She'll have to know at least a little about it."

"I remember hearing about it at the time," Julia said. "Just a little, but I didn't pay much attention. Billionaires and beauty queens aren't exactly in my wheelhouse."

"We'll get some more background information from Maggie Lu tomorrow."

***

The Little Duck was a cute breakfast and lunch restaurant that was modeled after the diners that were popular in the 1920s and '30s. It managed to be nostalgic and contemporary at the same time, and Meredith couldn't help feeling more cheerful when she walked in the door.

Maggie Lu wasn't there when they arrived, so Meredith and Julia sat at a table where they could see the door and watch for her. It was only a few minutes later that Maggie Lu came in. A smile lit her gently lined face when she saw them, and she hurried over to the table.

Meredith and Julia both stood up to hug her, and for a moment they all talked at once.

"You'd think we hadn't seen each other in years," Maggie Lu said, laughing as she finally sat down. "I hope I'm not late."

"Oh, no," Meredith said. "We were a little early. We wanted to beat the crowd."

Maggie Lu took a deep breath and then let it out slowly. "Mmm. I've been thinking about shrimp and grits ever since we decided to have lunch here. I can smell it now."

"It is good," Julia said.

"Just don't get in my way when it comes," Maggie Lu warned with a wink.

The waitress came to bring them menus and take their drink orders and then left them to make their choices.

"I can't decide," Meredith said on a sigh. "Maybe one of these gourmet grilled cheese sandwiches."

"I'm headed straight for dessert," Julia announced. "Then I'll pick something for before that."

Once they'd given their orders, they had a chance to really talk.

Julia launched right into a description of their most recent case.

"Mmm," Maggie Lu said with a shake of her head. "That jewel theft was a long way back now. Good luck finding out much about it."

"We were wondering if you knew anything about the Van Ordens. Or if there was anything your Granny Luv ever said to you about them."

"I remember her talking about what a scandal it was back in the day when old Mr. Thomas married a twenty-five-year-old woman and they had a baby that first year. Then didn't that baby turn around nearly seventy years later and marry a twenty-six-year-old?" Maggie

Lu laughed low. "I thought about Granny Luv when that happened. I could just see her pursing her lips and shaking her head."

Meredith sighed again. "Maybe that's better than giving up on love altogether."

The smiles on her friends' faces faded.

"You seem a little down today," Julia said.

Maggie Lu nodded, concern in her warm dark eyes. "Are you okay?"

"Oh, yeah, I am." Meredith shrugged. "Really, I am."

"But?" Maggie Lu asked, and Julia gave her an expectant look.

"It's nothing."

"Mere," Julia said sternly.

"Really, it's silly."

Both of Meredith's friends stubbornly waited.

She looked down at her menu. "I've just been thinking about Ron a lot lately. He proposed to me on July 7, 1977."

"Today's the seventh," Julia said, realization in her eyes.

"Yeah. Seven, seven, seventy-seven."

Maggie Lu reached over and took Meredith's hand. "You miss him, I know."

"I do," Meredith said, "but maybe not enough."

"What do you mean?"

Once more, Meredith sighed. "I loved him so much. I never wanted anybody else in my life. Now though..." She shrugged, feeling sudden tightness in her throat and the sting of tears in her eyes. "I feel lonely sometimes. Not lonely for friends or family, not like that, but lonely for someone special. Someone I can be special to.

Somebody…" She shrugged as she trailed off, not sure she was making herself very clear.

"There's nothing wrong with that," Julia said.

Maggie Lu nodded. "And losing someone you love doesn't mean you don't have the need to love somebody else either. Julia's right. There's nothing wrong with that. I know that after my Darwin died in the war, I missed him so much. But I thought it would be good for my children if I focused on them while they were growing up. I don't think Darwin would have wanted me to be alone the rest of my life, and I know he would have understood my being lonely, but I had kids to think of. Yours are grown."

"And I don't think Ron would have wanted you to be alone forever either," Julia told Meredith. "Just because you're older, that doesn't mean you don't need to be loved."

"Why, look at these Van Orden men," Maggie Lu said with a twinkle in her eye. "Both of them marrying women they could have been grandfather to. Age didn't stop them."

That made Meredith laugh. "Well, I don't plan on robbing any cradles just yet. But sometimes it is hard to be single in a couples world."

Maggie Lu nodded.

"I guess it is," Julia said. "I'm sorry if Beau and I have made you feel left out."

"No, not at all," Meredith assured her. "You've both been wonderful, and I certainly don't want you to feel like you're responsible for my social life. But it would be nice to have somebody at my side instead of being a third wheel all the time."

Maggie Lu gave Meredith a little nudge with her elbow. "You haven't seemed to be attending events by yourself these days. Wonder why that is."

Meredith laughed, knowing there had to be a sudden touch of color in her cheeks. She knew they were thinking of Quin Crowley, a friend of theirs who had escorted her to different events from time to time.

"Okay," she admitted. "Quin has been on my mind lately. He's just so...nice."

"And not bad to look at either," Maggie Lu said. "For an old man."

Meredith snickered. Maggie Lu was older than Quin by at least ten years.

"Yes, he is nice to look at. And he has such nice manners. Even here, it's getting more and more rare to see a real Southern gentleman."

"So why don't you go out with him?" Julia asked. "And I don't mean only as friends."

The waitress came to refresh their drinks and tell them their food would be out soon.

"Anyway," Meredith said brightly once she was gone, "we were talking about the Van Ordens, and I think—"

"No," Julia said, "we were talking about why you don't go out with Quin."

Maggie Lu raised one eyebrow. "And exactly why was that now?"

Meredith groaned. "I don't know. I want to and I don't want to. And I'm afraid if I do, it still won't be what I'm looking for and then I will have been disloyal to Ron and ended up getting nothing out of it anyway. Aren't I supposed to be happy with or without anybody?"

"You're happy, aren't you?" Maggie Lu asked.

"Yes. I'm happy. I like my job, I enjoy my family, I don't have a spare minute most of the time. I'm happy. But that doesn't mean I don't miss what I had with Ron. It doesn't mean I don't wonder what it would be like to be in love again."

"Then I guess you'll have to jump out there and see," Julia said. "There's nothing wrong with that."

"Maybe, but then I wonder if I have time for anybody or anything else. Maintaining a good relationship takes work."

"Anything worth having does," Maggie Lu said. "But I understand what you're saying. You're the one who has to decide what you want to do about Quin, if you decide to do anything at all."

"If you're looking for somebody to take Ron's place," Julia said, "then it's probably a good idea to tap the brakes for a while."

Meredith nodded. "I know. But maybe there's someone I could share my life with again."

"Well, give yourself time to think about it," Maggie Lu said. "Don't mistake missing Ron because it's the anniversary of when he proposed to you for being in love with Quin."

Meredith smiled. "I would never do that. Maybe this anniversary has made me think about it a little more than usual, but it's been on my mind for a while. Now I have to decide what I want to do about it. And I suppose Quin will have to be willing to take a chance too."

"From what I've seen," Julia said, "I think he is."

"He hasn't ever said anything, has he?" Meredith asked her.

"No, but I have eyes, don't I?"

"And so do I," Maggie Lu said with a chuckle. "I think all he's waiting for is a little encouragement from you."

Meredith winced. "No pressure, right?"

"None," Julia assured her. "Take your time, relax, and think about what you really want. You can leave things exactly the way they are if you like."

"I know."

Maggie Lu reached over and patted her arm. "But you don't have to."

Meredith squeezed her hand in return, glad she had such good friends to talk things out with, even if they did sound silly when she said them. "I don't want to make a fool of myself."

"You won't," Julia said. "Just don't let fear keep you from doing what you really want to do. Whatever that is."

"Amen," Maggie Lu added. "And here's our food, right on time."

The waitress served their meals and after they assured her there was nothing else they needed, she left them alone again.

"Now can we get back to the Van Ordens?" Meredith asked after she'd taken a bite of her grilled cheese sandwich. "Or do we have to talk about my moody indecisiveness again?"

Her friends laughed and started eating their own meals.

"I'm trying to think about what else I've heard about the Van Ordens," Maggie Lu said after she finished gushing about the shrimp and grits. "I know they made their money from several wars, starting with Thomas Van Orden's father's time in the Spanish American War. Thomas married into money later on and really built up the company then. I expect that was when the family started rubbing elbows with politicians and the like."

"Besides the jewel theft," Meredith said, "did you ever hear of any scandals or anything about the family?"

"You mean besides the cradle robbing?" Julia asked archly.

"Besides that."

"I'll give it some thought," Maggie Lu said. "I think Granny Luv had somebody on her side of the family who worked for them, if I'm remembering right. I'll have to see if I can find anything about that for sure. And I'd be surprised if there weren't articles on the Van Ordens from time to time in the papers over the past hundred years. With a big company and money like theirs, there must have been something."

"There's always something," Julia agreed as she added more mayo to her club sandwich. "And you know, I think I must have heard about David Van Orden marrying Vanessa back in the late nineties sometime. The story sounds so familiar."

"Speaking of sounding familiar," Maggie Lu said, "I saw that article in the paper a few days ago about a one-hundred-year-old mystery. It mentioned the Van Ordens and that Magnolia Investigations had been recommended, so I'm sure it's the same case you're working on."

"That's the one," Meredith said. "I guess you never know where a recommendation is going to come from."

"The article said Magnolia Investigations was one of the agencies that was recommended. Something about you being very good with historical mysteries. What's the name of the lady who wants you to look into this?"

"Lydia Cooper."

Maggie Lu pushed her coffee cup toward the edge of the table so the waitress would know she needed a refill. "That's the name in the article. I didn't know there were online groups for people who wanted to ask real private investigators and historians about how to research things like this."

"I think there's a group for everything." Meredith took a bite of her sandwich and then a sip of her coffee. "I'm glad they advised her for a case as old as this to hire a professional."

"It looks like we have a lot of research to do on the Van Ordens before we really know where to start looking for answers," Julia said. "I hope you don't mind us calling on you, Maggie Lu, if we have more questions about some of these things."

"Not at all. I love looking into things like this." Maggie Lu speared a shrimp on her fork. "But not until I finish up this wonderful lunch."

***

When Julia and Meredith got back to the office, they found two clients waiting for them. One was concerning a fraud case they had been working on. The other was completely unexpected. Carmen came into Meredith's office to tell them about him.

"I told him he should have an appointment," she said, her lips pursed, "but he said he would wait. I told him it might be a very long wait, but he didn't want to come back later. Do you want me to tell him he still needs to make an appointment? You have an opening on Friday."

Julia looked at Meredith, eyebrows raised.

"Do we both need to talk to Mr. Bates?" Meredith asked. "You have everything on that case in your office already, don't you? Why don't you see him, and I'll talk to this new client? If either of them needs both of us, we can always confer once the other one has gone."

"That should work." Julia looked at Carmen. "Did you get a name for our new client?"

"He told me his name is Spencer Robinson," Carmen said. "He said he's from Atlanta and that he wants to talk to someone about a case. He wouldn't say what kind of case."

Meredith sighed. She really wanted to get to work on the Van Orden case. She supposed she ought to call it the Cooper case since Lydia Cooper had hired her, or the Brandon case since James Brandon was the one who had presumably been falsely convicted of the jewel theft, but they had been the Van Orden jewels, and the Van Ordens had been the most influential players in the story. Whatever she called it, the case would have to wait just a while longer.

"Give me a few minutes and then send him in," she told Carmen. "I don't want him to think we generally drop everything we're doing just because somebody walks in off the street."

Julia smirked and walked to the door. "You can show Mr. Bates to my office right away."

Once she was alone, Meredith got out a new file folder and a blank copy of the information sheet they generally filled out for new clients. Then she read over the newspaper article about Lydia Cooper's quest to clear her great-grandfather. Just as she reached the concluding remarks expressing hope that her efforts would be successful, Carmen announced Mr. Robinson.

"Good afternoon," Meredith said, standing and extending her hand. "I'm Meredith Bellefontaine."

"Spencer Robinson." He gave her hand a warm, firm shake. "Thanks for seeing me. I realize you and your partner must be very busy."

She couldn't help smiling at the young man, who was maybe in his midtwenties. He was tall and fit and had dark eyes and neatly trimmed dark hair. And he had that unmistakable precise way of carrying himself that said he was or had been in the military.

"Please sit down." Meredith indicated the chair on the other side of her desk and reseated herself. "How can I help you?"

"I read an article in the *Tribune* about a woman who wants to find out about a jewel theft that took place in 1918. It said she was planning on hiring you to investigate that for her. Did she?"

"I'm sorry, but I can't give out that kind of information. Is there something we can help you with?"

"According to the article, that theft involved Thomas Van Orden."

"That's true."

"Well, I'm interested in investigating the Van Ordens too."

Chapter Three

"You want us to investigate the Van Ordens?" Meredith asked. "Regarding what?"

"I want to know what kind of people they are," Spencer told her, setting a thick file folder on the desk. "How they got their money and what they do with it. That kind of thing."

Meredith raised one eyebrow. "That's a pretty big question. What's this for?"

"Do I have to tell you?" He tightened his jaw. "I'm willing to pay whatever your fee is, but does that mean you have to know why I want the information?"

"I suppose not. We won't do anything illegal for you. That's absolutely out, so don't even bother asking."

"I wouldn't expect you to. I don't want that. I just want to know who they are. That kind of thing."

"I think there's only one left," Meredith said, "and she's only a Van Orden by marriage."

"Vanessa, right? She runs everything now."

"That's my understanding. We haven't started our research on her yet."

"So Lydia Cooper is your client, right?"

Meredith couldn't help a slight grin at the mischievousness in his eyes. "All right, I'll admit it, we are looking into that theft for her, but that was back in 1918. You don't want us investigating the Van Orden family that far back, do you?"

"Actually, I do. I'd like to know what they're up to now, business-wise anyway, but I want to know about back then too. I want to know why there aren't any more Van Ordens, and where the money comes from and where it goes. I want to know what kind of people they were."

"I see."

Meredith looked him over for a moment, wondering if he might be an investigative reporter or something along those lines. Or maybe he wanted to write a book about the family or even a novel based on them.

"Have you done any research on them on your own?" she asked.

"Some, but I haven't found out much. I've looked into some newspaper articles that have been printed over the years, even back as far as 1899." He opened the folder and took out a stack of papers. "These are all the ones I've found."

Meredith took them eagerly. "Would it be all right if we made copies of these? They'd be a big help in the investigation. And, since you've already done this much work, it'll save you some money."

"Oh, those are for you. I already have copies of my own. I thought you'd want them."

"Very much. Thank you."

"I have another question," Spencer said, a touch of uncertainty in his tone now. "Is it possible for me to help in the investigation? I know that's probably unusual for a client to ask, but I'd really like to be involved. It's only that I don't know the best way to go about it without getting myself into trouble. Since you and your partner are professionals, I figured I could see what you do and maybe take on some of the grunt work for you. As you say, it would be cheaper for me too."

"I don't know."

Part of Meredith thought it would be wonderful to have somebody around to do whatever she and Julia didn't feel like doing. And a guy like him would certainly make her feel safer when she had to ask unpleasant questions from time to time. But the other part of her was wondering if that might not be a huge mistake in the long run. Would they be responsible for his safety? What if he did something illegal? Would they be liable?

She took a deep breath. "You'll have to let me discuss that with my partner. I'm actually not sure what we are and aren't allowed to do professionally. I'm fairly sure we can't do that. My husband was a private investigator before he died, and he never would allow any of his clients to be involved in the investigations."

"There's an article in that stack about the jewel theft," Spencer said. "You know, if there's a possibility you want it for your other case."

She shook her head. "You're certainly helpful if nothing else."

"Oh, I am," he said earnestly. "I really am."

"All right, I get the idea, but really, I can't give you an answer yet. For now, though, let me get some basic information from you."

She got his full name, address, and phone number.

"I was born in Atlanta," he told her, "but my great-grandfather came to this country from the UK right after World War II. He lived in New York City until my grandfather was born and then the family moved down south."

"And you're still in Atlanta I see. Did you come down here to Savannah because of the article about the jewel theft or were you already here?"

"Actually, I was already here. As you can see, I was doing some research on my own."

"You're not a writer, are you?" she asked. "Some of these industrial dynasties have fascinating family stories. I'm sure they'd make good reading."

"I'm sure they would, but no, I'm not much of a writer. I admire anybody who can come up with an entertaining story, but that's not something I was gifted to do."

So much for the journalist theory.

"What business are you in?" she asked him.

"I manage a hardware store. Actually, it's our family business. My great-grandfather bought it when he moved to Atlanta, and the family's run it ever since."

"That sounds like a good business to be in."

"Yeah, it is most of the time. When times are bad, people need to fix what they already have so they don't have to buy new. And when times are good, they usually want to add on and renovate. We're good either way."

"I'm surprised you have time to be away from the store."

"Usually I don't, but we have some great employees, and my dad really runs the place anyway. I've helped out there ever since I was old enough, but I really started learning the business once I got out of the Marines three years ago. He keeps telling me he's going to retire early and play golf every day, but I can't see it. He's still pretty young and in good shape. I expect him to be around for at least another thirty or forty years."

"Do you like working with him?"

"I can't imagine working for anybody else. He always takes the time to teach me the right way to do things and to help me out when something goes wrong. I know I can always turn to him if I need help."

"Sounds like he's a great dad."

"Yeah," Spencer said with a little bit of a shrug. "They don't often make them like that anymore."

Meredith shuffled through the stack of newspaper articles he'd given her, searching for the one about the 1918 jewel theft. It certainly would be helpful to be looking for information that applied to two cases at once, especially if one of the clients provided that information for her.

"I do have a question for you," she said after a moment. "If we're unable to let you participate in your investigation, does that mean you don't want to hire us?"

"No," he said after a moment's consideration. "But I'd like it better if you did. The truth is what's important to me, but I'd like to know what you find when you investigate the company."

"What is it that you think is going on with the Van Ordens?"

"I can't say for sure. But there are a few things I've dug up that make me think they may not be entirely aboveboard in the way they run things. You look over those articles. It's usually not anything tremendously big, or at least it's not things that a lot of companies don't generally get away with because of all the money that's behind them. But taken altogether, there seems like a pattern, and it's not a pretty one."

"I'll admit I've heard that kind of thing about them too. Little things, for the most part, from what I can tell. It's the ones that involve the more powerful politicians that disturb me the most."

He nodded eagerly. "Like when that property was rezoned so they could put a manufacturing plant there, even though the area had previously been a historical district. Van Orden Munitions had to pull some pretty hefty strings to get that done."

"We'll certainly check out what we can. Is there anything else you want to tell me about? Anything that'll point us in the right direction here? That is, if you want to hire us. And, at this point, it would have to be with the understanding that you can't be part of our investigation except for providing us with any information you already have and letting us know if you want us to continue and for what period."

He huffed and then nodded. "Okay, I really do want you to investigate. And I really do want you to ask your partner if I can help. Yeah, I understand if that isn't possible, but I'd rather be right in the middle of everything."

"Yes, I can tell."

She didn't ask him anything else, but he certainly seemed to have a more-than-average interest in the Van Ordens or at least in Van Orden Munitions.

Mr. Bates left Julia's office only a few minutes after Spencer left Meredith's, and then Meredith and Julia both got fresh cups of coffee and sat down to discuss their respective conferences.

"I don't think there's much to the Bates case," Julia said with a sigh. "He's sure his two brothers-in-law are syphoning money from the company they own together, but he couldn't give me any real evidence of that except that the two of them went in on a timeshare a month or so ago."

Meredith rolled her eyes. "I still think most of his problem is that he doesn't know the first thing about running a motorcycle shop or managing finances, and they do. I remember when we talked to him before. He's making money, but he thinks they're making more. I think this is much more likely to be family rivalry and a lack of communication rather than any actual malfeasance."

"Well, if he wants it checked out, we'll check it out. What about your guy? What's his story?"

Meredith filled her in on what Spencer Robinson had told her.

"It's odd that he should come to us about the Van Ordens," Julia said, "especially since Lydia Cooper just hired us to look into that jewel theft they were involved in."

"He said he came to us because of that article in the *Tribune*, so it's not that odd, but there's something about him that makes me wonder."

Julia gave her a strange look. "What do you mean?"

"Oh, nothing bad," Meredith assured her. "I don't think so anyway. He actually seems like a very nice young man, but he didn't want to tell me why he wants to have the Van Ordens investigated. He said he wants us to look into the family history and what they've done with their money and how they earned it in the first place. And he gave me a stack of newspaper articles about them, just to get the investigation started."

"Sounds like a very helpful young man if nothing else." Julia took the copies Meredith offered her and thumbed through them. "These go way back."

"He said he wanted us to go way back too. At least as far back as that jewel theft in 1918."

"Wow. Okay."

"And he wants to help in the investigation."

Julia stared at her. "What?"

"Just what I said." Meredith gave her a significant look over the rim of her coffee cup. "He very much wants to be in on everything with us. I told him I didn't think we could do that, but I said I would talk to you about it and get your opinion."

"Absolutely not. We can't possibly be responsible for someone who has no training and no credentials and whom we know nothing about. No. Just no."

"I agree. And I was wondering too, what would happen if he did something illegal or got into trouble some other way or, heaven forbid, he was hurt or killed. We wouldn't want to have even a possibility of being liable for that, right?"

"Right." Julia shook her head. "No, we have to tell him we can't possibly let him work on the case with us. If that loses us a client, so be it, no matter how convenient it might be to work on two related cases at the same time."

"Well, I already told Spencer that Ron never had any clients help with any investigations. I'm sure he would have mentioned that to me if he had, so I hope Spencer's not really expecting us to say yes. But he did say he still wants to hire us anyway, so we can go ahead and get started."

"Good. I'm ready." Julia flipped through the copies of newspaper articles again. "I think the most efficient way to go about his case and the Van Orden case is to start with the jewel theft. It applies to both cases, and we can start with the articles we have here."

"I agree. Let's divide and conquer. I'll take half, you take half."

Julia took two new legal pads out of the bottom drawer of her desk and gave one to Meredith. Then she stacked up the copies of the articles and split them equally between the two of them.

"Pick your poison," she said.

Meredith chose the one that was closest to her and started sorting.

"Ah," she said after a few minutes. "Jackpot."

She pulled out an article dated October 14, 1918. The headline was bold and imposing.

VAN ORDEN JEWELS STOLEN—ARREST MADE

"Oooh." Julia turned sideways so they could both read it.

Wealthy industrialist and philanthropist Thomas David Van Orden, owner of Van Orden Munitions & Manufacturing, reported to police late last night that a valuable collection of jewels was found to be missing from the safe located in the study of the elegant Van Orden mansion. Though Randolph M. Perrimot, Mr. Van Orden's estate manager, speaking to the Tribune *on his behalf, declined to reveal any specific figure, it is well known that the jewels were tremendously valuable, perhaps even into the millions of dollars, according to some sources. Many of them had belonged to Van Orden's late wife, socialite Catherine Van Orden, nee Palmer, and had been passed down to her by his mother, the celebrated Mrs. Carolina Shay Van Orden.*

Although the investigation is ongoing, Savannah police have arrested Mr. Van Orden's private secretary, a Mr. James

Dortort Brandon, regarding the theft. "According to inter-
views with the principals in the matter, Mr. Brandon had the
greatest opportunity to make away with the valuables chiefly
due to his position of trust with Mr. Van Orden," Police Chief
Benjamin S. Bryant stated. "The most obvious motive for the
theft is personal gain; however, at present a specific motive
has yet to be established. The whereabouts of the jewels has
also to be ascertained, but those of us on the police force are
confident we will be able to locate them and return them
safely to their rightful owner."

"Wow," Meredith said. "He's just been arrested, and they've
already got him convicted."

"I'm sure Mr. Van Orden was pretty powerful back then. It
could be that nobody considered questioning his version of the
story. Even the police."

"What else does it say?"

They read on.

Chief Bryant admits that there is some difficulty in pinpoint-
ing the actual date and time of the theft. "Mr. Van Orden
informed us that he does not regularly examine the contents
of his safe due to the confidence he has in the security of the
safe itself and in the people he has in his employ. However, he
is certain the theft had to have taken place sometime between
the morning of September 22, when he placed some valuable
papers in the safe, and yesterday afternoon, when he removed
his will from the safe in preparation for drafting a new one.

This, sadly, was made necessary by the death of his son, Matthew Andrew Van Orden, following the tragic loss of the Troopship Otranto *following her sinking off the western coast of Scotland on the 6th of this month. Mr. Van Orden maintains that, apart from Mr. Brandon, it would have been very difficult for anyone to have opened the safe without being noticed by him or someone on his staff, as only he and Mr. Brandon have access to his private study, the location of the safe."*

"I wonder how they knew that," Julia mused. "Why Brandon as opposed to anybody else who worked in the place, particularly this Perrimot guy who was in charge of the whole estate. Just because nobody else was supposed to be able to get into the study?"

Meredith shrugged. "Looks that way. And maybe because Brandon was involved on the business side of things and didn't have anything to do with the estate? I don't know."

"Well, I certainly don't know what difference that makes as far as who had access to the jewels and who might benefit from stealing them."

They read over the rest of the article, taking notes on anything that seemed pertinent to either of the cases they were working on. When they were done, Meredith looked at it again.

"I wonder if there's an article about Thomas Van Orden losing his son in that shipwreck. That must have been very hard for him, especially if his wife died when Matthew was born and he didn't have anybody else."

"I'm sure it was." Julia started going through her half of the articles, and then she abruptly stopped. "Here's something on it."

Meredith scanned the article. "'Memorial for Van Orden Son to Take Place,'" she read. "It looks like he was supposed to have a very lavish service. Is there anything on that anywhere? He was a nice-looking boy."

Matthew Van Orden looked very young in the photograph. He was wearing a navy uniform, but there was little more about him she could tell. He wore a hat, so she couldn't tell if his hair was light or dark. His eyes were sort of a medium shade and, in black and white, it was impossible to tell the exact shade.

"It's sad," Julia said, studying him too. "Sad for him and sad for his father. Thomas Van Orden must have started wondering what good all his money would do him when he had nobody to leave it to."

"Maybe that's why he married again so late in life." Meredith scanned the article. "Matt was only twenty. What a shame."

"It was. This article names two other young men from Savannah who were on that ship too. Matthew's friends. I guess they all went down together."

Meredith didn't know what to say to that. It was too sad.

Julia started going through her stack of articles again. "Wouldn't it be easier if we at least sorted them out by decade instead of pulling out random ones?"

"Makes perfect sense."

They did exactly that, starting with a stack for anything from the 1800s and moving up by decade through the 1900s and the 2000s.

"Looks like Spencer did his homework," Meredith said when they were done with the preliminary sorting.

"He's awfully interested in the Van Ordens. What do you think he's up to?"

"I don't know. I thought he was a journalist or something, look-ing for a good story. Turns out he helps run his family's hardware store in Atlanta."

Julia raised her silvery eyebrows. "And you say he was military?"

"Yes. Do you think that's the connection? Van Orden deals mostly with the military."

"Could be. I noticed two or three articles that indicated Van Orden was under investigation, but they always seem to come up clean."

"Investigation for what?" Meredith asked.

"I didn't do more than glance at them, but I think people were wondering about the money they were raking in from government contracts and exactly what went into negotiating those very favor-able contracts. But, again, they never seemed to be actually prose-cuted for anything."

"Maybe Spencer has something against the company because of that. If that's still going on, I mean."

"It's possible, I suppose. But he was interested in that jewel theft too, which really had nothing to do with the company or the military."

"True," Meredith said, "but those gems were bought with Van Orden money." A thought struck her. "You don't suppose he's on the hunt for the jewels, do you? After all, they were never recovered. At least that's what Lydia Cooper told me."

"I never thought of that."

"If that's the case," Meredith said, "he's going to have to look pretty far for them. All the way back to 1918."

Chapter Four

October 8, 1918
Ballycastle, Ireland

Aileen Byrne walked along the grim, rocky beach, drawing her shawl more tightly over her head and wishing for another layer of stockings under her wool skirt. The whipping wind tried to snatch the basket out of her hands, and she clung more tightly to the rough woven handle. It wouldn't do to lose the bread and fish she'd ventured out for. Not on a day like this.

A half dozen or more curlews skittered on their long legs across the wet rocks ahead of her, looking unsure whether or not to take flight. Besides them and the ever-crashing gray waves, nothing else moved. The waves and the birds made the only sound.

Aileen forced herself to move faster. It wasn't just the cold that hurried her along. Da would be waiting for his tea, and she had picked up a letter from Bran and a large spool of cord while she'd been out. Da would be wanting both.

She worried over Bran as she walked, wishing she knew already what he had written, but it was addressed to their father, and she didn't feel it right to open it herself. But she *hoped he wasn't writing to tell them he wouldn't be home on his leave next week as they'd planned.*

Da would have her read the letter to him anyway, so she didn't much fret over it now. He always thought a letter was good diversion for him as he wove one of the fishing nets he made. He was working on a very large one just now, one that ought to buy them a taste of beef or mutton when he was paid for it. That would be like a holiday all in itself.

She wasn't far from the cottage when she heard something rustle in the brush above the rocky beach. She stopped for a moment, thinking it must be the wind, and then passed on. She stopped again when the rustle was accompanied by a moan.

"Who's there?" she called, clutching her basket against her chest.

There was no answer, and she forced herself to come closer. Perhaps it was some beast that had taken shelter there. But it hadn't sounded like a beast. It had sounded like—

"A man," she breathed as she pulled back the brush.

He was curled up there, taking whatever shelter he could against the cold. A young man, dressed like a common laborer, pale faced and blue lipped and shivering.

"Please, sir," she said, "you cannot sleep here. You must not."

She shook him by the shoulder, and he moaned again.

"Sir," she said more forcefully, "you must go back into the town. You cannot—"

She broke off when the touch of her hand to his forehead told her he was burning with fever.

"Oh, sir," she murmured.

She looked toward the town where she'd come from many steps ago and then toward her own cottage not so many steps away. She pressed the back of her hand to his too-warm cheek and knew he wouldn't be able to walk even those few steps. She looked toward the cottage once more and then pulled off her shawl and laid it over his head and face and the upper part of his body.

"Poor, thin coat that you have, sir. I don't know how much it will help, but I'll be as quick as I can."

The raw wind added to her urgency, and her run home was swift.

"Da!" she called when the stone cottage came in sight. "Da!"

He was sitting at his net making when she pushed open the door, barely enough light coming through the small window to let him see what he was about.

"What is it, girl?" he asked, scowling and holding his wide netting needle poised to make another pass through the cords.

"You must come, Da." She left her market basket near the fireplace and went to him. "There's a man lying above the beach. He seems very ill, and I couldn't move him myself. Please, Da."

She tugged his arm, and he shook her off.

"Half a minute now," he said, securing a knot. "We can't have the whole net to unravel. Now what's this you say? Where's your shawl on such a day?"

"I'll get another," she said, grabbing his heavy coat and thrusting it into his hands and then seizing her summer

shawl from the peg by the door. "Please, Da. He's very bad off."

"Yes, yes," he grumbled, struggling into his coat. "Better get a blanket from me bed, and I'll get me flask."

His flask was already in his coat pocket, but Aileen grabbed the blanket from his bed and the one from her own and then flew back out the door and toward where she'd left the man. Da was twice her weight and bulk, but he kept up with her, his heavy brogues slapping the path behind her until she stopped at the stranger's side and moved the shawl from his face.

He was still now.

"Oh, Da," she whispered, and then she dropped to her knees beside him, begging God and all His angels to bring him help.

"Get those blankets over him," Da said, pushing her aside. "Come now, boyo. Now's not the time to give up the ghost. Not in front of me own daughter here."

He slid one hand behind the man's head, lifting it a little as he put the flask to his lips. Aileen caught a quick breath and laughed a little when the stranger coughed and tried to turn his head away.

"Here now," Da told him sternly. "There's little enough of that to drink much less waste. Take it down, lad. Take it down like an Irishman."

They got enough whiskey into the stranger to bring a little color to his lips.

"There he is," Da said, giving Aileen an encouraging look. "No need to worry ourselves, now. I daresay that's brought him round. Help me now."

He took one of the blankets off the man and spread it out beside him. Then he rolled the man onto it and swaddled him up like a baby. That done, he heaved the man over his broad shoulder and lifted him up.

"Hurry now," he told his daughter. "I'm not what I was when I was his age, and I don't have it in me to stand about like this."

Aileen snatched up her other shawl and the woolen cap that had evidently fallen from the man's head when he'd collapsed, and she hurried back to the house. She had a quick moment to lay her own bedding out before the fire before Da brought the stranger in and laid him down on it. The man didn't move until Da gave him another drop of whiskey.

"Please," he gasped hoarsely. "Can't—"

A fit of coughing took him, and Da sat him up and swatted him on the back.

"There now, boyo. You're all right now. We'll have you warm and well before you can say what's this."

"Gently now, Da," Aileen said, carefully lowering the man back to the blankets. "Would you rather have some tea?" she asked the stranger. "Some soup?"

The man made another hoarse attempt to talk and had to be satisfied with nodding.

Aileen brushed the dark hair from his forehead. "You rest now. We'll see to you."

She rummaged around and found some of Bran's clothes and gave them to her father.

"You'd better get those wet things off him and put him in these. They ought to fit him well enough. I'll make the tea."

She set the kettle on the fire and put some broth from yesterday's supper on the stove. Then she cut a slice of bread from the loaf she had just bought. The stranger probably wouldn't be able to eat any yet, but she'd try all the same.

It took only a few minutes for Da to wrestle him out of his sodden clothes and put the dry ones on him. He was a little taller than Bran, but not by much, and not as broad. He was a nice-looking man, she thought, with a square jaw and firm lips and a nose that was perfect in its ordinariness. She glanced at his left hand as it lay on top of the blankets and then blushed when she realized Da had noticed.

"It's a common thing to wonder," she said, a touch of temper in her tone. "It doesn't mean I'm after marrying him."

Da laughed, and she blushed more, hoping the man was as insensible as he looked. No ring didn't necessarily mean that he wasn't married or engaged or planning to be. It didn't mean he was a good man or a man worthy of her heart or that he'd want it if she threw it at his feet. And it certainly didn't mean she intended to snatch him up just because he looked sweet-faced and helpless lying there.

The kettle started to sing, and she grabbed up the wet clothes, tossed them into the empty washtub, and then went to make the tea.

He started when she put her hand lightly on his shoulder, his striking blue eyes wide and terror filled.

"Who are you?" he gasped, pulling away from her.

"Shh," she said. "You're all right here. You're safe. Would you like some tea?"

He looked around the dim cottage as if he was remembering what had happened, and then he calmed and swallowed hard. "Yes. Thanks."

She looked at him for a moment, puzzled. There was something in his low voice that was different from what she was used to hearing. He wasn't English or Scottish. He certainly wasn't Irish. There was something soft in his tone that was unlike any of that.

"You're American," Da said, coming to stand over them, teacup in hand. "I should have known it from the very start. I met one of you Yanks before. In Dublin when I was hardly a boy."

The stranger narrowed his eyes at Da. "I don't much like being called a Yankee."

"Sure, sure," Da said, a twinkle in his eye. "No harm meant. No harm at all."

The man smiled faintly and tried to lever himself up onto his elbow. Then he huffed, frustrated because he couldn't do it.

"Just lie still," Aileen told him, only half scolding. "I'll get you another pillow to prop you up, and then we'll see about your tea."

"Thank you, miss," he said, and she wondered if that was what all Americans sounded like.

She allowed her expression the slightest warmth. "I never met anyone from the States before. I always wanted to."

"It's our loss, I'm sure."

The teacup she was holding rattled in its saucer, and she had to steady it in her other hand. She also had to ignore her father's smirk.

"Here," she said, abruptly putting cup and saucer both into Da's hands. "I'll get the pillow."

Between the two of them, they got the stranger propped up enough to help him drink some tea without spilling it all down his front. She was pleased that he managed to drink the whole cup, but she wasn't pleased to find that he was still feverish.

"I have a bit of broth for you, sir," she said, "and then we'll have some wet cloths on your forehead to cool you down."

"I'm all right now," he said. "Now that I'm warm and dry. Thank you, Miss...?"

"Miss Byrne," she supplied. "Aileen Byrne."

"Miss Byrne. Thank you. I think you and your father saved my life."

"Oh, it was nothing," Da said quickly. "Nothing at all."

"It was a great deal to me," the stranger said. "You have my thanks, Mr. Byrne."

"It was only right, lad, only right. I couldn't do less and call meself a Christian."

"We're happy to help you, sir," Aileen said. "Might we know your name as well?"

The stranger didn't answer her at first, and there was something troubled in his expression. Then he looked away.

"I don't know," he said, his voice almost too low for her to hear. "I just don't know."

"You don't know your name, lad?" Da asked.

The man shook his head. "I can't remember. I know I was on a boat. Sometime. I don't know when. There were other men."

"Were you a fisherman?" Aileen asked him, taking the hand that reached for hers. "A sailor?"

"I don't know. I can't remember. I don't—" He sank back into the blankets, his eyes screwed shut. "I don't know who I am."

"It's all right," she soothed. "It's all right. It will come back to you, to be sure. With time and rest, it will come back. I'm sure it will."

He held her hand more tightly, desperate now. "I can't go back. Don't make me go back."

"Back where?" She exchanged a worried look with Da. "Where don't you want to go to?"

The stranger sank back into the blankets and covered his face with his free arm. "I don't know."

"But you're from America."

His only answer was an uncertain shrug.

"It's all right. We'll have the doctor come look at you. He'll know what to do. Dr. Morton is—"

"No." The word was muffled against his arm. "Please don't. Please."

"All right," she said, her voice very gentle. "You can rest here until you're better. It's all right."

She feathered her fingers through the still-damp locks of his dark hair until his hold on her hand loosened and she knew he slept.

"It's all right," she murmured again, and then she pulled the blanket up to his chin and stood up.

"What'll we do, Da?"

"We ought to have the doctor out," he said decidedly, "and perhaps a constable."

"A constable? Whatever for? He's done nothing wrong."

"That we know of," Da said warily.

"The poor man, he doesn't even know who he is, and you'll have him hauled away to prison."

"Now there's nobody's said a word about prison, my love, but there might be someone who's looking for him. A wife perhaps."

"He's got no ring."

"Well, a mother then. Would you break his poor mother's heart?"

"No, I suppose not."

"Or even his mates. Suppose he was on a fishing boat and washed overboard, how cruel for his poor shipmates all weeping his loss and even feeling the guilt of not being able to save him, and here he is taking his ease before our very fire. Could you live with yourself?"

That teased a smile out of her, and she kissed his ruddy cheek. "I wouldn't want that, of course, but mightn't we wait, Da? Just a day or two and see? Perhaps he'll remember after a little time, and then we'll know what to do."

"Now, my love—"

"He seems so lost and frightened. Could we not wait?" Before he could object, she pressed herself into his arms. "Please, Da, just a wee bit of a while?"

"You have your mother's charm for getting your own way, Daughter, and I'll never say different, but I suppose there's no real harm in it. It'll be work looking after him, mind that, and I'd better not hear a word of complaint."

"Oh, he's not in such a bad way, is he? Just cold and hungry and worn through."

"What about that fever?"

"I wouldn't be surprised if it was gone by the morning."

"And the feeding of him?" Da pressed. "How are we to manage that with not overmuch for ourselves as it is?"

"We're not so bad off that we can't provide a meal or two, are we? And what about that grand net you're about to sell? I know you're to have a pretty price for it, and then things will be cozier for all of us."

"I've been some time working on that, as you well know, and it'll take me such another time before we have any more money coming in. And what then, me fine girl? What then?"

"Then God will give us His provision as He always has, and I'll stand by that to me last breath and after."

She stood with her hands on her hips and her chin raised to him, and abruptly he laughed and threw his arms about her and hugged her close.

"So He will, my love, as He does for all us poor sparrows, even the half-drowned ones."

That night, when her father was asleep and she sat watching the man by the fire, she wrote in the diary her mother had given her nearly three years before, when she turned sixteen.

I found a man on the beach today. The poor thing, he doesn't know who he is or where he's come from, but I do not fear his dying as I did when I first saw him, and I believe he will soon recover. He sleeps very soundly. Truly, I don't know if I could wake him even if I tried, but sleep is healing. I pray he will be more himself in the morning. If not, I do not know what we shall do with him. We can only trust God to guide us in this as in everything.

Chapter Five

"I CAN'T BELIEVE SHE AGREED to see us," Meredith said as Julia drove toward the corporate offices of Van Orden Munitions & Manufacturing the next day.

"Especially at such short notice." Julia turned toward the business district. "But, from what you told me she said, I have a feeling she's not just trying to help us out."

"No, probably not. She must have read that article about Lydia Cooper looking into what happened to her great-grandfather, and now she wants to know exactly what we know. This ought to be interesting."

Vanessa Van Orden's private office was on the top floor of the Van Orden Building, a shining twenty stories of steel and glass on a corner lot. Meredith and Julia had to get past the receptionist for the floor and then a private secretary before they were ushered into Mrs. Van Orden's office. The room was far from cozy, but it wasn't the cold abstract-art-and-white-everything-else kind of place Meredith had been expecting.

It was done mostly in cool greens and blues, in rich damask silks and soft linens. Even the furniture was a warm cherry styled in gently curved lines. There was nothing minimalist or industrial in the style here, and yet the room was somehow very businesslike all the same.

As soon as the private secretary ushered them in, Vanessa Van Orden stood up and came to them, one hand outstretched. She definitely had the look of a one-time beauty queen. High cheekbones, long lustrous hair, willowy figure, and all. It didn't hurt that she had the money and taste to make the most of her looks. She was wearing a plum-colored silk suit with a blouse of soft lavender underneath it. Meredith knew how much something like that had probably cost, but she did look stunning in it.

"Come in," she said with a soft Southern lilt, shaking Meredith's hand and then Julia's. "Please make yourselves comfortable." She indicated the two graceful armchairs that had been placed in front of her wide desk. "May I have Dinah bring you something? Latte? Chai? Anything at all?"

"Oh, no," Julia said. "Thank you. We don't want to keep you long. I'm Julia Foley. This is my partner, Meredith Bellefontaine."

Vanessa smiled at them both. "Thanks for making that clear for me. Now tell me exactly what you'd like to know. As I told you over the phone, Meredith, I have heard about Thomas Van Orden having his jewels stolen, but I really don't know much about it. Until I saw that article about it in the *Tribune*, I really hadn't thought of it in years. Since my husband and I first married."

"He told you about it?" Meredith asked.

"He mentioned it. Just the one time. It really was only a little bit of a joke. He had given me a rather extravagant gift for our six-month anniversary, a really magnificent diamond and ruby collar. Antique looking, you know. He told me he would have given me all the jewels his great-grandmother had had before the Civil War, but they had been stolen decades before and never found. He had some photographs of his father's first wife and even one of his grand-mother wearing some of them, but that's all I really know."

Julia leaned slightly forward in her seat. "You have pictures?"

Vanessa nodded.

"Would it be possible for us to see them?"

"I don't have them here at the office, of course. In fact, it might take a little while to find them, but if you like, I can have them scanned and emailed to you. Would that do?"

"That would be extremely helpful," Julia said.

"It certainly would." Meredith handed Vanessa one of her business cards. "You can have it sent to the office email address, if you would. We'd be very grateful."

"Not a problem." Vanessa smiled benevolently. "I'll send as many as we can find. Now what else can I do for you?"

"You said you'd seen the article about the theft."

"Yes. The woman's name was Cooper, I believe."

"That's right," Meredith said. "She's trying to find out about her great-grandfather."

"James Brandon."

"Yes. Do you know anything about him?"

Vanessa shook her head. "I never heard the name before I read the article. He went to prison for the theft, and now this Cooper woman is trying to clear him?"

"Do you think there are any records on him in your company files?" Julia asked her.

"What sort of records?"

"Anything specific about him. His address, what he was paid, when he was hired, what his position was. That sort of thing."

"Mrs. Cooper has told us what she was told about him," Meredith said, "but we'd like to get the facts straight from the source. In case she was told something that wasn't correct."

"That makes sense," Vanessa said, "and we're, of course, happy to do what we can. You understand, though, that some of those records would be well over a hundred years old. Like most long-established companies, Van Orden has had to deal with fire and weather damage as well as with records being lost or, intentionally or otherwise, destroyed. I didn't take over managing the company until after my husband passed away, and what he or his father before him might have done with records that old, I don't know for certain."

"That's perfectly understandable," Julia said.

Meredith nodded, immediately wondering what the woman had to hide. She was certainly making preemptive excuses for not having any information about James Brandon. Or maybe Meredith was being overly suspicious. Just because a woman was rich, well connected, and beautiful didn't mean she had done anything wrong.

"But I will have some of my people look into it for you," Vanessa said. "Whatever they find, I'll have that forwarded to you along with the photographs you asked for."

"That would be very kind of you," Meredith said. "Our clients would be most grateful for any help you can give."

"Clients?" Vanessa asked, the thinnest thread of tension suddenly in her voice.

Meredith immediately regretted mentioning there was someone else who wanted Van Orden Munitions investigated.

"Well, Mrs. Cooper is really interested in finding out about the theft and about her great-grandfather's involvement in it for her mother's sake more than anything else." She gave Julia a glance that, she hoped, would tell her to play along. After all, it was the truth, even if it wasn't all of the truth. "Mrs. Cooper tells us her mother has always felt shamed by what people said about her family's involvement in the theft. Mrs. Cooper hopes it will help her mother to know the truth, whatever it is."

"I see. Well, I'll have my people find out what they can."

"Would it be possible," Julia added, "for us to get a sample of Matthew Van Orden's handwriting? It doesn't have to be anything important. A Christmas card or a letter or even a form he filled out. Anything."

"For what?" Vanessa asked, the overhead lights bringing out the flecks of gold in her eyes.

"Our client says that her mother claims to have had a letter from him that said James Brandon was innocent and that the Van Ordens knew what was going on all along."

"Oh yes, the letter she mentioned in the article." Vanessa looked mildly puzzled. "What does she mean the Van Ordens knew what was going on?"

"We don't know yet. She hasn't located the letter, if such a thing exists, but it would help us in our investigation to know what it says and to have proof that it wasn't written by Matthew. Do you have any idea who might have written her a letter like that? Perhaps it was your husband, and she got the names mixed up."

"David? No, I don't think he would have written anyone about that. At least he never mentioned it to me. You have to remember, that theft was well before his time too." Vanessa thought for a moment. "Do you know when it was supposed to have been sent to her?"

"No," Meredith admitted. "We don't have much information about it at all besides what Mrs. Cooper's mother has said."

"She can't tell you?"

Meredith glanced at Julia, wondering how much she should say.

"Mrs. Cooper's mother is having some memory issues," Julia supplied. "That's why we don't have many specific details about the letter."

Vanessa immediately looked sympathetic. "Oh, how sad. No wonder Mrs. Cooper wants to lay this matter of the jewel theft to rest. The poor woman. I've always felt terrible for people suffering from loss of memory. It's like they're losing their lives piece by piece. I don't know if we can unearth anything that will be much help in finding out what you want to know, but I'd certainly like to do something for this poor woman. Do you think it would be all right if I sent her something? Perhaps something that will give her a little pleasure during her remaining days."

"That's very thoughtful of you, but—"

"I'd be happy to do something for her. If you'll give her contact information to Dinah, my private secretary, I'll have her send something along. She won't mind, will she?"

Meredith smiled. "I'm sure she'll be very happy for someone to think of her."

"I'm sorry she couldn't give you more details about this letter she's mentioned. It might clear this matter up right away."

"Mrs. Cooper says her mother can't remember what she did with it. If it actually does exist, Mrs. Cooper hasn't been able to find it."

"How disappointing. Has she had a chance to look very much yet?"

"If Mrs. Cooper's mother hid it in something, I suppose it could have already been sold or given away."

"Or thrown away," Julia said.

"Or maybe there never was a letter." Vanessa's smile was only slightly indulgent. "Being part of a family with wealth and influence for so many years has taught me to expect to be a magnet for gossip and speculation. Over the years, Van Orden has been investigated a number of times, and we've never been found guilty of anything. I'm not surprised to hear that this poor woman has delusional ideas about the company. Whatever she's imagined about us is just as unlikely as a man writing her letters years after his death."

"It is a pretty wild claim to make," Julia said. "But we'll look into it all the same. If we can at least rule out that there ever was a letter, that'll be a help."

"True," Vanessa said. "Dinah is an excellent researcher. And please assure Mrs. Cooper that we'll be happy to get her whatever information we can."

"Thank you," Meredith said. "I'm sure she'll appreciate that and all your kindness very much."

"Really, it's nothing. What else can I do for you?"

Meredith looked again at Julia. Though they hadn't gotten any information as of yet, things had gone well and Vanessa couldn't have been more cooperative.

"I think that's all," Julia said, standing.

Meredith stood too. "We really appreciate it."

"I wish all my visitors were as easy to please." Vanessa took her Louis Vuitton purse from a drawer in her desk and pulled out two business cards. She gave Julia and Meredith each one as she walked with them to the door. "Now if you think of anything else you'd like to know, feel free to give me a call. I'll tell Dinah to put you right through. Actually, you can ask her almost anything you'd want to ask me. If she can't find out for you, I'll be happy to see what I can do. Since I joined the family so long after the theft, I really can't tell you much about it personally."

"Anything you can find for us in your records would be a big help," Julia assured her.

"And of course my father-in-law and brother-in-law were gone well before I was born, so I'm useless telling you much about the family either. Of course, if you want basic names and dates, you can find that on the company website. The address is on my card."

Meredith held up the glossy card Vanessa had just given her. "We'll make sure to check it out. Thank you."

"Dinah," Vanessa said once she had opened her office door.

The efficient-looking young woman sitting at a tidy desk in the outer office immediately stood up.

"Yes?" she said in a low, slightly lisping voice.

"This is Mrs. Bellefontaine and Mrs. Foley. They are investigating a theft that took place at the Van Orden home in 1918."

Dinah's brows went up.

"They have a number of things they'd like to know about the company at that time, specifically about a James Brandon who worked here then. Get someone in records to find whatever we have on him. They also would like copies of some photographs the late Mr. Van Orden had. Call Anna and ask her to track those down for us too. Send someone over to pick them up and then scan them along with whatever information you find on Brandon and email them to these ladies as soon as possible. Rush job."

"I'll take care of it."

"Oh, and they're going to give you contact information for their client's mother. I want you to find me some gift suggestions for older women who are housebound."

"Right away," Dinah said.

"Excellent. They'll give you the specifics. Give them whatever they need. I have to get to my meeting. What else do I have this afternoon?"

"You have that fundraiser for the Delorme Foundation at seven," Dinah told her. "Nothing before that."

"Okay. See you tomorrow then." Vanessa nodded at Meredith and Julia. "Ladies, it was a pleasure meeting you." She strode toward the outer door and then stopped and turned, her sunglasses halfway from her purse to her face. "Did you tell Steve I'm on my way down?"

"He'll have the car waiting for you," Dinah assured her.

Looking pleased, Vanessa gave them all a little wave and swept out of the office.

"She seems very busy," Meredith said.

"She is." Dinah took a notepad out of the top drawer of her desk and nodded toward the chairs across from her. "Would you like to sit down again?"

"Thank you," Julia said.

"Now," Dinah said once they were seated, "if you'd like to tell me specifically what information you're looking for, I'll be happy to see what we can find for you."

Between the two of them, Julia and Meredith gave her the names and dates and other information they had.

"Anything about Brandon James," Meredith stressed, "and about that jewel theft. The only specific thing we have on it is this article from 1918." She gave Dinah a copy of the article Spencer had given them. "Vanessa said you could have someone look through your company records and send us copies of whatever they find."

"She also said that at her home there were photographs of some of the jewelry that was stolen. Pictures of Thomas Van Orden's first wife wearing them and of his grandmother too, from Civil War times," Julia added. "And something with Matthew Van Orden's handwriting on it. Doesn't matter what."

Dinah nodded, not slowing her neat, rapid shorthand. "I'll get you copies of whatever we can track down. What about the information for your client's mother?"

"Her name is Sheila Bryleigh," Meredith told her. "She's at White Oak Arbor, a memory care facility. I'm afraid I don't have the address."

"I can get it. Is there anything else?"

"You look far too young to have worked here when David Van Orden was still alive," Meredith said with a smile.

Dinah grinned. "I was two when he passed away. Sorry."

"Is there anybody still working here who would have known him?"

Dinah looked thoughtful.

"I realize it would be a long shot," Meredith added, "but it's possible that he might have mentioned something his father said about the incident that could help us. You never know."

"Uh, sure." Dinah thought for a moment more. "There's Mr. Jarvi. He manages all the manufacturing departments. He's been here since the eighties. He's retiring at the end of next month, but if anybody can tell you about David Van Orden, I would think he could."

"Jarvi?" Meredith asked. "That's an uncommon name."

Dinah nodded. "He's Finnish. Mrs. Van Orden says he's the best in the business and that she doesn't know what she'll do without him."

"Do you think she'd mind if we had a few words with him?" Julia asked.

"I don't see why she would," Dinah said. "Would you like me to ask him to come up?"

Meredith nodded eagerly. "That would be great."

Dinah got up. "If you'll come this way, you can meet with him in the conference room. If he's not busy, he ought to be here in a few minutes."

Julia and Meredith took seats at the long conference room table. Less than five minutes later, the door opened and a tall, elderly man came in.

"Mrs. Bellefontaine? Mrs. Foley?"

Meredith could tell by the slightness of his accent that he must have come to America when he was fairly young. He had to be in his seventies by now. She and Julia both stood to shake hands with him.

"Mr. Jarvi?" Meredith said.

"Please, call me Miko, and please, make yourselves comfortable." They all sat at one end of the table.

"Now," he said, "how may I help you?"

"We understand you knew David Van Orden," Julia began.

"Ah, yes, I worked for him for many years."

"Could you tell us what he was like?" Meredith asked.

The man frowned thoughtfully. "I was always told he was very like his father. I never met his father of course, since that Mr. Van Orden died so long ago, but I did see pictures of him. I was told the two of them were very alike in personality too. David Van Orden was a very private person when I knew him. Not unkind, but very businesslike. He was definitely master of the company and expected all of us to do as we were told. I've heard his father ran the business the same way. I have no complaints of him. I never saw anything but that he treated his employees fairly, and Mrs. Van Orden has taken her cues from him, even after all this time."

"Did he ever talk about his father or his family?"

"Not often," he said. "When I mentioned once that my grandfather had fought in World War I—he was one of only five hundred Finns who volunteered for the Tsar's army—Mr. Van Orden said that his older brother was lost in that war. I thought it was very odd that his brother was of an age to have gone, but he told me it was his half brother who was some thirty years older. It amused him, I think, the difference in their ages."

"It is an unusual situation, I suppose," Julia said. "We're doing some research on the jewel theft that took place in 1918."

"So, during the war then," he said. "Interesting. I'm sorry, though, I'm afraid I never heard Mr. Van Orden make mention of it when I knew him."

"I'm curious," Meredith said. "You've worked for the company for a long time."

"Almost forty-two years," he said proudly.

"I suppose you've had to deal with government regulations in many different ways. I understand the US military is your biggest customer."

"We do a considerable amount of business with them, true, but we also deal with other companies, supplying parts and supplies for them to make what they sell to the military as well."

"Interesting. Is there a particular company you deal with most?"

"None that you would recognize. Most people don't know such companies exist because, needless to say, their products aren't something the average person would buy, but they all supply the brave men and women of our armed forces with the things they need in order to keep us all safe and at peace."

For another few minutes, he told them about the company and about its goals and accomplishments. Then there was a genteel chime from the vicinity of his coat pocket.

"Excuse me," he said apologetically, and he took out his phone. "I'm very sorry, but I have a meeting I must get to now. If there's anything else I can do for you, please let me know. At any time."

They all stood then, and he escorted Julia and Meredith to the conference room door.

"One moment, and I will have my assistant escort you to your car."

"Oh," Meredith began, "we can—"

"Truly, it is only courtesy. And our offices can be quite a maze if you are unfamiliar with them."

He made a brief phone call, and a minute or so later, a man in his late forties, thin, balding, and bespectacled, appeared.

"This is Jack Jackson," Mr. Jarvi said. "He'll take care of you from here. Jack, please see Mrs. Foley and Mrs. Bellefontaine to their car. It was a pleasure, ladies, to meet you both."

He hurried off, leaving them with his assistant.

"This way, please," Jack said, gesturing toward the hallway they had originally come down.

"Have you been with the company long, Jack?" Meredith asked as they walked.

"Yes, ma'am. About fifteen years now."

"And how do you like working here?"

"Oh, it's an amazing place." Jack gave her a bright smile. "I've learned a lot."

"You must have if you're Mr. Jarvi's assistant. That's got to be a big job."

He shrugged a little sheepishly. "I'm a glorified gofer, but that's okay. I'm good at it. Sometimes I even help out Mrs. Van Orden."

"She looks like a very busy woman," Julia observed.

"She is," Jack said. "Between the company and her charity work, she's always off somewhere. I'd say if anybody knew everything there is to know about Van Orden, she's the one. She knows, start to finish, how everything here runs. Have you met her?"

"Just today." Meredith told him what the article said about the jewel theft and about Lydia Cooper wanting to know what really happened. "We thought we'd see what we could find out about the company in general while we're at it. It must be hard to deal with all the federal regulations and the investigations and everything I've read about."

"They're a nuisance," Jack said. "Mrs. Van Orden has much better things to deal with than frivolous accusations. Come this way, please."

By then they were at the elevator. Jack kept up his cheerful small talk until they reached the ground floor and then the front entrance of the building.

"Which way is your car?" Jack asked, still with a smile.

"It's just over there," Meredith said, pointing. "You don't have to bother escorting us from here."

"Oh, no, ma'am. I have my marching orders." Jack took Meredith and Julia each by an arm, and though he still smiled, his expression hardened. "We only have a few seconds now. There are cameras. Don't look nervous."

Chapter Six

SOMEHOW, MEREDITH MANAGED NOT TO react as they walked from the Van Orden building to the car.

"Don't ask me anything," Jack said, his expression pleasantly bland. "I can't risk it. Just check into KBMJ Industries."

"But—"

"Look, someone told me you might be asking questions. Because of that article in the paper. He said if I didn't want to say anything to him, I should tell you and let you get to the bottom of it."

"Who was this? What was he like?" Meredith was struggling to keep her attitude casual.

"He didn't give a name," Jack said. "He was young. Dark hair and eyes. That's all I know."

"Okay," Meredith said, "but—"

"You can't tell anyone I said anything." There was a flicker of fear in his pale eyes despite his faint smile. "That's all I can tell you."

They were standing next to the car now.

"Thanks for seeing us out," Meredith said as she opened her door. "And do thank Mr. Jarvi for us. He's been very kind."

"It's our pleasure."

He stood beside the car and gave them a little wave as they drove away.

"Well, that was odd," Julia said from behind the wheel.

"The hallways and elevators must be monitored." Meredith glanced back at the building. "I wonder what he wants us to find."

"No telling until we start looking into things, but that was very strange."

"Now I'm wondering if Spencer knows more about the company than he's letting on. He fits the description of the guy Jack was talking about."

Julia frowned. "If he knows something, why wouldn't he tell us? Why pay us to dig up something he's got already?"

"I don't know. Maybe we ought to ask him." Meredith got out her phone and called Spencer.

"Hey, that was quick," he said as soon as he answered. "Did you find out something?"

"We're just getting started, so you're going to have to give us a little time," Meredith told him. "But I would like to know something. Have you been to the Van Orden building?"

"Well, yeah. I thought I'd try to find out some things I want to know."

"And did you?"

Spencer huffed. "Fat chance. They were all very nice, but nobody would tell me much of anything. Nothing I didn't already know anyway."

Julia kept looking over at Meredith, obviously wanting to know what he was saying.

"Do you mind if I put you on speaker, Spencer?" Meredith asked. "Julia and I are in the car, and she needs to hear what you have to say too."

"Sure," Spencer said. "Hi."

"Hi, Spencer," Julia replied.

"Tell us who you talked to," Meredith said. "And what kinds of things have you been asking?"

He hesitated for a moment. "I talked to the receptionist at the front desk for a few minutes, but she'd only been there for a couple of weeks, so she couldn't tell me much. I talked to a couple of guys coming out to the parking lot after work. They said they work in accounting, and they didn't know of anything in particular. You know, nothing out of line. Another guy came up to us and that kind of scared them away, I think."

"Who was the guy? What did he say?"

"I don't know who he was. I didn't want to ask anybody for names or anything. I was just trying to find out what I could. He asked me what I was doing asking questions. I told him I was trying to write an article about the defense industry." He snickered. "Yeah, I know I told you I'm no writer. I'm not. But I thought that was as good a cover as any."

Great, Meredith thought, *he's going to step all over this investigation before we even get started.*

"And did he give you any information?"

"Not much. He told me I should make an appointment with the company's PR lady. I could do that, I guess, but all she would do is give me some slick brochures about how great the company is and how it helps the troops. That's not what I need to know."

"What was this 'not much' information this guy gave you?" Julia asked.

"It was odd, but after he told me about the PR lady, he asked me what I was looking for. I was afraid at first that he was going to tell me to leave, but he sounded like he really wanted to know. I told him I wanted to find out about some of the inquiries into the company over the years. I made up a story about wanting to write a piece that would get me hired at one of the big papers. I told him I'd make it worth his while if he could point me in the right direction."

Julia rolled her eyes. "It's pretty unlikely that you'd be able to walk into a company's headquarters and ask to see records of their illegal transactions."

"No," he admitted, "but I was hoping maybe somebody there might care enough about what's been going on with them for decades to want to have some of it come out."

"There have been rumors over the years," Meredith said, "and I hope we can uncover something that will help us find out if they're true or not, but we won't end up getting anybody to confide in us if you go there and start grilling people. You don't have any experience in investigations, do you?"

"Uh, no. Not at all."

"I didn't think so. You're paying us to see to this for you. Why don't you let us handle it from now on?"

"Of course I will. I went there before I hired you."

"What information did you get out of the guy you talked to?" Julia asked again. "The one who wanted to send you to public relations?"

"I told him you two were probably going to come ask some questions about the jewel theft since you were mentioned in that article, and I asked him who at the company would be likely to help with something like that. He said he didn't know who that would be but that he could find out. That maybe he'd like to talk to you himself."

"When was this?" Meredith asked.

"A few days ago," Spencer told her.

"Did you tell this guy you were planning to come talk to us?"

"No. I thought maybe it would be best if I didn't let him know that part of it. But I gave him my number and told him to call if he had any information for me."

Meredith glanced at Julia. "Spencer? What did this man look like?"

"I don't know. Kind of average, I guess. Forty something. Glasses. Balding. Just a guy."

Julia's eyes widened.

"It's Jack," Meredith murmured.

"Who's Jack?" Spencer asked.

"He works for Mrs. Van Orden and for the man who is in charge of all their manufacturing operations, a Mr. Jarvi."

"I've heard of Jarvi. How do you know Jack?"

"Julia and I went to see Vanessa today. That's where we're coming from right now. The oddest thing is what happened when we were leaving the building. Jack came with us, and when we were outside, away from the security cameras, he told us to look into a company called KBMJ Industries."

Spencer was silent.

"Spencer?"

"Yeah, I'm here. KBMJ. Right."

"You've heard of them," Julia said.

"Uh, do you think I could come talk to you for a few minutes?"

Meredith looked over at Julia. "What do you have for today?"

"All I have planned is working on this case. You?"

"That's what I was expecting to do too. So, yeah, Spencer, if you want to come to the office and talk, we can do that. When can we expect you?"

"Is right now okay?" Spencer asked.

"That'll be fine. We'll be there in a few minutes."

"Great. So will I."

Meredith ended the call and put her phone back into her purse. "He knows something about KBMJ."

"I think so too," Julia said. "And I'm sure Jack's the guy he talked to when he was over at the Van Orden Building too."

***

Spencer was already at the office when Julia and Meredith got there. He and Carmen were discussing the differences between Guatemalan and Mexican food.

"You beat us here," Meredith said. "That was quick."

He stood up. "I'm glad you had time to see me."

"Why don't we go into my office?" Julia suggested. "Would you like some coffee?"

"None for me, thanks," Spencer said. "You wouldn't have a cold bottle of water, would you?"

"I'll get you some," Carmen said, and she hurried off to the kitchen for it.

"Would you please get one for me too?" Meredith called after her.

"*No problema.*"

"Come on back," Julia said to Spencer.

They made themselves comfortable in Julia's office, and Carmen was right behind them with the water.

"Thanks," Spencer said, first pressing the frosty bottle to his forehead and then opening it to take a deep drink. "I can never stand coffee this time of year. Not much of anything else but water. At least not while the sun's up."

Meredith took a few sips of her own water. "You sounded like you were in a hurry. What's up?"

"I've been thinking about this whole thing," he said, looking from her to Julia and back again. "I said I didn't want to tell you why I wanted to investigate Van Orden Munitions. I guess I didn't want to influence you or something. Now I'm thinking I'm just making it harder for you to find out anything."

"The more specific you can be about what you want to know, the more likely it is we can get you a specific answer. Except for questions about the jewel theft for Mrs. Cooper's case, all we could do over at the Van Orden Building was get a little information about the company. Something we could have gotten off the website."

"Yeah, well, I guess it's time I told you why I want to know about Van Orden."

"It would be helpful," Julia said.

He took another deep drink of water, and the lines in his face turned hard. "Three years ago, I was still in the service. In Afghanistan. I won't go into everything. I couldn't possibly tell you how it was over there. Same stuff that's been going on for years. Anyway, me and five of my buddies were on a security detail and we were ambushed."

Meredith caught a breath. This wasn't going to be good.

"I'll keep it short," Spencer said. "Three of the six of us were killed outright. One was taken prisoner. Two of us held the enemy off until another squad came to back us up. I got a bullet in the leg, but it wasn't a big deal. My buddy took a shot in the head. He's still working on learning to read and talk again."

"I'm sorry," Julia murmured. "How does Van Orden play into all of this?"

"The reason we couldn't get out of that mess was because two guys' weapons malfunctioned. Sure, it happens. I'd heard about it before. Just here and there. Just a story you'd hear once in a while. Guys with their guns jamming at the worst time. Ammo that was no good. I started asking around. Looking around. Almost every time, the equipment came from Van Orden."

"That's not good."

"I'll tell you what's worse. Some of the guns we'd pick up after an incident with the enemy, they were just the same. The other guy's weapon would jam or blow up in his hands or whatever."

"Those were Van Orden too?"

"No." Spencer clenched his jaw. "They had different names on them, but they were all the same. You know what I mean. Like getting two cans of peas with two different brand names on them, but that were both canned in the same factory."

"And you think this might be where KBMJ comes in?"

"Maybe. Maybe Van Orden runs KBMJ on the side. You know, takes second-rate parts and supplies, stuff they can't or won't sell under their own name, and still makes a killing on the black market."

"It's possible, I suppose."

"It didn't happen every time. And the guys we were fighting got their weapons from all over. From the Russians. From the weapons we'd give the Afghan police. Those were Van Orden a lot of the time too. But the ones that weren't were the same, just marked different."

"Is Van Orden that big of a supplier for the military?"

"They're no Lockheed Martin," Spencer said. "Van Orden's a drop in the bucket, but it's a dirty drop if you ask me. I want to know what's going on. If they're selling garbage to the military, why do they keep getting contracts? Somebody's got to be fixing it for them in Washington. And they have to be selling weapons or at least parts and raw materials to KBMJ, who are selling them to our enemies."

A little shiver went down Meredith's spine. What were they getting into here?

"I understand why you were cautious about telling us this," she said. "You must have done some serious research about it."

Spencer shrugged. "I tried to tell others, but nobody wanted to hear about it. I talked to our representative in Congress about it, and he said all he ever heard was rumors but there's no hard evidence. He's not talking to the guys fighting over there, that's for sure. I'm hoping that if I can find a real connection between Van Orden and KBMJ, or if you can find it anyway, maybe somebody will do something."

"So you mostly want to get enough evidence to get a large-scale investigation started," Julia said.

"Yeah, pretty much. And, you know, maybe I have this all wrong. Maybe I'm taking a small problem that's due to human error or mechanical breakdowns rather than graft, but I still think someone should find out about this, even if there is no malicious intent."

"I suppose there is a certain amount of equipment failure no matter who the manufacturer is."

"Right. But I'm having trouble making myself believe that about Van Orden. Especially since they've been in this business for over a hundred years, and these questions have dogged them almost since the beginning."

"Really?" Meredith asked.

"You give those articles I gave you a good look," Spencer said. "There aren't many answers in there. Some of the writers are a little bit over the top about what they suspect, but there's no hard evidence. Nothing the Van Ordens couldn't explain away."

"And what do you think Jack is up to?"

Spencer exhaled and shook his head. "Your guess is as good as mine. He asked me some questions, but he didn't give away any information. He wasn't just blowing me off either. I don't know."

"He was definitely scared when he talked to us," Julia said. "Uncomfortable. He didn't want anybody in the building to hear what he told us."

"That was when he told you about KBMJ, right?"

"Right," Meredith said.

Spencer frowned. "Does he know you're working for me?"

Julia shook her head. "We told everyone we were there because of the jewel theft."

"I thought it was better not to bring up anything else," Meredith said. "It's one thing to investigate a hundred-year-old case where the principals are all dead. It's another to start making accusations about them not being entirely aboveboard in their dealings with the government."

A sly smile touched Spencer's mouth. "So the theft is the perfect cover for you being able to investigate what might or might not be going on now."

Meredith nodded. "Now that we know what you really want us to find out."

***

Meredith spent the next morning reading through all the articles Spencer had brought her, making notes, jotting down questions as they occurred to her, creating a general timeline for Van Orden Munitions and, from the information she had, for the Van Orden family. As he had said, there always seemed to be someone questioning the company's integrity and someone representing the Van Ordens always seemed to explain away any concerns. She was surprised how often there was some office holder—state, local, or federal—who stood by the family.

She'd have to check out these politicians, especially the ones who were long gone. Usually people who were involved in one shady deal were involved in others, and their sins eventually found them out. Whether or not they were punished for their wrongdoing was an entirely different question.

It was nearly lunchtime when her phone rang. COOPER L. K. popped up on her screen. She answered immediately.

"Lydia. How are you?"

"Not very good right now," Lydia told her, a definite unsteadiness in her voice.

"What's wrong? Are you all right?"

"I'm all right. It's my mother."

"She hasn't gotten worse, has she?"

"Oh, no, she's fine. But somebody has been searching her room."

Chapter Seven

"Searching her room?" Meredith swiftly turned to a new page in her legal pad to jot down the information. "When was this?"

"I'm not sure," Lydia said. "I'm at the facility right now. Mom's asleep, so I thought it was a good time to call. What should I do?"

"What have you done already?"

"Uh, not much. I thought something odd had happened, because all of Mom's things were in the wrong place. She's very particular about that. If one of the healthcare workers puts Mom's socks in the pants drawer or something like that, she gets very upset. And everyone here knows that. They're careful to do things the way she wants."

"Maybe someone new is working there," Meredith suggested, feeling a little bit of a letdown. "It would be hard, I'd think, to remember the quirks of every patient in the facility."

"Yes, I suppose, but this seems like more than that to me. If it was just laundry being put in the wrong place, why would someone have rearranged her winter clothes?"

Meredith started taking notes again. "Her winter clothes?"

"You know, sweaters, sweatpants, warmer tops, that kind of thing. Not that she has a lot of them. There's not a ton of room for extra things. But I could tell they had been rearranged. And her

78

sheets weren't tucked in the same way as the people here always do them."

"But, again, couldn't that be someone new?"

"Maybe," Lydia admitted. "I haven't noticed anyone new though."

"Maybe on the night shift or something."

"I suppose." Lydia didn't sound at all convinced.

"Have you—"

Meredith broke off when she heard a querulous voice in the background.

"Lydia? Is that Grandma?"

"I have to go," Lydia told Meredith in a hushed tone. "I'll be here a while longer. Please come by if you can."

"I'll be right there," Meredith said.

"Thank you."

Lydia ended the call, and Meredith put down her phone. White Oak Arbor wasn't very far to drive, but she hadn't planned on doing anything today other than finishing her examination of the Van Orden articles and starting internet research based on the questions she had listed for herself.

She went into the reception area. "Did Julia say how long she'd be out?"

Carmen looked up from her computer monitor. "She said she'd be back after she and Beau have lunch."

"What are you working on?" she asked Carmen.

"Oh, more on the Bates case." Carmen sighed.

"Good luck with that," Meredith said sympathetically. "Look, I'm going out to talk to Lydia Cooper at her mother's care center. I shouldn't be long, but I can't promise that. You can always give me a call if you need me."

"Right."

"If I'm not back pretty soon, go ahead and lock up for lunch. Put a note on the door letting people know when you'll be back."

"Got it. Thanks."

Meredith gave Carmen a wave and went out to her car.

***

White Oak Arbor was a pleasant looking single-story building that had four long wings stretching out from a large central hub. The front of the building was mostly parking lot with a generous amount of handicapped spaces and gently sloped pathways leading up to the secured front door. Behind it, as far as Meredith could see, was a grassy area, well shaded with white oak trees and full of winding paved pathways liberally supplied with park benches.

She stepped inside and was instantly greeted by a bright-eyed young woman who was probably in her midtwenties. The name tag pinned to her blouse read CAROL MONROE, ACTIVITY DIRECTOR.

"Welcome to White Oak Arbor," she said. "Are you here to visit one of our residents, or would you like to tour the facility?"

"I'm here to see Lydia Cooper, actually," Meredith told her. "Her mother lives here."

"Oh yes, you mean Sheila Bryleigh. She's in A-137. I'll take you over there."

"That's all right. If you'll just direct me, I'm sure I can find it."

Carol pointed to her right. "A-Wing is right over there. Room 137 is on the right side of the hall. The numbers are on the doors."

"Thank you."

Meredith started to walk that way, but Carol stopped her.

"I'm sorry, but all of our guests have to sign in."

She took Meredith over to a counter with a register book on it.

"If you'll just sign your name and put in the time and the room you'll be visiting, that'll be fine."

"Thank you."

Meredith did as she was told, filling in the spaces and taking the opportunity to see who else had visited recently. The page she was on was almost full, but this was a large facility. There were four wings, so she guessed there were a lot of people living here. It was sad to see how few visitors there actually were.

She glanced up the list, trying to see if anyone else had visited A-137 in the past few days. Lydia was there every day as far as she could tell, but there wasn't anybody else listed. She noticed A-139 and A-142 were listed, both from last evening. She saw A-113 in there as well, two or three times over the past week. All the other room numbers on the list were in different wings. She wished she had time for more than a quick scan of the names written there, but nothing familiar or unusual leaped out at her.

"You'll need to sign out too," Carol said when Meredith had stretched out the signing-in process as long as she credibly could. "Whenever you're ready to go. We love to have visitors stay as long as they like, so no rush. We'll be having board games at one o'clock, and you're welcome to join us."

"Thank you. I'll remind Lydia and her mother of that."

Meredith hurried down the hallway of A-Wing, unable to help glancing into A-113 as she passed it. She smiled a little to see a middle-aged man and a very elderly one sitting on a sofa watching TV. The sound wasn't turned up loud, but she could tell from the little she could hear that they were watching a baseball game. Father and son, she assumed, loving the way they sat close, the father clinging to the son's arm and both of them sitting eagerly forward as the game unfolded before them.

For a moment she wished she could tell the son he would be happy he had taken the time to be with his father while he could and that no matter what memories his father had lost, times like this were precious to him. But she walked on. As far as she could tell, A-113 was one of the rooms that got regular visits. The son probably already knew all that.

She walked farther down, past more than one person who sat in a doorway slumped in a wheelchair, looking at her hopefully and then looking down again as she passed by. It hurt her heart to see that.

Lydia stepped out of A-137, and her face lit up when she saw Meredith. "Oh, I'm so glad you're here. Please, come in."

Mrs. Bryleigh's room was light and airy, the furniture attractive and comfortable looking. From what Meredith could tell, there was only one large space, a combination living room and bedroom. The door just inside the entry was open slightly, and she saw that it led to a small, gleaming white bathroom.

Lydia took Meredith's arm and drew her over to the frail little woman sitting in a recliner in the corner nearest the large window. "Mom, I brought a friend to see you. Her name is Meredith."

Mrs. Bryleigh looked up at Meredith with a sweet-if-somewhat-vacant smile. "Did you come to play bridge with us? We'll need someone else too."

"I'm afraid I don't have anyone with me," Meredith said. "We'll have to play another day."

"Oh." Mrs. Bryleigh's face fell. "Well, that's all right. I have to go home soon anyway." She glanced at her wrist even though there was no watch on it. "My husband ought to be here any minute."

Meredith looked at Lydia, not sure what to say, and Lydia, standing out of her mother's line of sight, only gave a subtle shake of her head.

"Meredith is a private detective, Mom," Lydia said brightly. "Isn't that interesting?"

"A real detective?" Mrs. Bryleigh said, her eyes wide. "That must be very dangerous."

"Oh, not most of the time," Meredith told her. "And it can be very interesting. Did you ever have anything you were looking for and couldn't find?"

Mrs. Bryleigh gave Meredith's hand a confidential pat. "Oh, all the time. All the time. Poor Lydia always has to help me find things."

Meredith sat down on the floral love seat that was at a right angle to the recliner. "What sort of things? Maybe, since I am a detective, I can help you find what you're looking for."

Mrs. Bryleigh beamed at her. "Oh, do you think so? I would love that. There was a letter I got a while ago, and now I can't find it."

"Have you been looking for it?"

"No. I haven't had time. Not for a long time now. I have everything in its place now, and I wouldn't want to be unorganized. I was very upset, you know."

Meredith glanced at Lydia. "With your daughter?"

"No, of course not. Not with her. With the people who come in here."

Lydia immediately looked concerned. "What people, Mom? You didn't tell me someone had been here."

"Oh, there's always someone. They come in when I'm not watching, and then they look at my things."

"Has she told you this before?" Meredith asked Lydia, her voice low.

Lydia shook her head. "When was this, Mom? Since I was here last?"

"Sometime," Mrs. Bryleigh said. "I'll have to think of it."

"What kind of a letter was it?" Meredith asked her.

"About Granddad," she said immediately. "Mama always knew he didn't steal anything, and then Matt wrote and told me he didn't. I have to find that letter and tell her about it."

"Who's Matt?"

"He wrote that letter. I told you."

Before Meredith could figure out how to reply to that, a cheerful, heavyset woman in scrubs rapped on the open door and came into the room.

"Time for your physical therapy, Sheila," she said, grabbing the walker that leaned against the wall and opening it up.

"Is it time, Janet?" Mrs. Bryleigh asked.

"Yes, ma'am. Are you ready?"

Lydia was already helping her mother out of her recliner. "You go ahead, Mom. I'll be there in a few minutes."

"But I have company."

"It's okay, Mom. I'll take care of Meredith. I'll be down there in a little bit."

The nurse had Mrs. Bryleigh halfway to the door by then. "Keith is here today," she said encouragingly. "You like Keith."

"He's such a nice boy."

They moved into the hallway and were gone a moment later.

Meredith got up and shut the door. "Does she always think people are going through her things?"

"Just now is the first she's mentioned it," Lydia said, looking around the neat room. "I haven't told her what I told you about her clothes."

"Sometimes in places like this, the other residents get confused and get into other residents' things. Is that a possibility?"

"I suppose it is, but I haven't heard of anyone specific here."

"How long has your mother been living here?" Meredith asked.

"Almost eleven months. I really didn't want to have to put her in a place like this, but she started leaving burners on in the kitchen and getting into her medications when she shouldn't and going outside by herself when I didn't realize it. She gave us some pretty good scares."

"I know that must be a hard decision to make, but this seems like a nice place."

"It really is." Lydia's expression relaxed a little. "And I try to come see her most days. At least I do as often as possible."

"I noticed that on the visitors' register. I didn't see that anyone but you had come recently."

"No, I don't think anyone else has come by. My sister lives in town, but she hasn't had time to visit yet."

Meredith gave her a sympathetic smile. Eleven months, and the sister hadn't had time yet.

"Would you mind showing me what you mean about your mother's things being out of place?"

Lydia nodded and opened the top drawer of the dresser. "This is where we keep her underthings and socks and all that. None of this is actually out of place, but I can tell it's been riffled through." She opened the next drawer. "These are Mom's slacks and sweatpants and things. I know these have been moved, because I just bought her these pink sweats. I put them on top of the stack yesterday, and now they're in the middle."

"And your mother couldn't have gone through things herself?"

"She could have, but it would be unusual for her. She usually lets one of the girls get out something for her to wear every morning."

"And one of them wouldn't have done it?"

"They usually get whatever's on top. I typically arrange everything so they're in a rotation."

Meredith thought for a moment. "What about the laundry? Does the staff here put away her clean things?"

"Yes, but that's on Tuesdays. They wouldn't have done it between when I put those new sweats in her drawer and today."

Meredith looked around the room. "Anything else you noticed?"

Lydia took her into the tiny bathroom. "This."

She indicated a container of scented face powder, and Meredith was certain that was the source of the pleasant but overwhelming aroma in the room.

"Did somebody get into the powder?" Meredith asked.

"Somebody must have. It was new yesterday. Now it's nearly half gone, and some of it was still on the counter here, and there were traces on the floor."

Meredith looked where she indicated and saw white in the crevices between the tiles and against the baseboard. "Maybe whoever it was spilled the box and had to clean it up quickly."

"Maybe, but why?"

Meredith shook her head. "Anything else?"

"Everything else." Lydia opened the cabinet under the sink. "Everything is jumbled up and not the way I had them. The closet's the same way. And like I said before, her sheets were taken off and put back on, or at least they were rummaged through. They're not tucked in the way the staff usually does them. And one other thing."

Lydia went back to the dresser. On top of it, in front of the large mirror, was a quilted runner and, on top of that, was a framed family picture, a hinged wooden box, and a stack of books.

"This makes me sure somebody's been here." Lydia moved the top two books, uncovering a black book with *Holy Bible* and the name SHEILA PARKER BRYLEIGH stamped on the front cover in gold. "Mother was always very particular about the Bible. From the time I was a little girl, she always said that there should be nothing covering the Bible but the roof of the house."

"Your mother couldn't have moved those others?" Meredith asked. "Maybe she was reading them."

Lydia shook her head. "Mom hasn't been able to read regular-size print for the past five years. I read the Bible to her. I read it to her yesterday. And when I left, it was on top of the stack."

"I hate to ask this, but could someone on staff be going through her things? I've heard of that happening in some homes when residents have had their valuables taken."

"That's the thing. Mom doesn't have any valuables. She still wears her wedding ring, but other than that, I have all her jewelry at my house. All she has here are clothes and some toiletries. That picture of the family. Her TV and furniture are probably the most valuable things in the room, and they belong to the facility."

"And it wouldn't be very easy to smuggle them out." Meredith frowned, thinking. "Have you talked to any of the staff about this?"

"Not yet. I thought, with the investigation going on, I ought to talk to you first. I don't want to spoil anything by saying something that might tip somebody off."

"Good thinking," Meredith said. "Who would you expect to have been in here between the time you left yesterday and the time you got here today?"

Lydia considered for a moment. "I left before dinner. Mom wanted to hear the lady from her church who comes every Thursday to play guitar and sing, so I took her down to the common room and got her settled in the chair she likes. Some of her friends were already down there, so she didn't mind my leaving. After that, Carol or one of the other girls would have made sure she went into the dining room to eat and then either taken her back to watch the movie they were having or seen that she got settled into her room for the night, whichever she felt like doing after that."

"Do you know which she did?"

"She said she saw *It's a Wonderful Life*, but that's what she always says, so I'm not sure. I can definitely ask."

"Okay, we'll check that out. What about after she was back in her room?"

"Whoever was on duty last night would have checked to make sure Mom was settled in and helped her with her nightgown if she needed it."

"Does she usually need help?"

"She has her good days and her bad days," Lydia said. "I'll have to ask how last night was."

"And this morning?"

"Someone would have come to check on her, gotten her ready for breakfast, and taken her down to the dining room. I didn't have a chance to ask her what she did after that, because as soon as I got here, I could tell something wasn't right."

"What does she typically do in the mornings?"

"There are different things. There are small groups that go out to walk when the weather is good, but not usually when it's this hot. There are crafts. Some exercise groups that focus on gentle movement. People from the church visit, especially the residents who don't have family come by much. It varies, but there's usually something going on between breakfast and bedtime for anybody who wants to participate."

"So your mom might have been in and out of the room several times since you were here last. And for long periods of time."

"That's right. But Mom did say somebody had been looking through her things, so she must have seen whoever it was, even if it was just briefly."

Meredith picked up the Bible and flipped through the pages. There was nothing in it except for a couple of bookmarks and a piece of unfolded note paper, about three by five, that had some scripture references written on it. It was very faded, and she could tell the words had been written with an actual fountain pen.

"What are these scriptures?"

"They're some verses my grandma wrote down and kept in her own Bible before she passed away. Mom always keeps it in hers now, but that's another thing I meant to mention to you. That yellow bookmark used to be my great-grandfather's. Mom always kept it to mark the Twenty-Third Psalm. The other one, the one with the roses on it, that's one of mine. It was marking my place in Romans yesterday. Now all of those are in the back of the book, like somebody dumped them out and then stuffed them back in."

Meredith nodded and then turned her attention to the family picture. "What about this?" she asked. "If I was going to hide something thin, I might pick something like the back of a photo, inside a frame."

"I hadn't thought of looking there before, but now that you mention it, it sounds like a good idea." Lydia bit her lower lip. "I didn't notice anything," She came closer as Meredith examined the picture frame, and then she frowned. "I can't be absolutely sure, but I don't remember being able to see the white along the top edge of that photo before. Not when it was in the frame."

"Has your mother ever hidden anything in the back of a picture before?"

"Not that I know of." There was a touch of excitement in Lydia's eyes. "I can't stand it. Open it."

"Well, if somebody's already taken it apart, there won't be anything to see, but I think we ought to look anyway. Just to be sure."

At Lydia's nod, Meredith slipped off the back of the frame and then removed the piece of cardboard that kept the picture secure.

There was nothing else in the frame but the picture itself.

Chapter Eight

Lydia huffed. "Drat. I was hoping it was there."

"It could have been." Meredith looked around the room again. "If the person who was here found it, we wouldn't be able to tell." She removed the picture from the frame and looked at it a little more closely. "Does this look recent to you?"

She pointed out the top left corner of the photo. The tip of it was turned under.

Lydia frowned. "Yes, it does. Wouldn't it be more compressed than that if it had been that way for a long time?"

"Could be. And it could be that somebody was in a hurry to put this back yesterday, and that corner snagged on something and was flipped up as it was shoved back into the frame."

Lydia wrinkled her forehead. "So what do we do now?"

"Who would you normally talk to if you had a question or if there was a problem?"

"Carol, I guess," Lydia said. "If she doesn't know, she ought to be able to tell us who does. About everything but financial matters I think, and that's always the business office."

"She's the one I saw when I came in, right?"

"That would be Carol. She's usually somewhere out and about."

They found Carol playing checkers with an elderly Black man wearing a Falcons cap and the thickest glasses Meredith had ever seen.

"Are you looking for me?" she asked cheerfully when Meredith and Lydia came up to her.

"There's something we need to ask you about," Lydia said.

"When you have time," Meredith added, smiling at the man. "We don't want to interrupt your game."

"No, now, you can go on, Miss Carol," the man said. "I'm about to figure out how to beat you this time. Might take me a few more minutes."

Carol smiled. "All right, Mr. Anderson. I'll be right back."

She walked with Meredith and Lydia back to A-137, discreet enough to hold her questions until they were inside the room again.

"Is there a problem?" she asked. "Is your mother all right?"

"Mom's fine," Lydia assured her. "I'm not actually sure there is a problem, but we thought you'd be the one to ask if there was."

"That's why I get the big bucks."

Lydia glanced at Meredith, who gave her an encouraging nod.

"It just seemed to me that, when I got here today, things in Mom's room didn't seem...right."

Carol's warm expression turned serious. "What do you mean by not right?"

"It looks like someone's been in here," Lydia said, clearly uncomfortable. "Like things have been, well, searched."

"Is anything missing?"

Again Lydia hesitated. "I don't think so, no. Not anything I can be sure of."

"Okay," Carol soothed. "Why don't you show me specifically what you mean."

As she had done earlier, Lydia pointed out what seemed out of place in the room.

"When do you think this would have happened?" Carol asked.

"Sometime between when I left yesterday and when I got here today."

"Did your mother say someone had been in her room?"

"She said there was a woman, but she couldn't give me any details, so I'm not sure whether she might have gotten confused about someone on staff coming in or even another resident."

Carol gave her a professional smile. "Well, as long as nothing is missing."

"I'm sure this happens sometimes in this type of setting," Meredith said. "Have you had any other complaints?"

"No," Carol said quickly, and then she winced slightly. "Not actual complaints. Not really. There hasn't been any harm, you know, and as you say, it's not uncommon in facilities like ours. Our staff is trained to be on the lookout for residents who have wandered into the wrong rooms, but with so many living here—"

"So there have been occasions you've been told about."

Carol nodded. "As I said, nothing major. Nothing stolen. There's a gentleman in C-Wing who sometimes wanders into places he shouldn't. He says he's sure his wife has his credit cards hidden somewhere, but I'm afraid she's been gone for over twenty years. He's still trying to find where she hid those cards."

"Is there anyone closer to this room than that?"

"I hope you'll forgive me, but I can't really give you specifics. It's against our privacy policy. Unless an actual crime has been committed, we're not allowed to give out that kind of information."

"Is that what you think happened?" Meredith asked, disappointed at not getting anything helpful from her.

"It seems the most likely explanation, don't you think so?"

Meredith did think so.

"If you'd like," Carol went on, "we can check the register for last night and this morning. As you know, all nonresidents have to sign in and out, so if someone came to visit Sheila, we'd be able to tell right away."

Meredith hadn't seen anyone but Lydia sign in for A-137, but maybe she'd missed something. Perhaps now she could get more than just a glimpse of the register book.

Carol took them up to the front desk, and together they checked the register.

"I don't see anyone but you for the past few days," she told Lydia finally.

There weren't many visitors during the time period in question, and for A-Wing only those two Meredith had already noticed. The names were Evelyn Sanders and Sam Russell. Maybe she could make a casual visit to A-139 and A-142. Both of them were close to Lydia's mother's room.

"Are there security cameras in the hallways?" Meredith asked.

"Yes," Carol said. "It's not monitored security, because we have staff at the nurses' stations at the end of each wing twenty-four seven. But, really, this seems like a very minor incident. I realize it's unsettling for you and your mother," she said to Lydia. "We do everything we can to keep things like this from happening, and I'll make sure to let the staff know that they need to be especially careful not to let it happen again. Okay?"

Carol smiled, a definite indication that she expected there to be no more discussion.

"Okay," Lydia said with a questioning glance at Meredith. "I'm sorry to have bothered you."

"Oh, no bother," Carol assured her. "That's what we're here for. Now I'd better get back to Mr. Anderson before he decides to finish the game all by himself. You let me know if there's anything else I can do to help. We're always here for you."

"Thanks." Lydia sighed, and she and Meredith walked back to her mother's room. "I guess that explains it all right. I suppose if I hadn't found that letter by now, it's not very likely anyone else will have."

"Maybe," Meredith said, scanning the room again. "Do you know any of the other residents here?"

"Not really. I know Mrs. Carlton next door. Just a little bit, but she and Mom sometimes eat their meals together. I've had dinner or lunch with them a few times."

"How is she?"

"Better than most here, I'd say. I mean, like Mom, she has her good and bad days. She has some issues, but they seem fairly mild in comparison to everyone else. She does a lot better than Mom right now, I can tell you."

"Have you ever heard her mention anyone named Sanders or Russell?"

"Not that I can recall, but it's possible. Those were the names of people who signed in yesterday evening, right?"

"Right. Sanders was the one who supposedly went to visit A-139. Do you think you could introduce me to Mrs. Carlton?"

"Maybe. If she's in her room. If not, we can ask at the nurses' station at the end of the wing. Someone there ought to know where she is right now."

A-139 was right next door. Mrs. Carlton was a bright-eyed sparrow of a woman, tiny and frail looking, but there was a smile on her brightly colored lips and a big black-and-white polka dot bow in her maroon-tipped hair.

"Hello," she said when Lydia knocked on her open door. "You're Sheila's friend."

"I'm her daughter, yes," Lydia said. "My name's—"

"You're Lydia," Mrs. Carlton said, looking very pleased with herself. "I remembered that."

"That's right. I'm Lydia. This is my friend Meredith."

"Hello," Meredith said. "Are you having a good day?"

"I always have a good day," Mrs. Carlton said with a determined lift of her small chin. "That's always what I decide."

Meredith smiled. "That's a good choice to make. Did you have a good day yesterday? I understand you had a visitor."

"That's right, I did. Sheila came to see me for a little while and then we went to the movies."

"Was it only Sheila?" Meredith asked.

Mrs. Carlton shook her head. "No, there were lots of people there."

"No, I mean visiting you in here. Did anyone besides Sheila come visit you in your room yesterday?"

Mrs. Carlton huffed. "Like that ever happens. I don't know when Alexandria came to see me last. I think it's been years."

"Now, wasn't Alexandria here at Christmas?" Lydia asked. "I think I saw her with you at the Christmas dinner."

Mrs. Carlton huffed. "Well, that was at least two months ago. Maybe three."

"Is Alexandria your daughter?" Meredith asked.

Mrs. Carlton nodded. "I have three boys too, but I never much expected to see them anyway."

"But nobody came to see you yesterday?"

"Not anybody. Just Sheila for a while."

"You didn't talk to somebody named Sanders, did you?"

"Sanders?"

Meredith nodded. "I believe her name is Evelyn. Do you know somebody named Evelyn?"

"No." Mrs. Carlton frowned. "Except when I was still in school, but that was a little while ago. Why? Did she say she knew me?"

"No, we were just wondering."

"Where's Sheila anyway?" Mrs. Carlton looked at Lydia. "You should tell her to come over when she can. We can watch that price game they have on TV."

"She's at her physical therapy." Lydia glanced at her watch. "I'd better go over there now. I think I've missed most of it."

"Okay, but you tell her, all right?"

"I'll tell her, Mrs. Carlton. Thanks for letting us come by."

"It was good to meet you," Meredith told the older woman.

When they stepped back into the corridor, Meredith saw Mrs. Bryleigh and Janet coming toward them. Lydia waved, and she and Meredith stood there waiting for them to get to the room.

"I think you might be right about Mrs. Carlton doing fairly well," Meredith said, keeping her voice low. "Except for being a little shaky about dates, she seems pretty lucid."

"She generally is," Lydia said. "Do you think she would have forgotten a visitor if she had one?"

"I'm wondering about that."

Mrs. Bryleigh and Janet reached them then. Mrs. Bryleigh looked exhausted.

"You look like you worked very hard today," Lydia said to her.

"It's not very much fun when you don't come help me," Mrs. Bryleigh said with more than a hint of a pout.

"I'm sorry. I was talking to Meredith and I lost track of the time. We talked to Mrs. Carlton for a little bit too. She says you should come over and watch TV with her if you want to."

Mrs. Bryleigh brightened considerably. "Oh, that would be nice."

"I'm going to have to get back to work pretty soon," Meredith said. "But I was wondering if you happened to see the lady who visited Mrs. Carlton yesterday. Her name was Evelyn."

Mrs. Bryleigh merely looked bewildered.

"Did you see Mrs. Carlton's guest?" Meredith asked Janet.

"No, ma'am," Janet said. "But your mom had her hair and nails done after you left for the day, Lydia. I'm afraid they were running a little bit late, but I did see a couple of people in the hallway when we got back here. I didn't know which room they were visiting."

"Could they have come to visit Mom?" Lydia asked.

"Possibly," Janet said, looking a little bewildered herself. "One of them, a man, was heading down the hallway like he was leaving.

The other one was a woman. She was standing about where I am now, but Sheila's door was shut. She walked away when we got here."

"Did Mrs. Bryleigh seem to recognize her?" Meredith asked.

"She tried to go after her and asked her not to go. She said they hadn't seen each other since her mother's birthday party. The woman just kept walking."

Meredith gave Lydia a significant glance.

"Did she say anything?" Lydia asked Janet.

"I need to sit down," Lydia's mother said, moving her walker forward through the other three standing at the door.

"I'm sorry, Mom," Lydia said. "We were just trying to figure out if you knew the woman who was in the hall by your room yesterday."

Mrs. Bryleigh shuffled to her recliner and sank into it with a relieved sigh before she responded. "What woman?"

"Was she one of the ones you said had been looking through your things?" Lydia asked. "One of the ones you were mad at?"

"Who said I was mad? I'm not mad at anybody."

"Okay, Mom." Lydia sighed and turned back to Meredith and Janet. "I'm sorry. I don't know what she might have seen, if anything."

"There was a woman here yesterday," Janet said. "I can't say for sure who she came to see, but I didn't think anything of it."

Meredith turned to Lydia. "Could she have been someone your mother knows? Family maybe?"

Lydia thought for a moment. "I have a couple of cousins on my father's side. Mom didn't have any brothers or sisters, and I don't remember ever hearing the name Evelyn Sanders."

"But Mrs. Bryleigh thought she knew her," Meredith said, looking at Janet.

"Definitely," Janet said. "I didn't think anything of it. Sometimes our residents see a stranger and imagine that person is a loved one. Is something wrong?"

"Could you say for sure if you've ever seen her here before?"

Janet pursed her lips thoughtfully. "Nooo, I don't think so. But I didn't get more than a glimpse of her. She had long blond hair, if I remember right. Kind of tall."

"What did she have on?"

Janet shrugged. "Nothing particularly memorable. Jeans maybe. Seems like she had on a short-sleeved blouse. Not a T-shirt or a tank top. But she must have been heading out to the parking lot when we saw her, because she had on sunglasses."

Meredith didn't comment on that particular aspect of the description. Sunglasses weren't an uncommon way for someone to avoid being recognized, especially if that someone was a tall, uncommonly beautiful blond with striking green-gold eyes.

Chapter Nine

"Do you remember what time it was?" Meredith tried to keep her expression calm and neutral. "When did you see the woman?"

"After Sheila's daughter left yesterday. Before dinner."

"What about the man?"

"Oh, I barely saw him. But you could always check our visitors' registration if you want to get names. Our activity director, Carol, should be able to help you with that."

"We talked to her already," Meredith said. "Can you tell me anything about him?"

"Not much. He was halfway down the hall when we got here."

"The register says there was a man coming to A-142. Who's in that room?"

"That's Mr. Adams," Janet said. "He has a big family from what I've heard, but he doesn't get many visitors."

"Do you know Mr. Adams?" Meredith asked Lydia.

"No. I've seen him a few times going in and out of his room, but we haven't really spoken."

"Do you think we could talk to him?" Meredith asked Janet. "Just for a minute or two?"

"I don't know why not. He might be in the common room playing cards though." Janet frowned. "Is something going on? Why do you want to know about these people?"

Meredith looked at Lydia, and Lydia gave her a subtle nod.

"We think Mrs. Bryleigh's room might have been searched," Meredith told Janet. "Maybe yesterday evening. Maybe during the night or early this morning."

"No, probably not during the night," Lydia said. "Mom's a light sleeper. She would have woken up and thrown a screaming fit if there had been anybody in her room. Especially if that person had gone through her things and even untucked her sheets."

Meredith nodded. "I suppose you're right about that. So it would have to have been sometime during the day when she was away from her room."

"What makes you think there was somebody in her room in the first place?" Janet asked.

Meredith and Lydia went over everything they had found that made it seem like there had been an uninvited guest.

Janet stared at them for a moment, and then she snorted. "That's nothing. That's more than likely just Alice."

"Alice?" Meredith asked.

"I'm not supposed to tell tales," Janet said, lowering her voice. "But Alice has been known to go into other residents' rooms. She doesn't generally take anything, and we have no idea what she could be looking for. She always denies doing anything, but she's been caught at it more than once. We try to keep an eye on her, but we can't watch everybody all the time. She doesn't mean any harm."

"Does she live in this wing?"

Janet glanced around briefly. "Yes, she does, but really, please don't say anything. I don't want to get written up for talking about it, but I thought you ought to know it's nothing to worry about. Was anything taken?"

"No," Lydia said. "Not as far as I can tell. Mom doesn't have anything valuable here anyway. We're just concerned that someone might have been looking for a keepsake of Mom's. Nothing that would be of value to anyone but our family, but it's important to us."

"Like what?" Janet asked.

Meredith gave Lydia a covert warning look.

"Well, it doesn't matter," Lydia said, suddenly smiling. "As I said, I don't think anything was taken, and if it's just another resident, I'm sure there's no real harm done."

"We'd still like to talk to Mr. Adams, if you don't mind helping us find him," Meredith put in.

"Not a problem," Janet said, "and please, don't say anything about what I just told you. About Alice, I mean."

"Our lips are sealed," Meredith said. "Right, Lydia?"

Lydia nodded.

"Thanks," Janet said. "Let's go over to Mr. Adams's room and see if he's there right now."

"We'll be back in a few minutes," Lydia said, going into the room to give her mother a kiss on the cheek.

"Are you going to find those people?" Mrs. Bryleigh asked. "The ones who were here yesterday?" She pulled Lydia a little closer. "Are they looking for that letter?"

"We'll talk about that when I come back, okay?"

"Well, I won't let them come in this time," Mrs. Bryleigh said. "That woman tried to pretend that I knew her."

"It's all right, Mom. I'll be right back, and we can talk about it."

Lydia gave her mother a brief hug, and then Janet took them across the hall and to the room marked A-142.

"Mr. Adams?" she said, knocking on the door frame as she leaned in to look into the room. "Are you busy?"

Mr. Adams was a tall, lanky man with a large aquiline nose and a full head of white, curly hair. He looked up at Janet, obviously annoyed.

"I'm watching the baseball game. Y'all come back when it's over."

"We only need to talk to you for a minute," Janet said, going into the room.

Meredith and Lydia followed her.

With a huff, Mr. Adams put the game on pause and looked at them. "Well?"

"I'm sorry to interrupt your game, Mr. Adams," Meredith said with an ingratiating smile. "I was just wondering if you could tell us about the visitor you had yesterday evening."

"What visitor?" Mr. Adams snapped.

"Well, that's what we'd like to find out. According to the register, someone signed in saying he was coming to visit you. Didn't he come?"

"No. My grandson comes to see me on Sunday afternoons. We go to the baseball game if there is one."

"He never comes any other days?" Meredith asked him, looking over at Janet questioningly.

"No," Mr. Adams said. "He'd tell me if he was going to."

"Do you know someone named Sam Russell?" Meredith asked him.

He shook his head. "Did he say he knows me?"

"No. That was the name on the register yesterday. The one who was supposed to be coming to this room."

"Is Mike supposed to come see you on Sunday this week?" Janet asked. "Will you be going to the ball game?"

"He said so, but if they don't win today, it's not much going to matter what they do Sunday."

Without another word, he turned back to the television set and started the game going again. Clearly he was finished with the conversation.

Meredith thanked him, and with a shake of her head, Janet led them back over to Mrs. Bryleigh's room.

"He's pretty serious about his baseball," she said.

"What about visitors?" Meredith asked her. "Is he likely to forget having someone come to see him?"

"That's hard to say. We're specifically a memory care facility, so we try not to put too much pressure on any of our residents to remember anything. As you know with your own mother, Lydia, they have their good and bad days. Many of them are more likely to remember something that happened seventy years ago than something that happened yesterday."

Meredith thought for a long moment.

"Does Mr. Adams's grandson usually come get him on Sundays, like he said?" she asked Janet finally.

"Mike? Yeah, I think so. If there's a game anyway. If the weather is good and not too hot."

"Are you on duty this Sunday?"

"Oh yeah," Janet said. "No rest for the weary."

"Do you think you could ask Mike if his grandfather knows a Sam Russell? I mean, if he does, that'll pretty much settle that the man you saw was the one who signed in to visit his room."

"And if not?" Lydia asked.

"If not, we'll have to keep trying to find out who he was and what he wanted here."

"What about the other one? The woman?"

"Yeah, that may be more of a problem. Is Mrs. Carlton's daughter really as bad as she says about not coming to visit?"

"She doesn't come often, that's true enough," Janet said. "But no, her last visit wasn't as far back as Christmas either. I'd guess she visits Mrs. Carlton about once every month or two. She doesn't stay long when she's here."

"Does anyone else visit her?" Meredith asked. "Even just once in a while?"

"I know she had a niece and nephew come a couple of times. I'm not sure if that was an actual nephew or if he was the niece's husband. But they did come."

"Could the woman you saw yesterday possibly have been the niece?"

Janet's face puckered as she thought. "We get a lot of people in and out of here, so it's hard to remember all of them. But it seems to me that the niece had long dark hair. The woman's yesterday was blond. I'm sure of that much."

Meredith was careful not to look over at Lydia just then. If Janet thought there was something serious going on, she might clam up entirely until she had official permission to talk to them.

"We appreciate your help. Could you possibly do one more thing for us?"

"If I can."

Meredith took out one of her business cards. "You said you'd ask Mr. Adams's grandson if he knows a Sam Russell. Could you ask him about Evelyn Sanders too?"

"Okay."

"Could you ask Mrs. Carlton's daughter if she knows Evelyn Sanders or Sam Russell? Wait a minute." Meredith wrote the two names along with the related room numbers on the back of the card and then handed the card to Janet. "I don't know when her daughter might come by. You said she wasn't here often."

"I think the last time I saw her was in May." Janet gave the back of the card only a cursory glance and then put it in her pocket. "But yeah, I can ask her if I happen to see her. And I'll make sure to talk to Mr. Adams's grandson when he's here on Sunday."

"I really appreciate it. I'm not trying to pry into anyone's business. I only want to make sure that these visitors really did come to see the people they claimed to be visiting."

"Of course. And I'll let you know as soon as I have anything. But, you know, just between us."

"Sure."

"You already talked to Carol, right?" Janet turned to Lydia. "You told her about someone being in your mom's room?"

Lydia nodded.

"I'm sure she'll have a word with the staff about it, but my bet would still be on Alice." Janet patted her shoulder. "We want our residents and their families to feel like they and their things are safe here."

Lydia and Meredith both thanked her and waited for her to walk away.

"What do you think?" Lydia asked.

"It's hard to say. It could be Alice like Janet said." They walked back into Mrs. Bryleigh's apartment.

Lydia looked at the floor. "I should never have said anything about the letter in that newspaper article, should I?"

"Do you mean the letter about my grandfather?" Mrs. Bryleigh leaned forward in her recliner. "Did you find it yet, Lydia?"

"Not yet, Mom. Have you thought any more about where it might be?"

"Oh, no, honey. I know I put it somewhere safe so it wouldn't get lost, but that was a while ago. And Matt, well, he said it was important that nobody knew about it, just that he wanted me to know that Granddad didn't take those jewels."

"I understand, Mom." Lydia leaned over and kissed her mother's temple. "We'll see what we can do."

***

"We did some more searching once Janet left," Meredith told Julia once she was back in the office. "No luck."

"And Lydia's mother never mentioned this letter before she moved in to White Oak?"

"I don't think so. Lydia said her mother's been there for eleven months, and she started mentioning this letter a few weeks ago."

Julia leaned her elbow on her desk and propped her chin on it. "Of course that doesn't necessarily mean she hid the letter recently. And you have no proof that either of those people Janet saw were ever in Lydia's mother's room, right?"

"It seems a little far-fetched at this point," Meredith said, "but when I heard that one visitor was a tall blond, I couldn't help thinking of Vanessa Van Orden. Maybe her offer to send something to Mrs. Bryleigh wasn't so altruistic after all."

"What was it Lydia's mother said about the letter? That Matt knew what was going on?"

"Sounds ominous, doesn't it?"

"Might be enough to make someone like Vanessa worry." Julia tapped one neatly manicured finger against her lips. "But she doesn't seem like the type to do this kind of job herself, do you think?"

"It seems to me like someone with her money and influence would have one of her people do it for her. But maybe she did it herself exactly because it seems so unlikely that she would do it herself."

"She pretty much shrugged the letter off when we talked about it at her office."

Meredith nodded. "And she seemed very willing to help in any way she could about the jewel theft." She caught a little breath. "Ooh. I need to check and see if her assistant has sent us anything yet."

"Good idea. I was working on the Bates case, and I totally forgot about it." Julia turned eagerly to the laptop that was already open on her desk. "They're supposed to send everything to both of us, so let me look here." A few seconds later, her eyes lit. "Here's something from DinahBrownfield@VanOrdenMM. That has to be it."

With a click, she had the email open, and Meredith read it over her shoulder.

Dear Mrs. Bellefontaine and Mrs. Foley,

Here is some of the information you requested from us regarding James Brandon's employment record and other information regarding the theft of the Van Orden jewels in 1918.

We're still searching our records for additional information, but we thought you would like to have this to start with. We should be back to you soon with more.

Mrs. Van Orden wanted me to let you know she is happy to help you in any way she can to get the information you're looking for. She would love to know what you find out.

Best regards,

Dinah Brownfield,

Executive Administrative Assistant

Van Orden Munitions & Manufacturing

"Well, that doesn't tell us much," Meredith said. "What exactly did she send?"

Julia scrolled down to the attachments. "Let me download them and we'll see."

They were all images. Some were actual photographs. Others were scans of documents.

"Oh, look." Julia made one of the photos full screen.

"Wow," Meredith breathed.

The photograph was of a white-haired, elderly woman in a dark gown. She was seated before a heavy-looking velvet curtain with fringe on it, and to her left was a potted vine with delicate leaves and tendrils sitting on a Grecian column.

The woman had both hands resting lightly at her throat, effectively showing off what must have been a vast fortune in jewels. She wore multiple rings set with large precious stones. Both wrists were encircled by several wide bejeweled bracelets, and the diamonds and pearls in her earrings fell almost to her shoulders. Nestled in her upswept hair was a heavy tiara of diamonds and some large dark-colored stones—rubies or sapphires probably.

"Wow," Meredith breathed again.

"I know," Julia said. "And that necklace. What do you think those stones are?"

"I don't know. It's hard to tell in black and white. They could be any of the dark precious gems or even a combination of all of them. She must have been quite a sight to see in all that."

"You don't think she went out like that, do you?"

Meredith grinned. "Half of that would knock your eyes out, but she probably wanted to let everyone know how well off she was." She thought for a moment. "I wonder where she was from. If she was from the South, how in the world did she manage to keep those jewels in the family after the war?"

"Maybe she was from the North," Julia said with a shrug. "Or maybe they were extremely fortunate to come through the war with that kind of wealth and keep it afterward. Whatever it was, it was passed down to Thomas Van Orden."

"Does it say exactly who she is?"

Julia glanced at the file name. "This says Elizabeth Myrtle Hunt, 1862. I'm guessing this was Thomas Van Orden's grandmother."

"I'll look that up to be sure." Meredith made a note on Julia's nearly used-up notepad. "But you're probably right. She must have had quite a jewelry box to put all that in."

"Wait, here's another one."

Julia opened another picture. It showed the same woman in the same dress in the same location. The potted plant was gone, and the woman had her hands resting on top of the column. She was, if possible, draped in an even more magnificent array of rings and bracelets and earrings than she had been in the first picture. Around her neck was a golden collar studded with what must have been hundreds of diamonds, a collar so tall that she couldn't possibly have bent her neck enough to allow her to see the floor.

"Good grief," Meredith said.

Julia snickered. "I didn't think you could get more elaborate than that first tiara. I don't know how she kept from toppling over in this one."

This tiara was tall and imposing, more suited to a czarina at some state occasion than a wealthy American woman, no matter how grand a ball she might have wanted to attend.

"Okay, so they obviously had money, and whoever took those jewels made quite a haul. What else is in the attachments?"

Before Julia could answer her, the office phone rang. They both paused, waiting for Carmen to put the call through.

"It's for either of you," Carmen told Meredith when she picked up. "He said he only has a minute, and he wouldn't give a name."

"That sounds interesting. I'll take it." Meredith put the phone on speaker. "This is Meredith Bellefontaine. How may I help you?"

There was silence for a moment and then an audible breath.

"This is Jack."

Chapter Ten

MEREDITH CAUGHT A STARTLED BREATH.

"Jack. Jack from Van Orden Munitions?"

Julia's mouth dropped open.

"Look," Jack said, his voice just above a whisper. "I can't say much. Did you check out KBMJ?"

"We're working on it. Do you have any more information for us?"

"Only that Jarvi's a front. He thinks he runs manufacturing, but he only sees what he's allowed to see."

"Okay." Meredith quickly took notes. "Who runs it then? What proof do you have of this? What's going on behind the scenes?"

"Jarvi—" Jack huffed in frustration. "I have to go. I'll see what I can get for you. I want this blown wide open. It's gone on too long."

"But—"

"I can't get caught talking to you. I'll be back in touch when and how I can."

There was a click and a dial tone. Meredith hung up the phone.

"Wow," Julia said.

"Yeah. Wow." Meredith pushed the INTERCOM button. "Hey, Carmen?"

"Yes?"

"Will you find out what you can about the number that just called?"

"Okay."

"Anyway," Meredith told Julia, "I'd really like to go talk to him."

"If he's blowing the whistle on the company for whatever reason, he sure doesn't seem ready for Vanessa to know that quite yet."

"True. I guess all we can do on this end is find out as much as possible on our own and wait for him to call back."

Carmen came to stand in the office door. "The number belongs to Van Orden Munitions. He's the guy who wanted you to check on what they're doing, right?"

Meredith nodded.

"Isn't it pretty stupid for him to call right from their building? Anybody could overhear the call."

"Maybe he called from somebody else's office or somewhere in a maintenance area," Julia suggested.

"He sounded pretty jumpy," Meredith said. "Wherever he was. I wish I'd asked him to meet us somewhere we could talk."

"He doesn't seem brave enough for that." Julia frowned. "What did he say about wanting something blown wide open?"

"Just that. He didn't have time for much more. I'm wondering now what's set him off. He said before he's worked for Van Orden for about fifteen years. Why does he want them exposed now?"

"Do you want me to check on anything else?" Carmen asked.

"Not right now," Meredith said. "Thank you."

"*De nada.*"

Carmen went back to her desk, and Meredith looked at the photo of Thomas Van Orden's bejeweled grandmother that was still on Julia's computer monitor.

"For now I guess we see what else Vanessa had sent to us."

Julia opened the next photo. This one showed a heavyset middle-aged man in a dapper striped suit with a substantial gold chain draped from one side of his brocade vest to the watch pocket on the other side. He was shaking hands with a younger man, a man maybe in his midthirties. The younger man was slightly built and not very tall, and he was neatly if not expensively dressed, but there was an expression of pride on his thin, mustached face.

Julia read the name of the picture file. "'Thomas Van Orden—James Brandon—1915.'"

"So that's Lydia's great-grandfather," Meredith said.

"With Vanessa's father-in-law," Julia added with a snicker. "It's still crazy to think that she's only in her forties."

"She obviously knew what she was doing when she married David Van Orden and ended up with a fortune. But what else did she send us?"

"Matt's handwriting," Julia said.

The picture was of the inside of a faded birthday card. The saccharine verse was printed, but written under it in neat, decisive, masculine hand was *You're a champ, Dad. All the best and more, Matt.*

"It's not much," Meredith said, "but if we ever do find the letter, at least we'll have something to compare it to. What's next?"

Julia opened another of the attachments. "This looks like a paybook."

The image was of a tall, narrow ledger page with names listed in the left column in a spidery old-fashioned copperplate. It took only a moment for Meredith to find James Brandon's.

"April 16, 1915," she said. "He's listed as secretary to Mr. Van Orden."

"And he was paid a grand sum of fifteen dollars," Julia added. "Looks like that was for the week."

"That seems like so little."

"Not really. He wouldn't have been rich, but he was probably comfortable enough on that."

"Unless he lost a lot on gambling the way Lydia said he was accused of."

"True." Julia opened the next attachment. "This one is Matt Van Orden. It says 'Matt Van Orden—Calvin Bean—Tyler Porter.'"

The picture showed three young men in T-shirts and running shorts who had numbers pinned to their chests. They were all smiling and had their arms thrown over each other's shoulders. In the background was a stadium, and alongside them were men in straw boaters and dark suits standing at the side of the track.

"They look like they just finished a race," Meredith said. "I wonder which one is which."

"The one on the left is Matt, if the name of the file shows the right order, but I'm not sure if that's the case. The picture from the paper wasn't all that clear."

All three of them had lean runners' bodies and long muscular legs. They all looked as if they were still in their teens.

"Go back to the picture of Thomas Van Orden," Meredith said after a moment's consideration. "Can you put the pictures side by side?"

Julia obliged. "It's hard to tell much with these old pictures, but I'd rule out the one on the right. He doesn't look like Thomas at all."

Meredith frowned, unsatisfied. "Matt could look like his mother's side of the family. Are there any other photographs?"

Julia opened the next attachment, which turned out to be a picture of a woman dressed in a ball gown with enormous puffed sleeves and a low neckline.

"Look at that tiny waist," she said.

"Look at those enormous jewels," Meredith replied. "At least she's not wearing the whole collection all at once like the other woman was. Who is she?"

"Catherine Palmer Van Orden, 1896."

"So she's Thomas Van Orden's first wife. Matt's mother."

"Are you sure?" Julia asked.

"I saw her name in one of the articles Spencer gave us copies of. I have it in my notes to see if I could find pictures of her and Thomas and Matt, and I guess we have them."

"Except we're not sure about Matt yet," Julia reminded her. "Or…"

She opened the last of the attachments.

"Ah, there he is. Matthew Andrew Van Orden, 1915. At least that's the name of the file."

Meredith studied the picture. If it had been taken in 1915, Matt would have been about seventeen years old. He was dressed in a suit and tie, his dark hair slicked back, his expression serious. This was definitely the young man on the left in the earlier picture, and she could see a definite resemblance to Thomas Van Orden in the strong nose and chin. But there was something of his mother in him too, in the thickly lashed eyes and handsome mouth.

"It's too bad," she said with a sigh.

"What?"

"Too bad that he died in the war. I wonder what happened to his two friends in that picture."

"They probably went into the service too," Julia said. "Maybe they even joined up together. I hope they at least made it back home."

Meredith looked at the computer screen again. "Nothing else?"

"Nope. They sort of set the stage for us, but there's not a lot of information here that's going to help us solve this case."

"Maybe they'll come up with more soon. It hasn't been very long since we talked to Vanessa in the first place."

"I guess we could ask Dinah to see if she can find more information on the household staff at the time of the theft." Julia frowned. "Was there any information about them in those articles you went through?"

"Nothing specific. No names. All it said was that there was a butler, an estate manager, a cook, a housekeeper, and three maids."

"I'll reply to Dinah's message and ask her to find out who all was working at the estate at that time. Maybe they can come up with some names. If one of them suddenly bought a yacht and sailed off to Aruba right after the theft, we may have a lead."

"Good idea," Meredith said. "I can see somebody taking those jewels and keeping his or her head down until the case was considered solved and then later on taking off when nobody would make the connection between that and the theft."

"Your cell phone," Carmen called from across the hall.

Startled, Meredith hurried back to her office where she had dropped her purse when she came in. She saw the caller ID and answered before the call could go to voice mail.

"Quin. Hi."

"Did I catch you at a bad time?" Quin asked, a touch of concern in his baritone voice.

"Oh, no. I was in Julia's office. How are you?"

"I'm doing all right. Have you been busy?"

"It's been an intriguing day," she told him. "Did you see that article in the *Tribune* about the woman trying to solve a hundred-year-old jewel theft?"

"As a matter of fact, I did. I noticed you were recommended to her. Do you two have it solved yet?"

"Only getting started. Right now, we're trying to figure out who's who and who else besides our client's great-grandfather could have actually taken the jewels."

He chuckled. "Sounds like a challenge if nothing else. Good luck with it."

"What have you been up to?" she asked.

"I have a problem," he said with a sigh. "I'm hoping you can help me solve it."

"If I can. What's going on?"

"Well, I accidentally bought two tickets instead of one to this concert tomorrow night, and I was hoping you might like the extra one."

She couldn't stop a grin from spreading over her face. "You accidentally bought two," she said, trying to sound stern. "And you didn't realize it until now?"

"As a matter of fact, I did buy them very recently. A friend of mine was going to go with his wife, but she's not feeling well, and he hated for them to go to waste. I'd considered getting tickets earlier, but they sold out before I could, so I never mentioned it to you."

"And I'm supposed to drop everything at the last minute?"

"Only if you'd like to go," he said.

"Maybe," she said, knowing already that she was going to say yes. "The philharmonic?"

"Nope. Guess again."

She huffed. "I don't know. Tell me."

"It's a Beatles tribute band. They sing and play everything live. I've heard it's really an amazing concert. Like being there for the real thing sixty years ago. What do you think?"

"I think it sounds like a lot of fun," she said. "I saw a clip about one of those groups on TV a year or two ago. It's incredible how close to the real thing they sound."

"Maybe these are the same guys."

He told her the name, and she gasped.

"Yes! It's the same group! I'd love to see them!"

"So, is that a yes?"

"It's a definite yes and a big thank you for thinking of me."

"I think about you a lot," he said softly.

For a moment she didn't reply, didn't breathe. Then she told herself she wasn't fifteen anymore and not to be ridiculous.

"I hope they're happy thoughts," she said lightly.

"Always," he told her. "So what do you think? Would you like to have dinner first? We can go to that Italian place you like and then to the concert."

"That would be wonderful. Yes. What time?"

"The concert's at eight. If we don't want to rush through dinner, maybe I'd better pick you up at six. We can always take our time over coffee if we finish eating too early. Okay?"

"Six would be great." She took a deep breath. This was only a casual date. Nothing serious. "I'll be ready."

"Great. I'll see you tomorrow at six."

She clutched her phone in both hands once he ended the call, excitement and dread swirling through her in equal measure. *"I think about you a lot."* She could still hear the velvet smoothness of his voice when he'd said it. What was she going to do? What did she want to do?

She squeezed her eyes shut. "I'll go and have fun," she said half under her breath. "I don't have to make any big commitment right this minute. I'll go and have fun."

"Where are you going?"

Meredith felt her face turn hot, and she turned around to see Julia standing in the doorway, a mischievous smile on her face.

"Oh. Nothing important. Just going out tomorrow night. Not a big deal."

There was archness now in Julia's smile. "With Quin?"

Meredith laughed and sank down into one of the chairs in front of her desk. "Yes, with Quin."

"Where are you going?"

"You've heard of that Beatles tribute band, right? He has tickets for tomorrow night, and we're going to have dinner at my favorite Italian place by the river before the concert. It sounds like a lot of fun."

"Then why the anguish?"

Meredith bit her lip, and her face turned even hotter. "He said he thought about me a lot."

"I could have told you that already."

"Do you think it means…" Meredith winced. "What I think it means?"

"I think it means exactly that. He likes you and not in a just-friends way."

"I know. Now what do I do?"

"The best thing you can do is get back to work on the Van Orden case. You made yourself a list of questions after you read all those articles about them, right?"

Meredith nodded.

"Well, you sit down and start finding answers for all those questions and you make notes about the questions those answers raise. That should keep you busy until tomorrow night."

"Right. You're absolutely right. I need to get back to work and stop worrying about tomorrow night." Meredith sighed again. "But what am I going to do tomorrow night?"

"Just what you already decided," Julia said, giving her a brief hug. "Go and have fun."

***

In spite of her swirling thoughts, Meredith sat at her desk and made a determined effort to continue work on the Van Orden case. She wondered what was going on with Jack and what evidence he might have for them. Then she thought again about the pictures she and Julia had been looking at and who might have been in a position to steal those jewels besides Lydia's great-grandfather. She thought too about Lydia's mother's insistence that she had received a letter from Matt Van Orden that exonerated James Brandon. What must it have been like for Mrs. Bryleigh and her mother having to deal with him being branded a thief and a convict?

A moment later, she was dialing her phone. If anybody might have some information about the staff at the Van Orden estate or about James Brandon's family, it would be Maggie Lu.

The phone rang several times, and Meredith was sure it was about to go to voice mail, but then Maggie Lu answered.

"Meredith. How are you?"

Meredith wanted to tell her about her upcoming "real date," but she decided that would keep for another time. She had work to do.

"I'm doing fine. How are you? I hope I'm not interrupting anything."

"No, not really. I just this minute put a cake in the oven. It's the perfect time for me to put my feet up and take a break."

"Oooh. What kind of cake did you make?"

"Oh, girl, you'd like this one. It's just a lemon cake with a lemon drizzle on top, but I cook it in a pan that has 3D lemons and leaves on top, and it's the prettiest thing. Besides that, it's really rich and moist and fresh tasting. Remind me next time we all get together, and I'll make another one so you can taste it."

"I would love that. Sounds like I need your recipe too."

"I'll send it to you as soon as we're through talking. How's that? It's really simple, but you get a lot of bang for your buck. People think it's hard to do."

"I guess it tastes the same even without the fancy pan."

"Sure, but I like to impress the other church ladies."

Meredith chuckled. "There's that. Listen, if you have a few minutes, I'd love to ask you about a few things regarding the Van Orden case."

"Sure. The longer we talk, the more time I have to not go and clean up the kitchen."

"Great. You remember the article about the jewel theft and everything."

"Yes."

"Lydia Cooper is our client, and her mother is Sheila Bryleigh. Have you ever heard of her?"

"That name does sound familiar," Maggie Lu said. "Let me think a minute."

"Sheila's grandfather is the one who was sent to prison for stealing those jewels."

"Oh yes. I don't know how helpful this will be, but I do remember now. I was still in school, but I remember people talking about Sheila Parker, as she was then. They never said anything about her without saying how her grandfather died in prison. And then they wondered about 'that nice Mr. Bryleigh' from the high school going ahead and marrying her."

"Her husband was a teacher?"

"He was the football coach and a history teacher. Everybody liked him. I guess that helped Sheila in the long run, and the talk did eventually die off, but I know it was hard on her. I hadn't thought about it much, but looking back on it now, I'm sorry people added to the load she already had to carry. No wonder her daughter wants to find out what really happened in that theft. It would be a shame if Sheila died and never knew the truth."

"I think so too," Meredith said. "That's why I want to do all I can to solve this case, but so far we don't know much. One of the reasons I called you is because I'm trying to figure out who else might have had a chance to steal those jewels. I was wondering if you knew anything about who all worked at the Van Orden estate at that time. I know that's pretty far back."

"That was a long time ago for sure. I never did find anything on Granny Luv's relative who worked there. She also had a friend whose sister worked out there for a while, but I don't recall her name off-hand. And I couldn't swear right off when that was, whether it was before or after that robbery. But let me see what I can find out. I know one of them has a great-granddaughter who has a little restaurant in town. She and Charlene get together sometimes to gripe about the restaurant business."

Meredith snickered. Maggie Lu's daughter owned the Down-home Diner, and it was definitely a demanding job.

"I can give Charlene a call if you want," Maggie Lu added. "The great-granddaughter's name is Daisy Dupree, but that's about all I know. I can get her number from Charlene and then ask her what she knows about the Van Ordens."

"That would be a huge help, if you don't mind."

"Not at all. You've got me curious about it now too. If she's up for it, would you like me to arrange for you to talk to her? I guess you and Julia and I could go eat at her restaurant, and maybe she'd have time to talk to us for a few minutes."

"Oh, that would be great. Just about any time would work for me. Whenever you think would be good."

"Okay. I can't do it tomorrow though. That cake I have in the oven is for a church picnic at noon. I guess we could do it tomorrow evening, but I doubt I'll be hungry again by then. Not after one of our picnics."

"No, I can't tomorrow. I, uh, well, I guess I have a date."

Maggie Lu snorted. "You guess?"

"All right, I do have a date."

"With Quin? Or am I further behind than I thought I was?"

"Yes, with Quin." Meredith took a quick breath. "We're going to dinner and then to a concert."

"That sounds like a date to me," Maggie Lu said. "Now don't tell me you're nervous. It's Quin, you know."

"Yes, I know. But…it's Quin!"

"You're going to be fine, all right? Just see what happens. Either you'll realize you're only friends or you'll realize there's something more. Either way, you're okay."

"I know, but thank you for saying it. I guess I'm more excited and scared than I thought I would be."

"Come on now, it's not any different than the other times you two have gone out. As friends."

"But it could be. That's what's scary."

"Well, don't let it be scary. Go and enjoy yourself. You'll be able to tell if you really feel something for Quin if you'll just stay open to the possibility."

"I know you're right," Meredith said.

She still felt excited and scared and knew it was kind of ridiculous to feel that way over a casual date. But, after all, it wasn't the date. She was sure the date itself would be fun. It was the idea of finally letting go of the idea that Ron was her one and only and that maybe, just maybe, there might be room in her heart for someone else.

"*I think about you a lot.*"

She heard his low voice again, and it turned warm inside her heart. It was hard to imagine that he would say something like that if he wanted to only be friends.

"Meredith?" Maggie Lu said.

Meredith laughed breathlessly. "Sorry. What did you say?"

"I was wondering if you and Julia might want to go talk to Daisy after church on Sunday. But I guess you've got other things on your mind." She chuckled.

"Oh, hush," Meredith said good naturedly. "Sunday would be fine with me. I'll check with Julia and get back to you on the time, okay?"

"And then you can tell us all about your big date."

"Be nice to me," Meredith said, "or I'm not telling either of you anything."

Maggie Lu chuckled. "You go and have a good time, and keep your heart open. You don't want to miss out on something that could be wonderful."

"I know. I know. Thanks, Maggie Lu. And I'll get back to you about Sunday, okay?"

"You do that, and say hi to Quin for me."

"Definitely," Meredith said. "Talk to you soon."

She smiled as she ended the call. It was always good to chat with Maggie Lu. She was so down-to-earth and easy to talk to.

Meredith's thoughts turned to her plans for tomorrow night, but she shook her head and turned them again toward the case she was working on.

She got up and walked to Julia's office. "Hey," she said, leaning on the doorjamb. "Are you busy Sunday after church?"

Julia looked up from her computer screen. "Not really. What's going on?"

"I just talked to Maggie Lu."

"You did?"

"Yeah," Meredith said. "You know we were talking about finding out who else could have taken the Van Orden jewels, and I thought Maggie Lu might know somebody related to somebody who had worked for the family at that time."

"If anybody knows, it'll be Maggie Lu," Julia agreed. "And she said?"

"Evidently Charlene knows someone who's the great-granddaughter of someone who worked for the Van Ordens. Maggie Lu isn't a hundred percent sure exactly when they worked there. She doesn't even remember their names, but she's hoping we can talk to this woman on Sunday and find out a little more."

"Did you already set up a time to meet with this person?"

"Actually, she has a restaurant in town. That's how Charlene knows her. Maggie Lu had a great idea about us going to eat at that restaurant and hopefully getting a chance to talk to her for a few minutes while we're there. That way we can all three get a chance to hear what she has to say and maybe think of more things to ask her. What do you think?"

"Works for me," Julia said. "Beau can find something in the fridge he can heat up for lunch if he wants. He'll be fine. I'm sure there's a golf tournament or something on that he'll want to watch.

When he turns one of those on, Bunny immediately gets in his lap, because she knows he won't be moving for hours."

Meredith chuckled. "That's settled then. I'll text Maggie Lu and let her know we're on. I don't even know which restaurant it is, so she'll have to give me the details."

"That's fine. We can meet her there."

"That'll work. I'll get the information and let you know."

Meredith started texting as she walked back down the hall. Then, once she hit SEND, she got herself a fresh cup of coffee and started back to work on the case.

First she opened her email and the message Vanessa Van Orden's assistant had sent. She opened each of the attachments and studied them, again writing down the questions they brought to her mind.

Was there more to the jewelry collection than what was shown in the photographs? Maybe there had been a detailed list given to the police at the time. Would the Van Ordens still have record of that? She'd have to ask Dinah.

She looked at the picture of the three young men standing together. They were healthy looking, so it was almost certain they had all been in the war. She knew Matt Van Orden had been killed not very long after the jewel theft. What had happened to his two friends? If they were buddies, it seemed very likely that they would have been in and out of the Van Orden home several times. Could either of them have had anything to do with the missing jewelry?

She brought up a site that would let you search military records back as far as the revolutionary war, or so it claimed. There was a seven-day free trial, so she decided to give it a try. If it proved to be useful, there was no reason why the agency shouldn't subscribe to the service.

Once she got through the sign-up process, she put in the name Matthew Andrew Van Orden, his birth date, and his hometown of Savannah, Georgia. Soon she had his enlistment date and where he had been assigned for the short time he'd been in the military. At the end of the report, she found what she most wanted to know.

Killed when Troopship Otranto *sank near the Island of Islay off the Scottish Coast, 6 October, 1918.*

Meredith looked at her notes and sighed. He had been only twenty years old.

She brought up the track meet picture once more and jotted down the names of Matt's two friends. Calvin Benn and Tyler Porter. She started with Porter, assuming he was the same age as Matt and was from Savannah.

There were two men from Savannah with the name Tyler Porter, both born 1898, the same year as Matt Van Orden. She looked at both records and found that one had joined the navy and had been given an honorable discharge in 1919. The other...

She stared at the screen in disbelief.

Killed when Troopship Otranto *sank near the Island of Islay off the Scottish Coast, 6 October, 1918.*

Maybe he and Matt had signed up together and had ended up on the *Otranto* together. Evidently, so had Benn, but there was a slight difference in the information about him.

Believed killed when Troopship Otranto *sank near the Island of Islay off the Scottish Coast, 6 October, 1918.*

She read it over twice.

Believed killed.

Believed.

Chapter Eleven

"I JUST HAD A CRAZY idea," Meredith said as she hurried into Julia's office.

Julia didn't look up. "Wouldn't be the first time."

"I'm serious."

"So am I." Julia finally cracked a smile. "Tell me your idea."

Meredith perched herself on the edge of one of the chairs in front of Julia's desk. "I was looking into the military records for Thomas Van Orden's son Matt, and yes, I found out he was killed during World War I."

"Mmmkay. I'm not seeing the crazy in that idea."

"No, the crazy part is this. You know that picture of him and his friends at that track meet?"

"Yeah."

"I figured his friends had to be in good enough shape to go into the military too, being runners and all, so I looked them up. All three of them were on the same ship, the *Otranto*, that was wrecked off the coast of Scotland."

"Okay, and?"

"And here's the crazy part. What if one of them took those jewels?"

Julia's forehead wrinkled. "What?"

"They probably had access to the Van Orden home on many opportunities. The jewels could have been stolen well before the theft was discovered. Why couldn't one of them have taken them, knowing he'd be out of the country before he'd be found out and knowing he probably wouldn't even be suspected?"

"But why? It seems pretty likely that, if he and the other boy were friends with Matt, they would all have been reasonably well off."

"Maybe. Maybe not. Maybe the thief got in trouble gambling or something. It evidently happened to James Brandon, and that seems to have been enough to have him convicted of the theft. Or maybe he didn't think his allowance was enough for him. Or maybe there was a girl involved, either one who was in trouble or one who was very expensive to keep. There could be a lot of reasons."

Before she could say anything more, the office phone rang. Noticing that Carmen was on the other line, Julia answered it.

"Magnolia Investigations. This is Julia."

Julia got a funny look on her face and then hung up.

Meredith looked at her expectantly.

"Wrong number, supposedly," Julia said, jotting down the number from the caller ID. "A woman."

Meredith shrugged.

"A woman with a slight lisp."

Meredith glanced at the number and then checked her notes. "Calling from the same number Jack called from."

Julia's forehead puckered. "Could it have been Dinah? Vanessa's assistant?"

"Could be. Checking on who Jack was talking to?"

"Probably. I wonder if they know it was Jack or just overheard a few words before he took off."

"Hmm. Hard to say. I guess we'll know if he manages to call us back." Meredith shook her head. "Should we risk checking on him again at the Van Orden Building?"

"He might lose his job or worse for talking to us."

"True," Meredith said. "Maybe we'd better stay clear of the company offices for now and concentrate on the jewel theft."

"Good idea," Julia said. "Were there any questions about Matt's friends in those articles Spencer gave you? Any mention of alternate suspects at all?"

"None. And the jewels weren't insured, so there's no question of insurance fraud by Van Orden himself."

"Not insured? You're kidding."

"Nope. He told the police he didn't believe in it, not when he was well able to see to his own property himself."

"And evidently no one even thought to wonder about his son, seeing that he had so recently died in service to his country. But it could have been him." Julia frowned. "And if that's the case, then all that jewelry more than likely ended up at the bottom of the ocean."

"But that's where my crazy idea comes in. What if one of them didn't die in that wreck?"

Julia's frown deepened. "What?"

"According to the records, one of them, Calvin Benn, was *believed* killed. I guess that means they didn't recover a body."

Julia leaned forward a little in her chair. "Then he could have disappeared somewhere in Scotland or, really, anywhere in that part of the world, and lived comfortably the rest of his life."

"Unless, of course, he really did die in that wreck and the jewels are, in fact, at the bottom of the ocean."

"Or unless the boys had nothing to do with the theft at all."

"But one of them could have," Meredith insisted.

"Maybe it was one of the ones we know was killed at the time. And how would someone like that have carted around that much jewelry in the military?"

Meredith sighed. "Okay, maybe it's unlikely. I told you it was a crazy idea. It still makes me wonder."

October 10, 1918
Ballycastle, Ireland

Their American refugee slept the clock round and more. Aileen had found him in the evening of the day before yesterday, and now it was morning for the second time. In the time since, she had managed to get a bit of broth and water down him and he wasn't very feverish anymore, but he had rarely been awake. Even then, he had only looked at her as he clutched the blankets up to his chin until his black lashes fluttered back to his pale cheeks and he was once more asleep.

This morning she had gotten up before dawn as usual to stir the fire and start heating the water for tea and washing. She heard her father stirring in his little nook of a room, so she put some fish in the pan to fry up and put on the pot with yesterday's beans. Then she sliced a couple of pieces of bread and toasted them over the fire. They were just the right shade of brown when he came into the room.

"The best of the morning, my love," he said, giving her a smacking kiss on the cheek.

She shushed him, nodding toward the man who was still bundled in blankets on the floor before the hearth.

"Sorry," Da murmured, taking a seat at the little table before the window. "Has he said any more?"

"Not all this time," she said, dishing up his fish and beans and adding the toast to the side of the plate. "He just looks at me like he's afraid I'll eat him whole."

Da ate a few contemplative bites while she poured his tea and brought it to him.

"You know, my love," he said when she went back to plate up her own breakfast, "I heard something when I was in the village last night. You were already abed when I came home, so I didn't want to wake you, but I may know where our stray came from."

She glanced once more at the man on the floor and then hurried to the table with her plate. "What have you heard?"

"Well, you remember the letter we got from Bran day before last."

She nodded and ate a bite of fish.

"That bit about him coming across an old mate of his in Glasgow last month, the one who'd been in hospital for shell shock."

Again she nodded. "Do you think his mate truly got all the way to Glasgow from that asylum in Devonshire without anyone knowing who he was?"

"It seems so from what Bran had to say, and it was a good deed he did, identifying him to his captain so's the poor boy could be seen to. Well, old Mr. Blankensop who works at Houghton's said he got word this very week his grandson who's been missing these four months was found much the same, wandering the roads in Shropshire and not knowing his own name."

She put one hand over her heart. "Oh, but they've seen to him now, I hope."

"He's in fine hands now, my love, and not to worry. Blankensop says he's to come home as soon as may be, and he and Mrs. Blankensop will see he's given all the love and tending he needs to make him well again."

"Oh, good." Aileen ate a spoonful of beans and washed it down with tea. "And you think our man is in the same way as those?"

"It happens in war, Daughter," Da said, his face grim and his eyes sad. "I've seen it meself before. A man is wounded or he's just seen more of war and death than his mind can bear, and he slips away from himself. Things happen in battle, and he loses his papers along with his mind. Someone finds him and puts him in a hospital where he can be seen to, but they're overwhelmed with those who are sick in body and in mind, so it's no surprise when some of them wander away, wander to who knows where, and are lost."

"Oh, Da," she breathed, wanting to cry at the thought and for the man they were trying to help. "Do they never come to themselves?"

"Some do, darlin', not all I daresay, but some. Many, I hope."

"But how would he have got here then? And dressed as he was? They never gave him those clothes in any hospital."

"True enough," Da mused. "True enough. I suppose all we can do is talk to Mr. Blankensop about him and see who he'd recommend we send the boy to."

"But not yet," Aileen pleaded, resting her spoon on her plate. "Please, Da, there might be no need of that. Give him a chance to at least open his eyes and know where he is. You said you would."

"Yes, yes, I know what I said, but how can we—"

"Your word, Da. Don't you always keep your word?"

"All right then. All right. I have done." He shoveled a spoonful of beans into his mouth. "Keep your puppy if you will. And don't go shining those eyes at me. I have done, but I don't promise to never say I told you so when everything comes tumblin' about your ears."

She smiled and looked down into her teacup, knowing the best time to stop talking was when she'd won.

***

It was well past noon when the man on the floor began to stir on his own. Aileen was mending the hem of her old apron, but she immediately dropped her work onto the table and went to him.

"Good day to you," she said, giving him a gentle smile. "Would you like something to eat? Some tea perhaps?"

"Some water," he rasped.

She had tried to give him something to drink after she and Da had finished breakfast, but he hadn't been very responsive to her attempts and, fearing she might choke him, *she had finally given up. She hurried to put some water in a teacup and brought it to him. As gently as she was able, she lifted his head and gave him a sip.*

"Not so quickly now," she said, pulling back when he tried to down it all at once. "You'll wash clear away."

He smiled a little at that, and he seemed more lucid than she had seen him yet.

"Sorry. I guess I'm pretty thirsty."

"You are that, sir, but I can understand. You haven't had a proper drink since you've come here."

He struggled to sit up, and she helped him.

"Are you hungry?" she asked.

He had to consider for a moment. "Yes."

"We haven't much," she said. "Some fish and beans. I can toast you some bread and cheese if you'd rather."

"Anything would be very kind of you, Miss…?"

She really couldn't blame him for not remembering. "Aileen Byrne. I live here with me da."

The man looked around the small room and then, questioningly, back at her.

"He went to help Mrs. Marlin mend her chicken coop before it falls to pieces."

"I see," he said, looking around once more. "Uh, how long have I been here?"

"Nearly two days. How are you feeling now?" She put one hand on his forehead and then smiled. "You don't seem to have any fever."

"I feel a little clearer in my head now," he said.

They stared at each other for a moment more, and then, feeling her face turn warm, she got to her feet.

"I'll be getting you some food then."

"I don't want to put you out, Miss Byrne. I've imposed on you too long as it is."

"Christian charity, sir. You wouldn't want to deprive me of doing what's right, would you? Or do you think me and mine reprobates who're only after pleasing ourselves?"

"No, of course not, but—"

"And tell me," she said, letting a touch of mischief into her eyes, "where would you go?"

His shoulders sagged a bit at that, and she knew, at least for now, she'd bested him.

"I'll get your food."

She turned her back so he couldn't see her smile and went over to the stove. There was only a bit of the fish left, but there were still beans in the pot. She sliced some cheese and toasted it on a piece of bread and then brought it all to him.

"Thank you," he said, and he tucked in with more enthusiasm than she had expected.

"You must be mending well." She pulled up a chair beside him and carried on with her mending again.

"I feel like I've been beaten with sticks," he said ruefully, "but not much worse than that. Where am I?"

She knew she shouldn't be surprised. He didn't know who he was much less where.

"This is Ballycastle on the coast of Ireland. Does that sound familiar?"

He shook his head and took a bite of toasted cheese.

"Do you not remember anything?" she asked. "A place? Family? What sort of work you do?"

He shrugged and took a bite of beans.

"Do you remember what you said when we first brought you here?" she asked him finally. "You said you didn't want to go back."

He shook his head and then looked down at his plate.

"Back to what?" she pressed. "Were you hurt? You said you were on a boat."

"I don't know what I said," he murmured, spearing the last bite of the fish. "I don't know where I was."

He wouldn't look at her. What didn't he want to say? What didn't he want her to see?

"Were you hurt?" she asked again, putting her mending on her lap so she could clasp his hand. "We only want to help you. Isn't anyone looking for you? Isn't there somewhere you belong?"

Maybe she should let him be. If he didn't know, he didn't know, and it was no use browbeating him.

"I'm sorry." She gave his hand a gentle squeeze and then released it. "I know you can't remember. Perhaps you were in the war. Perhaps you were in a hospital after you were wounded and wandered away. It happens. Da says—"

"I heard some of what you and your father were saying before," he admitted. "Maybe that's what happened to me. If it was, what would you do?"

"Do? I suppose we'd make sure you were well, and then we'd find out where you belong. You didn't have anything on *you that would let us know who you are. We know you haven't any money. We couldn't turn you out to wander again, not until we find out more. Mr. Blankensop ought to know who we can talk to about it, Da says. Someone ought to be able to find out where you've come from, especially since you're an American."*

His hand tightened on his plate. "Don't do that. Don't, please."

He lifted his head, and the lost look was gone. The fear was gone. There was only determination.

"I won't go back. Just let me stay here a while. I'll see you're repaid for it. I swear before God I will."

She was caught for a moment, and his striking blue eyes pierced into hers, and then she swallowed hard.

"Sir, I—"

"Aileen, darlin'!"

She bolted to her feet at the sound of her father coming toward the cottage.

"You won't believe what I've heard down the pub." Da put off his greatcoat and cap, hung them on the peg by the door, and then came to warm his hands at the fire. "There was a ship that wrecked over off Islay a few days ago. A transport ship, mind you, and full of Americans."

"And well?"

"Don't you see, girl? Mightn't our American have come from it?"

She didn't dare look over at the man on the floor. "But Islay is in Scotland, not Ireland."

"Bosh, it's hardly thirty miles away by water."

She put her fists on her hips. "Are you saying he swam that then?"

"No, I'm not saying he swam it." Da scowled at her. "But there ought to be someone from that wreck who could say whether or not he was part of it."

Da had his back to the man, so only she could see the subtle pleading in his eyes. I won't go back. Don't, please. Could she send him back into what he couldn't bear to face?

"Sit down and have your tea, Da, and don't make such a row. Can't you see the poor man is worn out just from sitting up to take a mouthful of food?"

There was gratitude in the American's eyes as he set his plate on the floor and sank back down onto his pallet.

"There, you see?" Aileen grabbed her father's arm and guided him to the table. "Let him sleep now, and we can talk about this when he's stronger."

It was all I could do to keep Da from worrying the man about that wreck he heard about, *she wrote in her diary that night once her father was asleep.* Our visitor didn't stir again all the rest of the day as it was, but that meant I had no opportunity to speak to him again about who he was or where he was meant to be. Perhaps, though, the good Lord meant for him to be here. May He show me now what we're meant to do about him.

Chapter Twelve

"So how was your date?" Julia asked Meredith as soon as they drove away from Julia's house.

"Give me a second or two to figure out where I'm going," Meredith said, quickly checking the directions she'd written down.

"You're stalling," Julia said with a touch of a grin. "You know where the restaurant is. It's not far from Charlene's, and we've driven past it a million times before."

"Well, I never paid attention before."

"I'll tell you if you make a wrong turn. You tell me about the date."

Meredith kept her eyes on the road. "It was fine, okay?"

"Just fine?"

Meredith felt her throat tighten up, and she knew if she said much of anything right now she'd probably burst into tears. "It was good. Really. And I promise I'll tell you all about it once Maggie Lu gets there. She's going to want to hear about it too, and I don't want to have to go over it twice."

Julia huffed. "Okay, that's fair enough, but you know you're killing me, right?"

"We had a good time. Honestly. It wasn't a big deal. If you're expecting some huge revelation, this isn't going to be it."

Julia laughed. "Well, I'm still curious. But I'll hold my peace until we're all together."

"Besides, we're on a business trip. Any personal stuff will have to be on the side."

"Got it. I'll be good."

Julia caught her up on the Bates case, which was going absolutely nowhere, and soon they were at the restaurant.

Daisy's Garden was a cute little salad and sandwich shop in a narrow building that was once half of a row house. It was bright and cheerful and was, of course, sprinkled everywhere with daisy motifs, from the actual daisies in the centerpieces on the tables to the artistic depictions of them in the framed prints and on the wallpaper border near the ceiling and the nearly abstract ones on the plates.

Daisy herself was aptly named. Maggie Lu had described her to Meredith when they'd talked on the phone, and Meredith spotted her right away as Daisy waited on a large party of young women at a table in the corner. Her corn silk hair was in a long braid down her back and her dark eyes shone with humor as she talked with her customers. She looked as if she was in her fifties, about Charlene's age, and she seemed as bright and unpretentious as the flower she had been named for.

A couple of minutes later, Meredith's assumptions were confirmed when Maggie Lu came into the restaurant and immediately went to hug her daughter's friend. Daisy nodded at something Maggie Lu said to her, and then Maggie Lu came and sat down at the table with Meredith and Julia.

"That was Daisy, right?" Meredith asked her once they had had a chance to say hello.

"That was Daisy," Maggie Lu said. "I told her we'd love to talk to her when she had a few minutes. She said she'd be happy to stop by once the tables she's waiting on are done."

"I didn't think about how tied up she'd be," Meredith said. "I guess Sundays right after church are busy for most restaurants."

"But maybe you two didn't want to wait until some Tuesday at three o'clock to find out what you need to know."

Julia smiled at Maggie Lu. "We appreciate you helping us out."

"Again," Meredith added.

"That's what friends are for," Maggie Lu said. "Besides, I have a lot of fun trying to answer your questions, no matter how off-the-wall they are." She snickered. "It also reminds me how much junk I have in my closets and my attic that needs to be tossed out."

"Don't you dare," Meredith and Julia said at the same time.

Maggie Lu shook her head. "Well, all right then."

"Really," Julia said. "You've come up with all kinds of information we couldn't have found anywhere else. That's not junk, it's treasure."

"You two tell that to Charlene when she has to clean it all out after I'm gone."

"That's not going to be for at least fifty years," Meredith said.

Maggie Lu rolled her eyes. "Right. At least."

"Close to that anyway," Meredith amended.

The waitress brought them menus and took their drink orders, and the three ladies discussed what they were going to have for lunch. When the waitress brought coffee for Meredith and Maggie Lu and a Diet Dr Pepper for Julia, they ordered their meals.

"So," Maggie Lu said when the waitress was gone, "how was the date last night?"

Meredith winced.

"She doesn't want to talk about it," Julia said in a stage whisper.

Maggie Lu's brows went up. "Didn't you have a good time?"

"It was fun," Meredith said, scowling at Julia. "And I didn't say I didn't want to talk about it. All I said to Julia was I didn't want to have to tell her about it and then tell you about it once we got here."

"True," Julia admitted. "But you didn't sound like you were overwhelmingly happy about it either."

Meredith sighed. "It wasn't the date. Dinner was wonderful. We went to Bepponi's, which you know is one of my very favorite places. Then we saw the Beatles tribute band, and they were really fabulous. They looked and sounded just like the real thing. They even dressed differently for three different periods of the music. It was so much fun. We danced and sang. I felt like I was in high school again."

"So what was the problem?" Maggie Lu asked. "It wasn't Quin, was it?"

"No. Quin was great. You know how he is, so easy to get along with, and he treats me like I'm something special."

"Because you are," Julia said, squeezing Meredith's arm.

Meredith shrugged.

"And?" Maggie Lu urged.

"And I had a wonderful time, and I felt happy and comfortable and like I meant something to the man I was with."

"But?"

"But...he wasn't Ron." Meredith exhaled heavily. "He took me home and walked me to the door and we talked there for a minute or so, and then he reached over and touched my cheek, and I knew he was about to kiss me."

"And?" Julia prompted.

"And I got cold feet and told him good night and hurried inside."

"Ouch."

"I know." Meredith poured some cream into her coffee and stirred it up. "I feel so dumb now."

"Now, there's no need for that," Maggie Lu told her. "If you're not ready, you're not ready. Nobody says when you have to date again or even *that* you have to date again."

"I realize that. I thought I was. Actually, I still think I am. I mean, not anything serious. Not yet. But just a little good-night kiss? After we had had such a great time? And after already being friends?"

"Maggie Lu is right," Julia said. "You don't have to feel bad about not doing what makes you uncomfortable."

"But Quin—"

"I'm sure Quin understands. He's a widower too."

Meredith nodded, but she wasn't at all sure how he was feeling about last night. She hadn't even looked at him before darting into the house.

"You like him, don't you?" Maggie Lu asked.

Again Meredith nodded.

"Then talk to him about it. Pray about it. It'll be okay."

"You're right. I will. And we did have a great time."

Feeling better already, Meredith told them more about the dinner and about the band. She had just gotten to the drive home when Daisy showed up at their table with their lunch.

"Well, Maggie Lu. I know this tuna salad on wheat must be yours."

Maggie Lu beamed at her, taking the platter she offered. "You are so right."

"And the chicken salad?"

"That's mine," Meredith said.

"Then the club sandwich must be yours." Daisy put the last plate in front of Julia.

"Thanks."

"So these are your detective friends," Daisy said to Maggie Lu.

Maggie Lu nodded. "This is Meredith Bellefontaine and Julia Foley."

"It's good to meet you, Daisy," Meredith said. "Do you have time to join us for a few minutes?"

"I told my staff I was going to take a break. Let me grab myself a cup of coffee, and I'll be right back." She returned to the table a moment later. "Now, what is it you wanted to talk about?"

"I understand that you had some people back in the day who worked for the Van Orden family," Maggie Lu said as she added pickles to her sandwich. "Meredith and Julia are working on a case about something that happened in 1918, and we were hoping you might know something about who all was on the household staff back then."

"My great-grandfather had a sister who worked there. That was Aunt Joanie. She died a long time before I was born, but I remember seeing a picture of her." Daisy chuckled. "She was dressed as a lady pirate. I guess she was in her late teens then. She looked like a real corker."

"Do you know when she worked for the Van Ordens?" Julia asked.

Daisy thought for a moment. "She and her husband moved to Kansas when my grandfather was twelve."

"Do you know what year that was?" Meredith asked her.

"Let's see. Grandpa was born in 1907, so that must have been 1919."

"So we can say for sure that Joanie didn't work for the Van Ordens after 1919."

Daisy nodded. "Grandpa said her family never came back to Savannah."

Julia took a sip of her Diet Dr Pepper. "Do you have any idea when she first went to work for the Van Ordens?"

"Now that I don't know. Her only child was killed in a car accident when he was young, so there aren't any grandchildren or great-grandchildren I can get in touch with, but my dad's sister used to keep in touch with Joanie. They exchanged a lot of letters and Christmas cards and things. She took care of Joanie before she passed away. If anybody knows about Joanie's life, it would be Aunt Wendy."

"Do you happen to know why Joanie's family moved?"

"I don't guess I've ever heard. Aunt Wendy would know, I'm sure."

Meredith and Julia exchanged a glance.

"Do you think she'd mind if we contacted her?" Meredith asked Daisy.

"I think she'd enjoy it, actually. She's the president of her quilt guild, so she's pretty busy most of the time. The best way to get her is by email. Then she can get back to you whenever she has a minute." Daisy gave her a wink. "She'll be eighty-four next month, but don't tell her that."

She scribbled an email address on a napkin and handed it to Julia.

"When I get off work, I'll send her a message to tell her you're going to contact her. If she isn't expecting you, she'll think you're a scammer and she'll block your address."

"Good for her," Maggie Lu said. "Too many people out there preying on us older folks, like we haven't seen those same old tired scams they've been running for years."

"Amen," Daisy said, and then she turned to Julia. "If you'll give me your address or whatever addresses you'll be using to contact her, I'll send them to her so she can put them on her white list. That way you won't accidentally go to spam."

"Good idea." Julia took out a business card and circled the email address for Magnolia Investigations. "We'll make sure and use that one when we contact her, okay?"

Daisy tucked the card into the pocket of her denim shirt. "That's perfect. She'll be so excited to hear from you."

"We'll be very grateful for whatever she can tell us," Meredith said. "Is there anything else you've heard about the Van Ordens? Especially back in the early nineteen hundreds, but anytime, really. Anything at all."

"I saw you were investigating an old jewel theft concerning them. I had never heard about that before. I've heard of Vanessa Van Orden running things now, but all the old stuff? I don't know anything about that."

The bell over the front door jingled, and they all looked that way to see a man and a woman and their four children come in.

"If there's anything else I can answer for you, let me know." Daisy stood up. "I think my break just ended."

"Thanks for talking to us," Meredith said.

"We appreciate it," Julia added.

"I want your recipe for tuna salad," Maggie Lu called after her.

Daisy laughed and then hurried to see to her new customers.

"That was interesting," Meredith said when she was gone.

"I'm sorry she couldn't give you much information," Maggie Lu said, picking up her sandwich.

"Maybe not a lot of information," Julia said, holding up the napkin with the email address on it, "but she gave us a good contact. If her aunt Wendy is as sharp as she sounds, we could hit pay dirt."

"We should have asked Daisy where her aunt lives," Meredith said. "Then we could actually go see her."

"This is the first I've heard of an aunt," Maggie Lu told them. "So I don't know whether or not she lives in town."

"Maybe email's the best way anyway. We won't have to impose on her time when it might not be convenient for her. She can answer us whenever she feels like it."

"And we'll already have everything she says in writing," Julia said. "That's always helpful."

They all settled into actually eating their lunch instead of just nibbling now and then, and before long they were full.

"That was great," Meredith said. "I don't know why we never tried this place before, Jules."

Julia popped the last bite of her club sandwich into her mouth with a contented sigh. "I'll have to get Beau to come here too. He'd like that tuna salad."

Maggie Lu chuckled. "I don't know if Daisy'll give me her recipe, but I can't blame her if she wants to keep it secret. It's got to be a moneymaker."

Meredith chuckled. "I doubt she's going to give her secret to the mother of the competition."

Maggie Lu laughed and they chatted for a few more minutes, finishing their drinks, and then the waitress brought the check.

Meredith immediately offered her credit card. "We've got this, Maggie Lu."

Julia nodded. "Put your purse down."

Maggie Lu put one hand on her hip. The other still clutched her handbag. "You can at least let me give you cash for my part."

Meredith shook her head. "You're helping us out. It's the least we can do for taking up your Sunday afternoon."

Maggie Lu frowned at them, but there was a smile in her eyes. "I tell you what, when I find more about the Van Ordens in Granny Luv's things, you two will have to come over for cake and coffee."

"Deal," Julia said.

"Especially if it's your famous lemon cake," Meredith added.

"I don't know about famous," Maggie Lu said, no longer acting like she was going to open her purse, "but I can definitely make one of those."

"Perfect," Meredith said as the waitress brought back her credit card and the charge slip for her to sign.

They got up and, with a wave and another thank-you to Daisy, they walked out to the car.

"Thank you for lunch." Maggie Lu gave them each a hug. "I enjoyed the food and the chat. And, Meredith, I don't want you worrying yourself about Quin."

All their talk about the case had totally put him out of Meredith's mind. Now her guilty conscience reminded her of how their date had ended.

"I'll try not to," she said, "but I probably should give him a call."

"Probably," Maggie Lu said, giving her one more little squeeze. "It'll be all right. You'll see."

"Thank you."

"We appreciate you," Julia told Maggie Lu. "I honestly don't know what we'd do without you and Granny Luv's keepsakes."

"Keepsakes?" Maggie Lu asked.

"All the newspapers and other things she kept that have helped us with our cases," Julia said, a twinkle in her eyes.

"She'd be glad to know they were helpful."

"Do you want us to drive you home?" Meredith asked.

"I'd love it."

"I can't wait to see what Aunt Wendy can tell us," Julia said once they had dropped Maggie Lu off.

"Me neither," Meredith said, "but we'll have to wait at least until tomorrow to contact her so Daisy will have a chance to let her know we're not spam."

It wasn't a long drive back to Julia's house. Beau must have heard them drive up, because by the time Julia got out of the car and walked to the front door, he was standing there holding Bunny and getting her to wave one striped paw. Meredith grinned and waved back and then headed for her own house, knowing she wasn't going to be able to enjoy her Sunday afternoon without clearing the air with Quin.

Chapter Thirteen

ONCE SHE GOT HOME, MEREDITH changed from the rose-colored knee-length dress she had worn to church and into jeans and a T-shirt. Then she checked her email to see if there was anything important. After that, she got herself a cold bottle of water and made herself comfortable in a recliner. Finally, she took a deep breath and called Quin.

It rang twice, three times, and just as she was trying to figure out what kind of message to leave him, he answered.

"Meredith. Sorry about that. I was out back trying to destroy an ant bed that doesn't seem to want to go away."

She giggled a little at that, and it made her feel a little more relaxed. "They can be stubborn."

"Regular ants are bad enough, but fire ants? Ugh. I have no pity on them."

"Oh, me neither. They don't just sting, they're angry about it too."

"True."

Neither of them said anything for a moment.

"So what's up?" he asked finally.

For an instant, she regretted making the call. Then she decided to stop being childish and just talk to him.

"I wanted to tell you that I'm sorry about last night, Quin. I really am."

"Sorry?" he asked lightly. "Sorry you came?"

"No. Not at all sorry about that. I had a marvelous time. Everything was perfect."

"Perfect except for me."

"Quin." She took a breath and held it for a moment, trying to figure out exactly what she wanted to say. "Especially you. It wouldn't have been the same without you."

"Okay." There was an understandable amount of uncertainty in his voice. "But?"

"But nothing. I was thrilled when you asked me out. I've been hoping you would. I—" She steeled herself and then plowed ahead. "You didn't do anything wrong last night. It was totally me, not you."

"What do you mean?"

She pulled one of her sofa pillows into her arms, using it to shield herself from she didn't know what. Or maybe it was something she could hold on to for reassurance.

"I mean I haven't dated in decades. I'm not sure how to do it anymore, and I didn't want to make a fool of myself with you."

"You wouldn't have done that," he said, his voice full of tender understanding. "And I shouldn't have made the kind of assumptions I did last night. I'm the one who should be apologizing to you."

"No. Please don't think that. You were a perfect gentleman. I… overreacted. I'm not saying I'm ready for anything serious yet, but I do want to be more than friends."

He let out a relieved breath. "Well, thank goodness for that. I was about to have to turn in my 'I can tell when a woman's interested' card."

"I'm sorry. Really I am. I was overthinking everything at that point. I mean, the evening was so nice, and you were so nice, and I'd been wondering how you felt about me."

"I told you I think about you a lot."

"But you didn't tell me *what* you think."

"Hey, I'm supposed to be the attorney here. Not you."

"Okay, okay," she said, putting a smile into her voice. "I won't cross-examine you anymore."

"It's not easy taking that first step," he said. "We've known each other a while now, and I thought last night would be a good time. I'm sorry it wasn't."

"No, it was a lovely time. Please don't think anything else. I like you a lot, Quin. I'd like us to have another chance to see if we can be more than friends. If you're still willing to take a chance."

He was silent for a moment.

"Is this about Ron?" he asked at last.

"No, not really."

"But?" he asked again.

"But," she said, "it hasn't even been three years since he died. I still miss him every day, but at the same time, I think I'm ready to try dating again. Is that wrong?"

"Only you can decide that," Quin told her. "Does it feel wrong?"

"No, but…"

But what? She didn't even know herself.

"But you think it should feel wrong," he supplied for her.

She stopped for a moment, mulling that over, letting herself feel all the feelings that came with what he had just said. Then tears stung her eyes.

"Ron proposed to me on July seventh back in 1977. I can't help remembering that every July, but it doesn't make me sad like it did last year and the year before. It just makes me glad we had so much time together, and it makes me smile a little to remember how silly and awkward we both were when we first started dating."

"So I take it you were much improved last night compared to then," Quin said, a touch of humor in his voice.

"Definitely compared to when Ron and I first went out. And when he proposed?" She exhaled audibly. "When he proposed, even though I had an idea he was going to and I was thrilled when he asked me, I totally froze. He told me later I looked like I was standing in front of a sold-out opera house and was expected to sing an aria in Italian."

"And, of course, you know no Italian," he said with a chuckle.

"Not much beyond tiramisu and cavatappi," she admitted. "And I don't know Puccini from Gershwin."

"But you eventually said yes."

"I did," she said, "and only a few minutes later."

"Good."

"Last night, I went inside and heard you drive away, and I wanted to run out and wave you down right then and tell you how sorry I was."

"It did feel a little awkward. It's not easy to get up the courage to tell somebody you care."

"I know. And I hope you know that I wouldn't hurt you for anything in the world."

"I know, Meredith. That's why I figured I'd wait and let you call me when you were ready to talk about it. I'm glad you did."

"Friends again?" she asked hopefully.

"We were already friends," he said.

"Well then, maybe more than friends again?"

"Definitely. Uh, would you like to give it another whirl? I don't have any plans tonight. Would you like to watch a movie or something? Nothing elaborate, but I have popcorn and some great DVDs. We can pick up something for dinner if you like too."

"I'd love that. But nothing heavy, okay? For the movie, I mean. Something light and fun. I feel like laughing for a while."

"How about I let you pick?" he offered.

"No, you decide. Whatever you choose will be great, I'm sure."

"Okay. After last night's entertainment, I think I know the perfect choice."

"I hope it's the one I'm thinking of," she said, smiling now and feeling last night's embarrassment roll off her shoulders.

"I'm not telling you anything until you get here," he said. "What time works for you? Six? Seven?"

"How about six? I have a long list of things I have to do tomorrow, and I'd better get an early start."

"That's fine," he said. "I was wondering about it yesterday, but I didn't want to bring up anything work related. How's the case going? I guess you're still on that Van Orden jewel theft."

"That's right, but we have another client too. Kind of related to that."

"Kind of related?"

She told him about Spencer Robinson and what he had said about KBMJ-made arms.

"You be careful with this one," Quin said when she was through. "You're talking about a lot of money changing hands for this kind of thing. If Van Orden Munitions is dirty, and there's been talk about them since before I can remember, there could be foreign governments, rebel factions, terrorist groups, even our own elected officials involved somewhere down the line."

A shiver ran down her spine. "Don't think I haven't thought of that. We'll be careful."

"I hope so. And you know you can call on me if there's anything I can do to help, right?"

"I know," she said, feeling happily warm all over. "Thank you. I'll see you at six, okay?"

"Six o'clock," he told her. "I'm looking forward to it."

"See you soon."

She ended the call, thinking about what he had just said. She hoped Vanessa Van Orden wasn't actually up to anything. She had been nothing but kind and accommodating about Lydia's case. She was always contributing to this charity or that, helping those in need, supporting Savannah with her money and with her influence among her well-off friends.

Maybe the gossip was just a holdover from the early days of the company. Back in the late 1800s and early 1900s, most companies were allowed to do as they pleased as long as they made money enough to be successful. Several of the articles Spencer had given her were about accusations made in the press about what Van Orden was up to. All of them, upon investigation, had been dismissed as false.

The articles were still at the office, but she had asked Carmen to scan them into the computer so she could access them wherever she was. She was tempted to look them over this afternoon, but then she decided against it. This was Sunday. It was meant to be a day of worship and rest. She had done the worship and let it restore her soul. Now she needed some time off to do the same for her body and mind.

"Come on, GK," she said to the smoke-colored cat who sat at the end of the couch staring at her with fathomless green eyes. "Let's do the Sunday crossword puzzle."

***

"You look happy," Julia observed when she and Meredith met for coffee in her office the next morning. "I guess you talked to Quin."

"I did," Meredith said with a smile. "And he was wonderful about Saturday night. We ended up having dinner and watching a movie at his house last night and just relaxing."

"That sounds fun."

Julia didn't press her for more, but Meredith could tell she wanted to.

"And, no, he didn't try to kiss me again, but he did put his arm around me for a while. It was so nice."

It was nice. It had been so long since she'd snuggled up to anyone like that and just relaxed. GK was not a cuddler.

"What did you watch?"

"In honor of the tribute concert we went to on Saturday," Meredith said momentously, "we watched the Beatles in *A Hard Day's Night*."

"That sounds fun."

"It was perfect, actually. I told him I was in the mood for something fun and light, and that was just right. Some of their later stuff was really weird, but this was cute. Exactly what I was in the mood for."

"I haven't seen it in years," Julia said, "but I liked it too. And I'm glad things are okay between you and Quin."

"He's a pretty understanding guy. I don't think he much likes us looking into Van Orden Munitions & Manufacturing though."

"I don't blame him. It makes me wonder if we're not in over our heads. Looking into the jewel theft isn't a big deal, as far as I can tell. But I just wonder if Spencer should have gone to the authorities instead of us with his concerns about Van Orden."

Meredith frowned. "He did try asking about it while he was in the service, but evidently that went nowhere. It's got to be pretty disheartening for somebody putting his life on the line for his country to be brushed off like that."

"We need to be careful, whatever we do. I'll tell you who might be interested in knowing about this, if there is actually anything to know about, and that's Kevin Patterson."

"Ooh," Meredith said, brightening. "That's a great idea. He's new in the House of Representatives and he's eager to clean up some of the corruption in government. He should have clout enough to start an investigation if we get enough evidence to convince him there's something going on."

"Let's see what we find out before we make any big plans, okay?"

"Good idea. So what do you think? Can we go ahead and email Aunt Wendy today?"

"We ought to be good to go," Julia said, jiggling her mouse to wake up her computer.

Together they sent Daisy's aunt an email thanking her for her help and asking her to tell them anything she remembered Aunt Joanie mentioning about when she was working for the Van Ordens in the early 1900s.

"Ask if there was ever anything going on that she thought was odd or troubling," Meredith said as Julia typed out the message. "Anything at all."

"Right. And who else worked there, if she ever mentioned any names."

"And what period of time Aunt Joanie was with the Van Ordens, if she has any idea. And ask her if she would mind if we contact her again if we think of more questions."

"This is probably enough for now," Julia said, still typing. "Aunt Wendy sounds like a busy lady. We don't want to wear out our welcome on the first email."

"Exactly. This ought to be a good start."

Meredith paused as the phone rang, waiting for Carmen to put the call through.

"It's Mrs. Van Orden," Carmen announced. "She doesn't sound very happy."

Meredith and Julia looked at each other, eyebrows raised.

"You get it," Julia said.

Meredith put the phone on speaker.

"Mrs. Van Orden, this is Meredith. Good morning. I have Julia here on speaker with me."

"Good morning," Vanessa said tautly. "Meredith, I am really very busy most days, and this morning I'm even busier than usual."

"I'm sure you are. What can I do for you?"

"I would like to know who you have planted in my company and who's feeding you false information."

That startled a faint laugh out of Meredith. Julia raised her eyebrows.

"Mrs. Van Orden," Meredith said, "we don't have anybody planted anywhere. I don't know how you would ever—"

"I believe I have been more than generous with you and your partner in sharing company and family information at the expense of my own time and resources. And this is how you repay me?"

"Mrs. Van Orden—"

"Please, Meredith, spare me the denials. I really don't have time for them. I will tell you again that Van Orden Munitions & Manufacturing is completely aboveboard and has been for as long as it's been in existence. And I take offense, personal offense, at people like you who try to fabricate scandals in order to get publicity for your pedestrian little agencies."

"We never—"

"All I'm asking is that you leave me and my employees in peace. And tell the boy you've been sending around to snoop that if he comes back on Van Orden property for any reason, I will have him arrested. Am I understood?"

"Mrs. Van Orden, we have not sent any *boy* to your office or anywhere. We do not employ any men at this time. And if we did, we—"

"As I said, I don't have time to argue with you. Please don't make me take any unpleasant actions to make your harassment stop."

The call ended with a cold click.

"What was that about?" Julia asked. "I mean, yes, I heard, but wow. If she thinks there's a plant, she can't suspect Jack, because he's been with her for years. And as far as Spencer is concerned—"

She stopped, listening as the front door opened. As expected, Carmen came into Julia's office a moment later.

"Spencer Robinson is here," she said. "Do you want to talk to him, or should I ask him to make an appointment?"

Meredith pursed her lips. "Oh yes, we want to talk to him. We sure do. Can he come in here?" she asked Julia. "Or do you want me to see him in my office?"

"Oh, in here, by all means."

"Okay, Carmen," Meredith said. "Bring him in here."

"Good morning," Spencer said when he reached Julia's door. "I hope it's okay for me to drop by."

"I can't always guarantee we'll be available if you do," Julia said without a smile, "but you hit us just right this morning. Have a seat."

He took the empty chair next to Meredith. "I was headed out to do some more research of my own, and I thought I'd bring you copies of what I found this weekend." He had a small canvas backpack slung over one arm, and he put it in his lap to open it up. "More newspaper articles I found. Did you have a chance to look at the others I brought you?"

"I'd like to ask you something first," Meredith said.

Obviously, Spencer knew she wasn't very pleased at the moment. "Uh, okay."

Meredith gave him a stern look. "Mrs. Van Orden just called. She thinks you're working for us and asked us to stop you from coming over to her office to snoop."

Spencer winced. "Ouch. I promise, I haven't been there." He ducked his head a little. "Much."

"Spencer!"

"When were you there?" Julia asked him. "And what were you doing?"

"Yesterday afternoon," Spencer said. "I was in the parking lot hoping I'd be able to talk to Jack again, but I never saw him. He probably doesn't work on Sundays."

"And you didn't go inside?"

He shrugged.

Julia frowned at him. "Spencer."

"Only for a few minutes. I didn't ask for Jack or anything. I was just hoping to see him."

"You're going to ruin everything with him if you don't stay away," Meredith said. "If he's trying to give us information without anyone knowing about it, the last thing he needs is for some stranger to come looking for him."

"Okay, I'm sorry. I've just been trying to help."

"Well, don't. If Jack calls you with any information, let us know. Otherwise, leave the case to us or we're through. Right, Julia?"

"That's right," Julia said. "You're making this harder for us, and it's already a delicate situation as it is."

Spencer looked toward his feet and nodded.

"Anyway," Meredith said, "you asked whether I read the articles you brought before. I did. Now I'm trying to follow up on that information."

"Good." He handed her a stack of copies. "Add these into the mix. More about Van Orden Munitions and some reports on some of the incidents I was telling you about when I was deployed. They don't seem like much individually, but together they might make a pretty good case."

"These will certainly help."

"And," he added, "I was wondering if you have any news for me yet."

"Besides the little incident with Mrs. Van Orden a few minutes ago, we have more questions than answers so far," Julia said. "But we just contacted a woman who knew someone who worked for the Van Ordens back in the nineteen-teens. She may be able to answer a few questions for us about the household at the time and about who might have had an opportunity to steal those jewels."

"Good. What about the company itself?"

"We're trying to find out more. You'll have to be patient."

"It would be faster if you'd let me help," he said. "If I could go with you—"

"We'd all be in trouble," Julia finished for him. "What did we just tell you? You're helping out the most by giving us copies of whatever information you have. The more research you can do on this, the more quickly we can do the investigating."

He huffed. "Yeah. Okay."

"There was an incident last week that might interest you," Meredith said. "You remember Lydia Cooper, or at least the name?"

"Yeah, she's the one who hired you to find out about the theft."

"Right. Her mother's room was searched on Friday. We're trying to find out who could have done it and whether that person took anything."

"Why would anybody do that?"

"There was a mention in that article about a letter her mother claims to have gotten."

Spencer fumbled with the zipper on his open backpack, not looking at Meredith as he tried to close it. "The one she says was from Matt Van Orden?"

Meredith nodded.

"Nobody even knows for sure that there is a letter." He yanked harder at the stubborn zipper. "That poor lady doesn't seem to know what she's talking about."

He yanked again, and suddenly the backpack shifted in his lap, the contents spilling all over the floor. More papers, a couple of spiral-bound notebooks, a handful of pens, a couple of paperbacks, Meredith didn't know what all, scattered. The three of them scrambled to pick it all up.

"Man," he grumbled, quickly stuffing his things into the backpack again. "Sorry about that."

Julia handed him a pocketknife that had ended up at her feet on the other side of the desk. "I guess this is yours."

"Yeah," he said. "Thanks."

He stacked a handful of papers and then picked up a small, lidless box with a layer of cotton at the bottom. Eyes wide, he started searching the floor again. He soon found the lid to it under

Meredith's chair, and then he got all the way down so he could look under Julia's desk.

"Is this what goes in there?" Meredith held up an old-fashioned pocket watch that had skidded into the corner behind her.

"Yeah," he said, giving her a relieved grin as he reached for it. "Thanks."

She turned it over in her hand before she gave it back to him. "It's beautiful. Was it passed down to you by your family?"

"It's a keepsake," he said, quickly taking it from her and putting it back into the box. "But I want to know about what happened with Mrs. Cooper's mother. You didn't find any sign of that letter, did you? Do you have any clues about who could have searched the room?"

Meredith intentionally didn't look at Julia. She didn't want to give away anything she was thinking right then. She kept her eyes on Spencer and told him about her visit to White Oak Arbor.

"There is a possibility that another resident searched the room. Evidently there's someone in the same wing as Mrs. Bryleigh who's been known to do that. But there were two visitors who could have been responsible too. I have someone checking into them."

"Mrs. Bryleigh didn't know them?" he asked.

"I'm afraid Mrs. Bryleigh was confused at the time. At one point, she seemed to recognize the woman, but afterward she didn't remember seeing anyone at all."

He frowned again. "So I guess it wouldn't do any good for me to talk to her."

"No. It really wouldn't."

"The best thing you can do," Julia added, "is let us do our job, okay?"

"Yeah. Well, I have some research to do myself, so I guess I'll let you both get back to what you were doing before I interrupted."

He made sure his backpack was zipped and then stood up and slung it over one shoulder. "Thanks for letting me stop by to talk to you. Let me know if you find anything useful in those articles."

Julia patted the stack of papers on her desk. "I'm sure they'll be a lot of help. Thank you."

"Great," he said. "I'll see you both later."

Meredith heard him say goodbye to Carmen, and then the front door closed. She went into her office to look out the front window. Spencer walked past, still with the backpack over his shoulder, got into a bright yellow sports car, and drove away.

Meredith got herself a cup of coffee and went back to Julia's office. "I wish I knew what he's really up to."

"You think it's about more than Van Orden Munitions?" Julia asked her.

"Why would he be so interested in that letter? Lydia did mention that it says something about the Van Ordens knowing 'what was going on.' Could be he thinks that's tied to this whole thing about profiteering over the last hundred years or so."

Julia raised her eyebrows. "But would he have known about that part? It wasn't in the article about Lydia and her mother."

"True," Meredith admitted. "Very true. And there was that pocket watch."

"Okay, I know you noticed something about that before you gave it back to him. I could tell by how you wouldn't look at me."

"You know me too well," Meredith said with a lopsided grin. "He took it back pretty quickly, but I saw what was engraved on the back of it. It said 'To M-A-V with love and pride from T-D-V. Emory University, 1915.' He knows more than he's saying."

Julia thought for a moment and then her gray eyes widened. "M-A-V. Matt Van Orden?"

"It could very well be. His middle name was Andrew, if I'm remembering right."

"And *T* for Thomas Van Orden?"

Meredith nodded. "I think I remember seeing his middle name was David, and his second son's name was David. And I know Matt went to Emory University. It was in the copy of his obituary that Spencer gave us. Matt would have been seventeen or eighteen in 1915, so he could easily have been going to Emory then."

"But how would Spencer have gotten ahold of Matt's watch? Could it have been part of what was stolen in the jewel robbery?"

"Possibly." Meredith thought for a moment. "If so, maybe Spencer has a lead on what happened to the rest of the jewels."

Julia's mouth was set in a hard line. "And maybe this has nothing to do with his military buddies dying because of Van Orden Munitions."

"And maybe Vanessa Van Orden was telling the truth about being totally aboveboard in all her business dealings."

"Right." Julia turned back to her computer and started typing. "I'm going to send her private secretary an email asking her to find out if there was a pocket watch among the things that were stolen along with the Van Orden jewels."

"Good. Thank her for the photos and ask her if there's any kind of a list or a police report that would show exactly what was taken."

"Got it."

She had just hit SEND when the office phone rang. Carmen buzzed Julia's office a moment later.

"It's Janet from White Oak Arbor," she said. "She wants to talk to Meredith."

Meredith put Julia's desk phone on speaker. "Janet, how are you? My partner Julia and I have you on speaker."

"Oh, okay," Janet said. "I'm on my break, but I only have a minute."

"All right, we're listening."

"You wanted to know about those two people who signed in to visit Thursday evening. I asked Mrs. Carlton's daughter about Evelyn Sanders. Turns out she's Mrs. Carlton's niece. Her mother died recently, and evidently Ms. Sanders was feeling guilty for not having spent more time with her own mother, so she thought visiting her aunt would be the next best thing."

"Oh, I see," Meredith said, nodding at Julia. "So Evelyn Sanders was who she was supposed to be."

"Exactly," Janet said. "So that explains why she was here, even if Mrs. Carlton didn't remember her. She must have been a different cousin than the one I saw before, or she bleached her hair."

"And the guy?" Meredith asked, and then she had to think for a minute. "Uh, Sam Russell."

"That's a different story," Janet told her. "Mrs. Carlton's daughter never heard of him. Mr. Adams's grandson, Mike, says neither of them knows anybody named Sam Russell or Evelyn Sanders, and Mr. Adams says he's absolutely sure nobody has come to visit him besides his grandson. Not for a very long time. And, as far as I've seen, he's right. I've never known him to have visitors besides Mike."

"Thanks for letting me know. That helps us out a lot. Is there any way we can ask for all the staff up there to keep a special watch on Mrs. Bryleigh's room for a little while? Just to make sure nobody comes around who shouldn't."

"I can't do anything official for you like that," Janet said, "but I can ask some of my friends on duty if they'll keep an eye out for you. In fact, our director may have already asked the staff to do that if Sheila's daughter brought it up."

"We did ask the activity director about it. Maybe she passed along our concerns to the people in charge. I'll ask Lydia to make an official request for them to keep a closer watch on her mother's room too. But if you don't mind keeping your eyes and ears open for us too, we'd sure appreciate it."

"I don't mind at all. Sheila's a nice lady, and I don't like the idea of anybody taking advantage of her or any of our residents for any reason."

"We appreciate your help, Janet."

Julia looked at Meredith expectantly when she finished the call. "What about the man? Sam Russell."

"He didn't visit the person he registered to see." Meredith took a sip of her coffee. "Which means he could be the person who searched Lydia's mother's room."

"We don't have any kind of description of him, do we?" Julia asked.

"I'm afraid not. All Janet could really tell was that it was a man. She saw him walking away from Mrs. Bryleigh's room, but he was already pretty far down the hallway. Actually there's no reason to say he had anything to do with Mrs. Bryleigh at all."

"Except her room was searched, and he wasn't there to see the person he was supposed to be visiting."

Meredith glanced toward the hallway.

"And, yes, it could have been Spencer," Julia added.

Meredith considered for a moment. "I told you how evasive he was the first time he came here. He didn't want to tell me the reason he wanted us to check up on the Van Ordens. Then he explained about his experiences in the military. Was that true or just a convenient story so we wouldn't wonder about his motivation?"

"Given that Van Orden has had several inquiries about their business practices over the years, it wouldn't be much of a leap to make up a story like that. If he actually needed a story like that. Maybe along with everything else, we ought to be checking out Spencer too."

Chapter Fourteen

A BRIEF CHECK OF THE web page for the hardware store in Atlanta showed a picture of Spencer with his father and other members of the Robinson family. Nothing looked out of place with the Better Business Bureau there. A background check showed Spencer at the address he'd given them, his military service, and his educational record. Nothing Meredith found contradicted what he had told them. He had no record of problems with the police, nothing to make her think he wasn't exactly what he presented himself to be.

Except she couldn't help wondering what he really wanted. Had that article brought him here with the hope of cleaning out a nest of profiteering scoundrels? Or had he somehow come across that pocket watch and learned that there was a fortune in jewels somewhere that might be connected to it?

Meredith hurried back into Julia's office when her preliminary research was done.

"What if there's something in that watch that's a clue to what happened to the Van Orden treasure?"

"You mean, 'The light of a blue moon through the crystal will show the way' sort of thing?"

Meredith chuckled. "Something like that. You know what I mean. Maybe an inscription inside the watch case or even a slip of paper that had been hidden in there for the past hundred years."

"But where would Spencer have gotten the watch in the first place?"

"Who knows? We don't know yet whether or not it was part of what was stolen from the Van Orden home. If Matt took it with him when he went into the service, he may have lost it or sold it or had it stolen from him."

"Obviously, it didn't go down with the ship when he was killed in 1918."

"I've been looking at the new stack of articles Spencer brought us," Meredith said. "One of them was about Matthew Van Orden's body being recovered and brought back to Savannah to be buried in the family plot, but I guess his watch could have ended up anywhere."

"Do you think Spencer would tell us where he got it?" Julia asked. "Would it hurt anything to simply ask him?"

"Maybe not, but if he's got something up his sleeve, he probably has a ready answer for that too."

Julia sighed. "Especially if he thinks you saw what was engraved on it."

"He has to think I saw it, and he was quick enough to take it back from me. I don't know. Let's see what Vanessa's assistant comes up with for us as far as what was reported stolen in the jewel theft. None of the contemporary articles mention anything but the jewelry, but I suppose the watch wouldn't have been in the safe with everything else."

"There's the friend of Matt's who was only believed killed. What was his name?"

"Ummm, Calvin Benn."

"He might have ended up with the watch. Maybe he meant to take it to Matt's family when he got back to the States. If he lived and didn't come home for whatever reason, he could have kept the watch. Again, he could have sold it, lost it, given it away."

"Passed it to a descendant?" Meredith considered.

"Any of that."

Meredith took a legal pad from the corner of Julia's desk and started writing down some notes. "We need to ask Aunt Wendy if her aunt Joanie ever talked about Matt Van Orden or any friends who came over to the house to visit. We're assuming that this Calvin Benn was a close friend, but maybe they were just on the same track team. Still, I wish I knew what happened to him for sure."

October 14, 1918
Ballycastle, Ireland

Aileen didn't say anything until her father had bundled himself up against the biting wind and headed over to talk to Mr. O'Donough about helping with the slaughtering of O'Donough's old sow in exchange for a bit of the meat. Once the sound of Da's boots and walking stick faded away, she went over to the man lying before the hearth.

"I've only tea and porridge to give you yet," she told him cheerfully, "but I thought you might like to take it sitting at the table like a proper guest."

"I'd be pleased to, miss," he said.

She took his arm, meaning to help him stand, but he didn't lean on her at all. He looked a little pale when he finally got to his feet, but that was all.

She smiled up at him. "You're a fine tall fellow, I see."

"Whether that's good or bad, it's none of my doing," he said, sitting on the chair she offered. "Thanks all the same."

She set the pot on the table and filled it from the kettle that hung over the fire. Once she had dished up a bowl of porridge for each of them, she poured out the tea. As always, he took it gratefully.

"You've been very kind," he said. "I hope to pay you and your father back in time."

"Haven't you heard, man?" she asked. "Virtue is its own reward."

"No reason gratitude can't add to that reward."

He looked down, and for a moment she thought he was after some sugar for his tea, but she'd already told him they would have none until her father finally was paid for the grand net he was making. Before she could ask him what he wanted, he looked up at her again.

"What are you going to do about me?" he asked, his eyes piercing.

She had convinced her father to give him a little more time before letting anyone know he was here, but how long could that go on?

"I thought you might be gone when Da and I came back from mass yesterday," she told him as she cut each of them a slice of bread.

"Should I have been?"

"Depends on what it is you're doing."

"I'm not doing anything but trying to get my feet under me again and figure out who I am."

"Your hands were dirty." She gripped the knife a little more tightly, not quite brandishing it at him. "When we came back."

He glanced at his now-clean hands and then back at her. "They were."

"Why? What did you do?"

"And if I don't tell you?"

"Da will tell the authorities about you, and then they'll see you get back to…" She frowned. "Well, back to wherever it is you belong. They'll find out who you are, and then perhaps you'll remember and go home. Won't that be nice?"

His face darkened. "I won't go back. I've thought about this the whole time I've been here, and I won't go back. I can't go back. The only way I can make things right is to go on. From here."

"Make things right?" she asked, not putting down the bread knife. "What things? What have you done?"

She jumped when he suddenly took her hand, and his grip was tight as he leaned across the table toward her.

"I'm a thief," he said very low.

Somehow she had no breath to answer him nor any strength to pull away.

"But I can't go back," he told her. "Your father was right. I was in that shipwreck. I clung to part of a lifeboat that was crushed when our ship was hit by another, and I floated for a night and a day. A fishing boat finally picked me up. I bought some clothes from them and threw my uniform into the sea. I got them to drop me here after that, and I started walking up the coast."

"Oh," she said on barely a breath.

"But I hadn't expected it to be so far to the next town, and I hadn't expected to be so tired and hungry. If you hadn't found me, Miss Byrne, I'd be long dead by now, and what I did would go for nothing."

"What you did?" she said, finally able to snatch her hand away. "Your theft, you mean, heaven preserve us. Now that you've told me as much, tell me why I shouldn't call for the magistrate or the constables and have you taken in for it?"

"You don't understand," he said swiftly. "Yes, I stole, but not for the reason you're thinking. Not for myself."

She pursed her lips. "You remember your crime, but you expect me to believe you don't remember your name?"

"I remember. Forgive me, but I couldn't tell you my name. I can never tell you my name. I can't tell you where I'm from. But I can tell you why. Before you have me taken away, at least let me explain."

She crossed her arms over her chest and stuck out her chin, giving him his opportunity.

"You want to know why my hands were dirty yesterday?"

He studied her for a long moment, and then he took a leather pouch from one pocket of his breeches and another pouch from the other. They weren't large, but they seemed heavy. The pouches were worn and looked as if they'd recently been cleaned.

"You dug those up," she said. "While we were at the church."

"Yes."

"You buried them where I found you."

"Not far from there. I didn't want to pass out and have someone take them from me." He tilted his head a little to one side. "Would you like to see?"

In spite of herself, she couldn't help the sudden quickness in her breath, the sudden racing of her heart, and she nodded.

"Hold out your hands then."

Wary, she put down the knife and turned up both palms so she could cup them together. He opened one pouch and then the other and poured from them a dazzling shower of white and colored gems.

"Oh," she gasped. "Oh, heaven help us and forgive us, where did you get them?"

"I won't give you a name or a place," he said, "but I'll tell you the story. There is a man where I lived, a very rich man, as you can see. His riches came from the blood of tens of thousands of young men who went to the wars he supplied with shoddy goods and spoilt food and weapons that gave no protection. These jewels were bought from decades of profiteering by the man and his ancestors for as long as my country has had wars."

She let the jewels slide through her fingers and rattle onto the table.

"I knew I couldn't stop him. Even if I dared speak, I knew I would be the one who would be censured. He was powerful and had powerful friends, and who was I?" He drew an unsteady breath. "So, when I knew I would be going to war, when I knew I might never come back, I decided I would do what little I could to make some good out of what he had hoarded from his evil. I stole all the jewelry he had in his safe."

"It was all loose gems like this?"

"No. Most of it was in heavy gold settings, tiaras and rings, bracelets, collars, and earrings. It was too much for me to carry with me as it was, so I removed the stones from the gold and then used the gold to buy other stones, as much as I could to take with me."

She blinked at him, not knowing what to say to this. It was a wild tale, but she could see it all in his eyes, the anger and the purpose and the bare truth of it.

"What do you mean to do?" she asked finally.

"Not to go back," he said. "They'll give it all back, and all of it steeped in blood, and I'll be sent to prison. How will that make anything right?"

"And just how does stealing from this man make anything right? Do you think it'll stop him? Is it all his fortune?"

"No," he murmured, and there was genuine grief in his eyes. "But I can turn at least this much of his wrong into right." He scooped up a bright handful of the gems that lay between them on the table. "There must be some way I can get these to the people who can most use them to win this war, to help our soldiers, to confound enemy agents who infiltrate our operations on the home front, I don't know what all. It's just what I know I must do."

He took her hand, and she made only a half-hearted effort to pull away.

"You can't betray me now," he said, his voice low and urgent. "You can't let me be sent anywhere. I won't tell them who I am or where I'm from, but I'm not mad. I'm not shell-shocked, no matter what I pretend. If you'll help me, if you'll convince them to let me stay here until I come to my senses, you'll be helping our cause."

"Oh please," she breathed. "I don't know anything about this. I cannot—"

"Don't you have anybody in the war?" he pressed. "Anyone you care for? Anyone who might die without the kind of help I'm offering? I know it isn't much compared to all that's spent on defense, but it's something I can do, something we can do, to help. Even if we save a hundred lives, ten, one, wouldn't it be worth it?"

He returned the jewels he held to the pile and then spread them all across the table.

"How many lives lie there before you, Aileen Byrne?" he asked. "Maybe a few. Maybe many. Are all these jewels worth even one? If you could help me get them to those who might best use them, in whatever way might be needed, how much more could you help our fighting men than just sitting here in your cottage doing your mending and tending to your father and carrying on as you always have? Is there no one you care for who might live because this bought what he needed to feed him or clothe him or keep him safe?"

She thought at once of Bran. She didn't know what he was doing or exactly where he was, but his letters to Da came from Ireland or Scotland, sometimes from England. She knew he was involved in protecting the country from enemy spies. She knew he hunted them and was hunted by them, and in his rare visits home in the past three years, he had told some hair-raising tales of his narrow escapes. Tales, she was certain, he'd made less grim and desperate than they had in truth been so she and Da would be spared at least some worry. How much would it help and safeguard men like Bran and the unit he worked with if this small fortune were at their disposal?

The man was still staring at her, urging her to understand, urging her to help. The jewels lay spread across the table, glinting and beckoning. They were stolen, but if he had told her the truth, if they had come from blood and profiteering, and if he truly meant to take what had been earned with evil and use it now for good, could she turn him down?

"I won't betray you," she said finally, reminding herself that he could as easily have kept silent. He could have kept these gems and lived comfortably on their worth rather than give them up to help in the war, and not a soul would have known. "Not yet."

"Not yet?" His dark brows curved up pleadingly.

"There is someone who will be here in a few days. If you will tell him what you have told me, he will know what's best to do. If you speak the truth, he will know how to help you and how to use this treasure where it will help most."

"I swear it's all true."

"Perhaps." She took one of the small bags and put half of the gems into it. "For now, we'll keep things as they are. I won't say anything to me father, and you'll not either."

"No." He scooped the rest of the jewels into the other bag and put both bags into his pockets. "Of course not."

"And you'll keep those to yourself, if you're wise."

He smiled. "I had them awhile in the lining of my coat. For a time, I had them inside a canvas belt I wore next to my skin. That's what I had on when the ship went down. One of the men in the fishing boat that picked me up had a couple of tobacco pouches he was willing to sell me at an egregious price. I put them in those when I could do so discreetly and then wore them for a time around my neck. That was until I buried them down the road a little way."

"And got them back too," she said.

"Right."

"As I said then, keep them to yourself. Da won't mind helping out a poor fellow with shell shock until something can be done about him, and I imagine I can convince him to leave things as they are until our visitor arrives. After that, we'll both abide by what he says. Fair enough?"

"Fair enough. And thank you. I can't say I knew exactly what I'd do when it came down to it," he admitted. "I couldn't do more than pray God would show me which way to go. I didn't think He'd answer me with a shipwreck."

"I doubt that was God's shipwreck, but as He often will, it seems He's made some good out of it." She looked at him for a long, hard moment, and then picked up the bread knife once more. "And if you're playing me false, Mr. Whatever-Your-Name-Is, you'll have Him to answer to."

"I realize that."

There was something in his simple solemnity that steadied her.

"For now, we ought to call you something," she said. "You can't go on being 'the American' forever."

"No," he said, and another smile touched his lips. "I suppose we ought to figure out a name for me. You can tell Mr. Byrne it was your idea if he asks."

"And what do you fancy then?" she asked unable to keep from smiling herself.

"Drew would work," he said after a moment's thought. "That ought to do for a start, yes?"

"I like it," she said. "There was a boy called Drew McAdams lived in Ballycastle not so long ago."

"Where is he now?" the man asked her.

The wistful memory swept over her. "He went to the war. He had only a widowed sister at home anymore, and she hasn't heard from him since two years now. It seems there's little chance of him coming home and complaining that you've taken his name."

"Just his first. There'll be time enough to think of a second when it's needed."

"As you please," she said and then she narrowed her eyes. "I suppose your tea and your porridge have both gone cold by now."

He put his hand around his cup and gave her a wry grin. "It could be hotter."

She made more tea and put the porridge on the stove to warm again. "There's one last favor I'd like to ask of you, if you'd oblige me," he said when she returned his warmed breakfast to him.

"If I can. What is it?"

"You can let me do something to help you. You know I'm all right, and I'll never really get my strength back unless I'm up and around. Surely there are things I can do to make your work easier for you. I suppose you have a peat fire."

"Turf," she corrected him, "and we have enough cut and stacked for the winter, thank you."

"There must be something I can do to be of use."

She thought of her least favorite chores.

"You could haul the water," she told him. "And shovel out the fireplace when it's needed. Clean the fish when we have it. Scrub the pots."

"Nothing worse than I did in the service," he said. "And it's better than lying back doing nothing."

"I don't know," she said with a laugh. "I've often thought that would make for a lovely day now and again."

"Now and again," he said, aping her brogue as he repeated the phrase, "but not all the time. And that doesn't seem so bad."

"Not to start," she agreed. "But I'll think of more."

"And I'll be happy to oblige, Miss Byrne."

He gave her that wry grin once more and then tucked into his porridge with a good will.

Be wary, girl, *she wrote in her diary that night.* You wouldn't be the first nor the last to be deceived by a fair face and a silver tongue. He's confessed to a crime. Does that make him an honest criminal? Or is he merely telling a pretty tale? I remember the many times an enemy agent has tried to convince Bran he was on our side. Could this be another one? I'll tell him nothing of Bran. Bran will see to him when he comes.

Chapter Fifteen

"ANYTHING NEW?" JULIA ASKED AS Meredith checked her email the next morning.

"We got a brief one from Vanessa's private secretary. They'll look for an itemized list of what was stolen in 1918, but it isn't very likely there was one or, if there was, that it survived. Vanessa doesn't remember ever hearing that a pocket watch was part of the theft."

"I'm glad Vanessa cooled off enough to cooperate with us again. Maybe they'll turn something up."

Meredith sighed. "I was hoping we'd hear something from Daisy's aunt Wendy this morning. I don't see anything."

"Give it time," Julia said. "Daisy says she's a busy lady. We can't expect her to drop everything just because we have a case."

"True. Anything new on Bates?"

"Nothing. I've checked everything I know to check. I can't prove a negative, but I sure haven't found any sign that Bates is being ripped off. Of course, he might think he has been when I give him the bill after telling him that."

Meredith snickered.

Julia was telling her everything she had done on the case, when the front door opened and someone told Carmen good morning.

"Maggie Lu!" Meredith called, and she hurried out into the hallway. "Come in. We didn't expect to see you this morning."

"I hope you don't mind my stopping by," Maggie Lu said, coming into Meredith's office. "Hello, Julia."

Julia smiled. "Hi. Coffee?"

"Oh, no, I've had mine. I'm going to the library, but I thought I'd drop off something I found for you in Granny Luv's things last night." Maggie Lu chuckled. "I was looking in my attic for a teapot she used to have. I saw one just like it on one of those antique shows, and that one was worth a lot. I thought if this one was made by the same company and not just a knockoff, I might have a little windfall."

"And was it?"

"I'm afraid not. It's cute, but it's not the real thing. But I did find something important all the same." Maggie Lu took a folded piece of newspaper out of her purse. "After I found that teapot, I noticed there was another box that was marked *china*, and I don't remember ever looking inside that one. I opened it up and found this."

She spread the paper on Meredith's desk.

Van Orden Maid Vanishes

Meredith blinked at the headline. "What on earth?"

Maggie Lu nodded significantly. "Go on and read it. This girl, her name was Anita Grambs, she wasn't actually a maid, from what I can tell, more like a cleaning girl. This says she was at the Van Orden home late to help serve dinner for a large party. She helped clean up afterward and then walked home as usual. But she never made it home."

Julia snatched up the paper, scanning it swiftly. "I'd sure like to know what happened."

"Me too," Meredith said. "What was her name again?"

"Anita Grambs," Maggie Lu told her.

Meredith typed ANITA GRAMBS, SAVANNAH, GEORGIA, DISAP-PEARANCE into her search engine.

"There are a couple of mentions of her disappearance on that date," she said after looking at the results. "Both of them on sites about haunted Savannah. This site claims she's one of many who were taken over the years by a swamp creature. The other says she fell victim to a serial killer who stalked the streets around the turn of that century. They don't explain how a man who was hanged in 1902 could have killed a young woman in 1911, but I guess that's not important on sites like this."

Maggie Lu shook her head. "I guess if it's on the internet, it must be true."

"There had to be some kind of follow-up on this story," Julia said.

"I didn't find anything," Maggie Lu told her, "but I thought you two would be interested. I looked at some of the other papers that set of china was wrapped up in, but it was all from the same day's news. There wasn't anything else about the Van Ordens or Anita Grambs in there."

Julia pursed her lips. "Thomas Van Orden offered a thousand-dollar reward for any information about her and says he regrets, 'in view of the lateness of the hour,' not sending her home in his own carriage. Like that ever happened."

"Maybe she was found later," Meredith said, hoping rather than expecting that to be true.

"I'll see if I can find anything in a later paper at the library," Maggie Lu said. "But I have to get going now. I only wanted to drop that off for you."

"We appreciate it." Meredith walked her to the front door. "Stop by anytime. Even if it's only to say hello."

Maggie Lu hugged her. "I will."

Meredith went back to her office when she was gone. "Do you think there was something going on with the Van Ordens that night?"

Julia shrugged. "No way to know without more information. She could have eloped and moved to Canada for all we know."

"Or ended up buried under the new swimming pool."

Julia raised her eyebrows. "Did they have a new swimming pool that year?"

"I don't know. It's possible."

"And it's possible that, if she was killed that night, it was by someone totally unrelated to the Van Ordens."

"Yeah, I know." Meredith refreshed her email page and caught a quick breath. "Oh, we have something from Aunt Wendy."

"Open it."

"She says she's happy to help us," Meredith said, glancing over the message. "It's been a long time since Aunt Joanie passed on, so she'll have to think about what she might have said about when she worked for the Van Ordens." She read further on. "Joanie worked for them after she left school, which Aunt Wendy thinks was about 1898 until she moved away in about 1919. Umm, she says Joanie was their maid and she reported to a very strict housekeeper who ran everything belowstairs."

"Hmm," Julia said, "I wonder if she ever heard Joanie mention Anita Grambs. We'll have to ask her."

"Definitely." Meredith continued reading. "Oh, listen to this. 'She did mention Mr. Matthew, as she called him, and he had two friends who would come spend weekends from time to time and summers now and then. I know she told me their names, but I'm afraid I can't remember now. I'm so sorry, but my memory isn't what it was. I remember they did racing, but I can't remember what kind. Sprinting, I think.' That has to be Calvin and Tyler."

"No doubt," Julia murmured. "What else?"

"She says Aunt Joanie used to tell her about where she worked when she moved to Kansas. She kept house for an accountant and his wife and took care of their little boy and girl. 'It was so different from the Van Orden house, she always told me. Mr. Chambers was always glad to come home, and the family was happy to see him. I don't remember them quarreling, not like Mr. Van Orden and Mr. Matt.'" Meredith shook her head. "Wow."

"Yeah. Does she say more about that?"

"She says the two of them argued all the time after Matt became a teenager, according to Joanie. 'She told me once that Mr. Matt told his father he couldn't stay there anymore. At that house is what she meant. He said, "I can't stay here anymore and let you keep on." And after that he joined up and she never saw him again.'"

"Keep on with what, I wonder," Julia said. "Could it have been the profiteering and all that?"

"Could be. Anyway, she says she doesn't know what else to tell us, but if we want to ask more, she's very happy to help." Meredith started typing a reply. "I want to know if Aunt Joanie ever mentioned anything illegal or underhanded."

"She might not have ever said even if she knew," Julia said. "Servants were supposed to be deaf and dumb."

"I'm going to ask anyway. And I'm asking her if Joanie knew anything about Anita Grambs."

"Good. Ask her if Joanie ever mentioned Matt's pocket watch or said anything about his funeral. Ask if she went and what it was like."

"All right," Meredith said, "but I don't know what that would tell us."

"I'm just trying to figure out what kind of man Thomas Van Orden was. If they quarreled and never made up, and if he loved his son, it should have shown."

"The description of the funeral that was in the newspaper article certainly seemed to have been ostentatious enough."

"I'm sure," Julia said. "But that could have been all for show."

"Could be." Meredith kept typing. "We'll see what Aunt Wendy says. It ought to be very enlightening."

October 17, 1918
Ballycastle, Ireland

Aileen smiled as she watched the American shoveling out the hearth. Drew, she reminded herself. It was a nice name. It suited him. He looked up at her suddenly, giving her the wry little grin that always warmed her heart.

He frowned when she laughed abruptly. "What is it?"

"I think you've more soot on you than in the pail."

"What do you mean?"

"Why, your nose is blacker than my kettle."

He wiped it with the back of his hand, spreading ashes onto both cheeks and making her laugh more.

"You'd better take the pail out before you're black all over," she said, shooing him away with both hands. "And don't come back till you've had a good wash."

"I may not come back at all," he said with a scowl, but he shoveled the last of the ashes into the pail and stood up.

"You'll be back, lad," Da said from where he was finishing the net he'd been so long working on. "There'll be mutton in the stew tonight, and you won't want to miss our girl's mutton stew."

"No, sir, I won't." Drew's smile was white in his blackened face. "I'll be back as soon as I've had a good wash."

"He's made things easier for us both," Da said when he was out of hearing. "I shan't like to give him up."

She wouldn't like it either, but she didn't dare say that aloud. Not to Da.

"Bran will be home," she said instead. "Today or next. He can best tell us what to do with our guest. For now, he's done no harm."

"Aye. He may not know his own name, but he's a gentleman, I can swear to that. I hope we don't do wrong by not having a doctor see to him. It might be there's something can be done to bring him back to himself."

"I don't think any doctor can make him remember any more than he does already," she said with a sad shake of her head. It was the truth if nothing else. "But you can't deny he seems content as he is."

"Ah, the blessed freedom of a clear conscience," Da said with a grin. "If he can't remember his sins, he can't be burdened with them."

"God forgive him of them," she said, "whatever they be and amen."

Drew had shoveled the ashes out of the stove before he'd seen to the fireplace, and she was grateful for it as she began cutting up the mutton that would feed them at supper. She didn't say anything of it to Da, but Drew had given her the money for it.

He had shushed her when she asked where that had come from and sent her off to the market. It wasn't American money, and it was only pennies. She assumed, for want of a better explanation, that he'd traded whatever American money he'd had to one of the fishermen for the clothes he'd been wearing when she found him. Maybe they'd been good enough to trade him a few pennies so he wouldn't be totally without means once he'd reached shore.

However he'd come by it, he'd been openhanded with it. Please God, *she prayed silently,* let him be what he claims to be.

It was a wicked world, she knew it well, and she'd known this man for far too short a time to be hurt by him, but she had a feeling she would be hurt more than just a little if he betrayed her trust. Please, God.

She frowned when she heard a knock at the door. Surely Drew knew he could come and go as he pleased by now. Maybe he was carrying something and needed her to open the door for him. She couldn't imagine what that could be, but she hurried to the door with a smile.

"Couldn't you manage it your—" Her smile faded into embarrassment. "I beg your pardon, sir, I was expecting it to be someone else."

"Your brother, Bran, perhaps?"

The man swept the cap from his head, a look of polite apology on his round, mustached face. His accent was English, his bearing military. Was he someone Bran worked with?

Her smile came back. "You know Bran? Has he sent you?"

The man glanced around and then nodded toward the door. "I'm supposed to meet him here." He tapped the side of his nose. "Important business, you know. Hush hush."

"Oh, yes. Yes, of course. Do come in from the cold."

She stepped back to admit him, turning to her father as she did.

"Da, this gentleman's come to see Bran."

Da glanced up, looking only slightly annoyed as he made another pass with his netting needle and then swiftly began knotting the cords to keep the net from unraveling. "I'll be not a moment, sir. Me daughter can give you tea, if you'd like."

"Splendid," the man said. "Thanks awfully. My name's Turner. I suppose you're Miss Aileen Byrne. Bran speaks of you often."

She hurried with the tea, and in a moment her father joined the man at the table.

"My son is well?" Da asked him. "He's supposed to be here soon."

"Yes," Turner said. "We thought this would be a quiet place to meet. No one would likely find us here." Once again, he tapped the side of his nose. "Can't be too careful."

Aileen forced herself to not look at the door. Where had Drew gone? What if this man was looking for him? What if Drew was actually an enemy spy? Someone who'd come after Bran, and Turner was here to stop him?

"How is my son, Mr. Turner?" Da asked genially. "It's been some while since we've seen him."

"Oh, splendid, sir, splendid." Turner beamed at him. "Don't know what we'd do without him in our unit, to tell truth."

Da's eyebrows bunched together. "I can imagine so. No more than a few days ago, we had—"

"There's your tea, Mr. Turner," Aileen said, jumping up to get the kettle. "It's a cold day, and I haven't had a moment to build up the fire."

He looked her over with a smile. "I noticed you'd just cleaned your hearth. It's a wonder you're not covered with soot."

"I was after starting the stew."

She was reluctant to mention Drew until she had a chance to talk to Bran about him. Maybe Drew had better make himself scarce until Bran came home.

"And then I was going to go after the turf for the fire. But you're right." She smiled brightly. "After your walk here from *the village, you'll be wanting to warm yourself while you're waiting. I won't be a moment getting it."*

He caught her arm before she could get to the door. "Who else is here?"

"Here now," Da said, starting to his feet.

Turner had his free hand in his pocket in an instant, and Aileen could see the clear outline of a pistol now.

"Stay where you are, Byrne," he said coldly. "Stay right where you are." He tugged Aileen into a chair. "Sit down if you want your father to stay well."

She sat. "What is it you want?"

"You needn't worry," he told her. "As I told you. I've come to meet your brother. Do as I say, and I won't harm you or your father. Now tell me, who cleaned out that hearth? Was your brother already here? Is he out there somewhere?"

"No," she said. "We haven't seen him. We haven't heard from him but for the letter he sent saying he was coming here."

"What else did he say?" Turner demanded. "What did he tell you?"

"Nothing. He said he was coming for a visit for a day or two. That was all."

Turner looked at Da, eyes hard.

"That was all," Da said. "What do you want of him?"

"Never you mind that. If he's out there, I expect he'll be in before long. If he's not yet arrived, I don't mind waiting." Turner smiled tautly. "We can all wait."

"You're here for Bran," Aileen breathed. "You're one of the men he's after."

"True, Miss Byrne. And he's the man I'm after. He and his men have spoiled too many of our plans, and I've been sent to see to him."

"You'll have to kill me first," Da said, glaring furiously.

Turner shrugged. "If you like."

Aileen caught her breath at what she saw over his shoulder and then fixed her eyes on the pocket in his woolen coat. Then she reached over and took her father's hand.

"Keep your eyes on me, Da," she said, making every word distinct. "Don't look anywhere else. We don't want that gun going off. Keep your eyes on me, and don't give him any trouble."

Da looked puzzled, but he did as she asked.

Turner chuckled. "You'd best listen to her, sir. Behave, and I'll do my errand and be gone. No harm to you."

"You'll kill my son and say no harm to me?" Da growled.

"Da," Aileen said. "Look at me. Just look at me. Don't listen to this English traitor."

Turner snorted. "Ha." Then he said something in German that sounded like a curse. "Vat?" he said, his words heavily accented now. "I am no Englander."

Da started to say something, then his eyes flicked up over Turner's head. The German noticed it, Aileen was sure. He tensed to stand, but instead there was a heavy thud and then the crack and boom of his pistol.

Aileen shrieked as Turner's face hit the table, and the acrid smell of gunpowder curled into the air.

"Drew!" she cried as the American swiftly fished the gun from the German's smoking pocket.

"It's all right," he said, putting down the fireplace shovel and holding the gun on the man instead. "He can't hurt you now. Sorry about the bullet in your floor."

"Oh, Drew," she breathed, clasping her trembling hands together.

Da was white as a sheet. "Where'd you come from, lad? Heaven help us, how'd you do it?"

"I was washing up, and I saw him coming toward the cottage," Drew said. "If he was someone from the village, from the authorities, I didn't want him to know I was here until your son got here. I knew from your descriptions that he couldn't be Bran, so I made myself scarce." He gave Aileen a rather sheepish grin. "I hope you'll forgive me this once, but I was listening at your bedroom window, trying to decide what I ought to do. Once I realized who he was, I crawled through. I'm afraid all I had was your shovel. I hope I haven't dented it."

Aileen set her teeth. "I hope you've bent it right in two."

"I expect we ought to tie him up or something till your brother gets here," Drew said, still keeping the pistol on the unconscious man. "He's pretty slippery. But I have to say, Miss Byrne, you were marvelous. I know you saw me behind him, but you kept his attention on you."

"And mine," Da said ruefully. "And I still nearly spoilt the thing."

"No, sir. It worked out just right. You and your daughter just sit there and—"

The front door banged open, and a tall figure filled the opening.

"Drop the gun."

"Bran!" Aileen cried.

"Drop the gun," Bran repeated, his voice dangerously low. "Do it now, man."

Drew held the gun in front of himself and carefully put it on the table.

"Now put up your hands and turn around."

Drew obeyed him.

"It's all right," Aileen said, going to her brother. "He saved us."

Bran frowned. "Get the gun, Da, and keep it on him."

Da shook his head, but he picked up the pistol and held it lightly in his hand. "Listen to your sister, lad. Didn't the man just save our lives?"

Bran looked Drew up and down. "Back up to the wall," he ordered, gesturing with his gun. "Go on."

Drew did as he was told, and then Bran went to the man sprawled over the table.

"Who's this?"

"He said his name was Turner," Aileen said. "But I think he's German. He came here to kill you."

Bran took a handful of the man's sandy hair and lifted his head. Then he smirked. "Dressler. I should have known it."

"Is he dead?" Aileen asked, her voice none too steady.

"He'll be all right. He's got a skull like cast iron."

"You know him."

"We've been hunting this one for nearly a year now."

"And he's been hunting you," Da said.

"I know it. I didn't think he knew about you or about this place, but then I realized he did." Bran exhaled heavily. "I should have expected something like this. He's one of their best." He narrowed his eyes at Drew. "Who's he and why's he here? Da, get me some of your cord."

"Me cord? Why would—" Da grinned, went over to where he'd been working, and cut two sturdy lengths of cord. "Use 'em in good health, Son."

"Just keep that gun on the other one."

Bran slipped his gun into his waistband, tied the unconscious man's wrists and ankles and then used the man's own belt to secure him to the chair. Then he patted down his prisoner's pockets, took an envelope from inside the man's waistcoat, and put it in his own with a grim smile.

"Now you," he told Drew. "Sit down."

Again, Drew obliged.

"Now, I want to know who you are," Bran said. "And I've no patience for lies at this point."

"Please, Bran," Aileen said, going to Drew.

"No, get away from him now. Go on. I shouldn't like you too near a desperate man."

"Da," Aileen protested.

"Do as he says now, girl," Da said sternly, still with the German's pistol pointed at Drew. "Perhaps he's right, and we've been too trusting. Neither you nor I know what we've got ahold of here. Bran's the expert in this. I say we let him decide what ought to be done now."

"But, Da—"

"Don't tell me what he's done. Tell your brother."

"Can't we all sit down?" Aileen asked.

Bran pressed his lips into a hard line, but he dragged the German, chair and all, into the corner. Then he grabbed the chair Da had been using while he worked and pulled it up to the table. Warily, he nodded for Aileen and Da to sit.

"So tell me," Bran said, sitting himself down where he could keep his eyes on his unconscious prisoner. "What's your friend here done?"

As Drew looked on, still silent, Aileen told her brother everything that had happened from the time she'd found Drew almost dead near the path to the cottage until he'd bashed the enemy spy on the head with the fire shovel.

"He saved us," she said with a stubborn lift of her chin. "And you as well, Bran." She nodded toward the German. "Wasn't that man meaning to hold us here until you came home, expecting to kill you the moment you did?"

"True enough, I suppose," he growled. "And yet you say he's a thief? A deserter?" One of his black brows went up as he looked Drew over. "Haven't you anything to say in defense of yourself?"

Drew lifted both hands, spreading them wide, showing they were empty. "If you'll allow me."

Making no sudden moves, he used his left hand to take one pouch and then the other from his pockets. Then, keeping his eyes on Bran's wary ones, he emptied them both on the table.

Aileen knew what to expect this time, but the sight of all those jewels, glinting and gleaming in the dimness of the cottage, still took her breath away.

"By all the saints," Da said after he'd listened to Aileen's story without a word. "And you've said nothing of this all the while?"

"I'm sorry, Da," she said. "I didn't know what I ought do. I thought Bran would best know."

Bran kept his eyes fixed on Drew. "And you mean to turn all this over to us? To use against the enemy?"

"That's the plan," Drew said. "I think, rather than using the jewels to buy arms or supplies for the troops, they'd do more to help what you do. Espionage. Code breaking. Giving agents whatever means necessary to protect our intelligence and access theirs. It's the soundest way I know to cut down on our casualties and end this war as quickly as possible." The gems made a scraping sound as he pushed them with both hands to Bran's side of the table. "It's what I came here for."

Bran looked at him for a long moment, and Aileen held her breath. Did Bran believe him? Would he let Drew help?

Or would he simply turn Drew over to the Americans to be punished for desertion?

Finally Bran patted the left side of his chest, rattling the envelope he'd just put there. "Do you know what this is?" he asked Drew.

Drew shook his head.

"It's a list of our agents in France and Germany. Men and even a few women who'd be killed if they were found out. The Germans broke our last code a few weeks ago. This is written in a new one, but that code was stolen as well, four days ago. The woman who took it disappeared. Our friend Dressler stole this list two days ago, knowing I'd have no choice but to come after him. He's supposed to meet his partner a mile or two up the coast. A submarine is meant to pick them up with their plunder. As you say, he meant to make away with me and then have her and himself wafted back to the continent and then to Berlin before anyone caught up to them."

Aileen swallowed hard. "He said he was going to let us go once he killed you."

Bran snorted. "I'm sure he would have. After he'd quietly cut your throats."

"Why do you tell me all that?" Drew asked him.

"His partner in this—she's called Arabella—has never seen him. She and I have met before." There was a sudden mischievous glint in Bran's dark eyes. "But she doesn't know you. What would you say, man, to some on-the-job training?"

Aileen seized her brother's hand. "You can't expect him to do something like this. Not right away."

Bran turned hard eyes on her. "Either he's with us or he's against us. I don't know a better nor a quicker way to find out."

"I've had some high school German," Drew said, "but I've forgotten most of it. She'd spot me right away."

"No. She's French, not German. A collaborator. The only language she and Dressler have in common is English."

Drew tightened his jaw. "Tell me what I need to do."

He and Bran talked long into the night. It seemed that Dressler would be their reluctant guest until his partner had been apprehended and then both of them would be sent to the authorities for questioning. Bran mentioned feeling sure his superiors would welcome Drew's contribution of valuables as well as of his intellect and effort, to advance their work and, he hoped, shorten the duration of the war.

Aileen brought them tea one last time before she headed to her bed, her heart full of pride and fear for them both, knowing they would face death many times before their work was done, amazed that Drew had come to them for just such a time. She believed that he had. She believed he was taking what the owner of those jewels had meant for evil and doing what he could to bring good out of it.

He'll be going with Bran now, *she wrote in her diary that night.* If they can stop the woman they're after and come home alive, what then? I hate that they must do these things, but I thank the dear Lord that there are such men who'll give their all to keep us safe. But what then?

Pray God, Bran will one day come home and we'll have peace. But Drew? I hardly know him. Da would laugh if he

knew how I fear for him now. I ought to laugh at myself. What is he to me more or less than any of the brave ones who fight for us? But how can I bear it if I never see him again?

In only these few days, he's crept into my heart, and I know I'll grieve for him when he's gone. And if he comes back? What then? Holy God, keep him in the hollow of Your hand.

Chapter Sixteen

Meredith and Julia got an email from Aunt Wendy the next day.

> *I'm really enjoying writing to you. I truly wish that Aunt Joanie were still here to tell you exactly what you want to know, but maybe what I can remember will be some help to you all the same.*
>
> *I do remember her talking about Anita Grambs. Aunt Joanie always brought her up when she wanted me to be extra careful, especially when I was out late. "I'll never forget poor Anita," she always said. "It takes only a minute for somebody to snatch you off the street."*
>
> *She didn't talk much about what actually happened to Anita at the time, but she did say there had been a large dinner party that night. That's why Anita was working so late. Evidently there were some very important people there. She said there was a senator, but she didn't give me any names.*
>
> *My mother always said Anita must have overheard something she shouldn't have, and that's why she disappeared, but I always thought that was just talk. But Aunt Joanie never contradicted her about that. She was very quiet*

about what the Van Ordens did back then. I always thought she knew more than she would admit to.

I don't know much more, I'm afraid, but it does sound as if the Van Ordens may have had some shady things going on, which would make what Mr. Matt said make a lot of sense.

Speaking of him, you wanted to know what Aunt Joanie said about his funeral. I remember her talking about how grand an occasion it was, huge banks of flowers and a flag over his coffin. She went to it, of course, feeling that she ought to, but she said it felt very strange, like a big show.

She said maybe it would have felt different if she could have seen him one last time, but once they got him out of the water and back to Savannah they couldn't have an open coffin. It seems so sad now, even with all the well-known people that came for his father's sake.

Oh goodness, I have rambled on. There are so many things she said that I haven't thought of in years. I hope this helps. Let me know if you have any other questions. I can't guarantee I know the answers, but I'll try.

Wendy

"That's interesting about the funeral," Meredith said when she and Julia had both read it. "Thomas Van Orden must have been very well connected."

"And what politician would miss the opportunity to show-case his patriotism when there was a military man's funeral to go to?"

"The more things change, the more they stay the same," Meredith observed with a sigh. "Aunt Wendy didn't give us more information about Anita Grambs like I had hoped, but I'm betting Joanie would have heard something if Anita had turned up alive somewhere or even if her body had been found. And she very likely would have passed that on to Wendy."

"Yeah," Julia said. "If she regularly used Anita as an example, having her found dead would have been the icing on her cautionary cake. I guess all we learn from her story now is that it can be dangerous to be around very influential people."

"So where do we go from here?" Meredith sat down in front of Julia's desk and grabbed a notepad. "I think most of my questions are about Spencer at this point."

"Exactly. What does he really want? Is he after Van Orden because of profiteering? Or is he after those jewels?"

"And where did he get that watch?" Meredith asked, starting a list. "And was he the one who searched Mrs. Bryleigh's room the other day?"

"And, if he did, did he find the letter?"

"Right," Meredith said, struggling to keep up. "And if the mystery man at White Oak Arbor calling himself Sam Russell wasn't Spencer, who was he?"

"I can tell you right now, it wasn't me."

Meredith caught her breath and turned to see Spencer standing in the doorway to Julia's office, backpack and all.

"Sorry," he said. "I didn't mean to startle anyone, but there was nobody at the reception desk or in the front office, so I thought I'd try back here."

"Come in," Julia said, still looking a little startled. "I think Carmen must be away from her desk for a moment. Can we get you coffee or anything?"

"No, I'm fine, thanks." Spencer took the chair next to Meredith. "Anyway, you were talking about that letter the lady said she got from Matt Van Orden. You think I took it?"

"I didn't say that." Meredith picked up her notepad and held it where he couldn't easily read what she had written. "I was only wondering if you could have been the person who checked in at the care center but didn't actually visit the room on the sign-in sheet."

"I'd think Vanessa Van Orden would be a more likely suspect," Spencer said tightly.

"Maybe so. But this person was a man, so it couldn't have been her."

"She could have sent somebody to do it for her, couldn't she? She's got money enough."

"I suppose. But since you're here, maybe it's time you answered a few questions."

Spencer shrugged. "Okay."

"What do you know about Lydia Cooper and her mother?" Meredith asked, watching his eyes.

Again he shrugged. "Only what was in the paper. What you've told me."

"Have you ever been to the White Oak Arbor Care Center?"

"No. No reason to."

"And you don't know anything about the letter Mrs. Bryleigh says she got from Matt Van Orden?"

"Again, only what was in the paper. I'd like to know about it though. If it says something about what was going on with the Van Ordens at the time, that might be important. And it might be something Vanessa Van Orden would like to suppress."

"Maybe," Julia agreed. "But what about you? What are you after in all this?"

Spencer frowned at her. "I told you about what happened when I was overseas. I want whatever Van Orden is up to to be exposed and shut down."

"And that's all?"

Meredith looked at him, watching his face, waiting for an answer. His expression showed nothing but exasperation.

"What else is there?"

"There are the jewels," Meredith said. "They were worth a small fortune in their day. They'd still be quite a haul today."

"The jewels?"

"They were never recovered. If someone could track down the right information, he might find a nice little treasure he could sell off a bit at a time without anyone being the wiser."

Now Spencer looked angry. "That has nothing to do with my interest in the Van Ordens. I told you why I want them investigated. If that's not good enough for you, I'll take my business elsewhere."

"You're not our only client regarding the Van Ordens," Julia said evenly.

Meredith nodded. "In this matter, we have an obligation to Lydia Cooper as much as to you to follow whatever leads we have, to question anyone who might have information, to find out the truth, whatever it is."

"All right," Spencer said, only slightly mollified. "And exactly what have I done that would make you suspect me?"

"You have Matt Van Orden's watch."

He pressed his lips together. "You must be very observant."

"I do try to be," Meredith said, "but we're working on a case with Thomas David Van Orden and Matthew Andrew Van Orden. They naturally spring to mind when I see the initials TDV and MAV. And I read in Matt's obituary that he'd gone to Emory University. It didn't take much to draw the conclusion. But that still leaves the question about how you came to have it."

"I didn't do anything illegal, if that's what you're thinking."

"Where did you get it?"

"It was passed down to me. A keepsake, like I said."

"How did that happen?" Julia asked him.

"My grandfather gave it to me. Before he died."

"How long ago was that?"

"About ten years ago now," Spencer said.

"And where did he get it?" Meredith asked. "Do you know?"

"From his grandfather, he told me."

"The one from Ireland?"

Spencer nodded.

"So that was your great-great-grandfather," Julia said. "That's going pretty far back. And were you ever told where he got it?"

"To be honest, I don't know much about him. Actually, part of all this in having you check out the Van Ordens has to do with that watch. I've been trying to figure out how that connects to my great-great-grandfather. I'd like to know not only who he was but how he ended up where he did and why. I've tried the usual methods, but I don't know if an ancestry site is going to be able to tell me a lot, especially when I don't much know where to look."

Meredith was intrigued. "Tracing someone only as far back as a great-great-grandfather shouldn't be all that hard. But it sounds like you have a complicated family history."

"Yeah, you could call it that."

"You know who your great-grandfather was," she said. "Why don't you know about his father?"

"Well, I know something about his father," Spencer admitted. "But his father didn't know who he was himself."

"Was he adopted?" she asked.

"In a way," Spencer said. "When he was in his early twenties."

"But somebody had to have taken care of him when he was a child, whether or not that person was one of his actual parents."

"To be honest, we have no idea about all that. That's part of what I want to try to find out now."

Meredith was getting more and more intrigued. "Maybe you'd better tell me the story in your own way, and then I'll know what to ask you about it."

"Maybe that's best. We're fairly sure he was twenty or twenty-one in 1918. That's the earliest we have on him. Nobody really knew where he came from. He remembered he'd been on a boat, but that's all he knew. My grandfather always said he must have been in the service even then, but there was no actual evidence he had been. Not at that time."

"Does that mean there was later?"

"Definitely, but I'll get to that. I'm talking about 1918, which is as far back as his known history goes. Evidently, things were a lot more lax during World War I than they got to be in succeeding wars. Some men who were shell-shocked just wandered off, off the battlefield or even out of the hospitals where they were being cared for. There were many of them who had been so traumatized by what they'd seen and done or who had severe injuries, particularly head injuries, that they couldn't remember who they were or where they'd been or which outfit they belonged to."

"Did that happen to your great-great-grandfather?"

"Yeah." Spencer gave her a wry grin. "You might as well call him Drew. It's a lot easier than saying 'great-great-grandfather' all the time. According to my grandpa, he always went by Drew. But what his real name was or where he came from, nobody ever knew."

"But shouldn't you be contacting someone in Great Britain about this? I mean, if he was British—"

"That's the thing. He wasn't British. He was American. He showed up in a little village called Ballycastle, which is on the northern coast of Ireland. Nobody knows how he got to such a remote place. They figured he had to have been in the war one way or other, but nobody they contacted in the American forces over there could identify him. They thought maybe he'd gotten on a boat from Scotland or England or even Wales and come over that way and then wandered around until he ended up there."

"That's quite a story. Was he in uniform when he was found?"

Spencer shook his head. "What my grandfather was told was that he had on what a laborer would have worn at the time, no matter where he was from in Britain. They don't know how long he might have wandered before someone took him in."

"Someone?"

"My great-great-grandmother's family, as you might expect."

Meredith returned his grin. "It's a logical conclusion."

"There's not that much to tell after that. He stayed in Ireland. His son came to America after the war. The rest of our family history is here in the US. And he came from the US. They were always sure of that, if nothing else."

"But you never knew who he really was." Meredith considered for a moment. "You're right about the record keeping back then. There must have been a lot of men who were injured or traumatized and who didn't know who they were, and a lot of families back at home who were told their loved ones were killed or believed killed."

She was thinking of Calvin Benn at that point. *Believed* killed. The *Otranto* had sunk between Scotland and Ireland. Could he have made it to the Irish coast alive? He was American, he'd been on the ship with Matthew Van Orden, and he'd had Matt's watch. Could he have been the amnesiac who showed up in Ballycastle, Ireland?

"And when someone like that never came home because he didn't know he had a home to go to," Spencer said, "what could his family do but believe he was dead?"

"Did anybody ever say that he wanted to know where he'd come from?" Meredith asked. "Did he want to know who he was?"

"I don't think I ever heard about him trying to find out. He might have, but it's nothing I ever heard my grandfather or anyone else mention. Maybe after a while he just accepted things as they were. I would have loved to ask my great-grandfather about it, but he died about three years before I was born. And I wish I had talked to my grandfather about it more than I did. He used to tell me stories, and we'd guess who he might have been and why he ended up in

Ireland, but Grandpa died about ten years ago. I was still finishing high school and didn't have much time for family then. I'm sorry I can't ask him all my questions now."

"That is a shame. Did he leave behind a diary or letters or any documents of any kind that refer to Drew? I know they would be from after he showed up in Ireland, but they might give us some clues."

"There's not much of anything actually. There's one picture my great-great-grandparents sent to my grandfather when they made their grand trip to France in the late seventies. Of course, they were in their seventies by then too, so it would be hard to make a certain comparison to pictures of Drew when he was only twenty. Grandpa always said his grandfather never liked to have his picture taken."

"I'd like to see that one anyway, if I could," Meredith said. "Every little bit helps."

"I was hoping you'd say that."

He opened the notebook and handed her a faded Polaroid photograph of an older couple in Paris. The setting sun was behind them, so they were more in shadow than in light, but they were holding hands and leaning forward to just touch their cheeks together as they gazed into the camera, the space between their bodies perfectly framing the backlit skeleton of the Eiffel Tower behind them. It was a charming picture, but there wasn't much she could tell from it. Could it be Calvin Benn?

"I see what you mean about making comparisons from that," Meredith said, handing it back. "Is there anything else?"

"There's really only a couple of things." Spencer took out a hard-sided notebook and opened it up. From it, he took out a carefully preserved document and spread it out on the desk. "What do you think?"

It was a letter, Meredith thought at first, and then she realized she was wrong. It was a citation. She turned it slightly so she and Julia could both read it.

It had the king's coat of arms at the top, and below it was written THE WAR OF 1914 - 1918.

"This shows a Second Lieutenant A. Robinson was mentioned in a dispatch for 'gallant and distinguished services in the field.'"

"A. Robinson?" Meredith asked. "Not D?"

"A for Andrew, of course," Spencer said.

"'I have it in command from the King to record His Majesty's high appreciation of the services rendered,'" Julia read. "That's quite an honor, isn't it?"

"It's not a medal," Spencer said. "But it's a commendation. And then there's this."

He took out another piece of paper. This one looked much newer. It was a letter dated June of 1969.

It was from a major general and addressed to Andrew Robinson at an address in York, England.

"This thanks him upon his retirement for his work in British intelligence during both world wars and after," Julia said, "not only in devoting his time and effort, but in exhausting his personal resources to the cause. That's pretty impressive."

"Yeah." There was pride in Spencer's expression. "He must have done a lot of things that I don't know anything about. I was—" He took out the watch and put it on the desk. "This was where I started from. I decided I was going to see if I could trace this down and figure out how it connected to my great-great-grandfather. I checked out the records for Emory in 1915. It blew me away when I saw MAV was Matt Van Orden. Then I saw that newspaper article about the theft back in 1918, and I knew I had to find out how Drew got the watch. It couldn't have been his own, because I know Matt is buried in the Van Orden family plot."

"True," Meredith said. "But I have an idea about who Drew might have been. Can you bring up that track meet picture, Jules?"

"Sure."

Julia tapped a few keys, and then the picture of Matt Van Orden and his two friends in their track clothes came onto her computer screen.

Spencer frowned at it. "Who's that?"

"That's Matt Van Orden on the left," Meredith said. "Next to him is Calvin Benn, and Tyler Porter is on the right. They all joined up during World War I and were reported killed when their troopship sank off the coast of Scotland."

Spencer's frown deepened. "And?"

"Except Calvin was reported missing, *believed* killed. Maybe, somehow, he ended up on the Irish coast not knowing who he was or where he'd come from."

Spencer leaned closer to the screen, peering at Calvin Benn. Then he got out the Polaroid of his great-great-grandparents in 1970s Paris.

"No," he said finally. "Drew isn't Calvin. He's Matt."

Chapter Seventeen

"He's what?" Meredith gasped.

Julia squinted at her computer monitor. "I can't tell."

"Look at his nose." Spencer pointed at the picture of Drew. "Now look at Matt's. Yes, it's slightly different because he's seventy-something in the Paris one and not seventeen or eighteen, but I can see a resemblance."

"I think he's right," Meredith said. "Look at Calvin's nose. It's a totally different shape. And look at Matt's eyebrows. They're finer than Calvin's and they curve up when he smiles just like Drew's in the Paris picture. So that's his own watch that was passed down to you. Wow."

"Then who's buried in Matt's grave?" Julia asked. "Calvin?"

"How would that have happened?" Spencer asked. "If they brought him home, he must have been identified by something."

"Things weren't all that well organized back then," Meredith said. "There might have been some kind of ID on the body that said he was Matt Van Orden, but remember what Aunt Joanie said about Matt's funeral?"

Julia nodded. "She said it was a closed casket 'once they got him out of the water.' Sounds to me like the body must have been in bad shape by then. You have two young men the same age, the same build, both dark haired, and the military makes a positive identification, I can't imagine even the family would dispute it by then. It could be that Matt's father wasn't up to looking at what was left of what he thought was his son."

"But how would Calvin have gotten Matt's ID?" Spencer asked. "Unless he took it from Matt for some reason, or…"

His eyes widened as he trailed off.

"Or Matt put his ID on him," Meredith supplied. "I can only guess at this point, but maybe Calvin was already dead by then. And Matt didn't want to go back home. Ever."

"But why?" Spencer pressed. "Why?"

"Aunt Joanie told Aunt Wendy—"

"Wait. Wait. Who are they?"

"Sorry," Meredith said. "I forgot we hadn't told you about them. Aunt Wendy is the aunt of one of our friends. She used to take care of Aunt Joanie, who was her great-aunt. Joanie worked for the Van Ordens in the early part of the twentieth century. She knew Thomas and Matt Van Orden. Wendy's told us a few things she remembers Joanie saying about the family."

"Man," Spencer breathed.

"One thing I remember she said was that Joanie mentioned Matt and his father arguing a lot. She said—" Meredith frowned. "Can you open her email, Julia? I want to get this right."

"Sure," Julia said.

"This is the part," Meredith said once the email was on the screen. "Aunt Joanie remembered Matt saying 'I can't stay here anymore and let you keep on.' What do you think that means?"

"I don't know," Spencer said. "It could be anything."

"And it could be the same thing you wanted Van Orden Munitions investigated for. Something Matt knew his father was involved in. Something he couldn't support."

"Profiteering. Man. Then he could have written that letter to Mrs. Cooper's mother. And if he did, and if he assured her that her grandfather didn't steal those jewels…" Spencer blinked at Meredith.

"And what about that letter from the military?" Julia asked. "It mentions him 'exhausting his personal resources.' If he was washed up on the beach in a place like Ballycastle with nothing but the clothes on his back, what personal resources could he have had to exhaust in the war effort? What could he have carried with him but the Van Orden jewels?"

Meredith felt her heartbeat quicken. "It makes perfect sense. He had an opportunity to disappear, to get away from decades of corruption and death that his family had been involved in, and use some of that dirty money to help make things right."

"But he couldn't have known there would be a shipwreck," Spencer protested.

"No, of course not. Who knows what his plan might have been originally, but the wreck was exactly what he needed so he could disappear."

"And he let James Brandon take the fall for the theft? I don't care how noble his reasons for taking the jewels might have been, that was a pretty underhanded thing to do."

Julia winced. "It was. It doesn't fit in with what else we're thinking about Matt."

"I wish we had found that letter Lydia's mother claims she got," Meredith said. "It would probably fill in a lot of holes. Maybe he wrote it years ago and for some reason it didn't get to Lydia's mother until much later."

Julia frowned. "But if he had written it during the war or right after, Lydia's mother hadn't been born yet. Lydia's grandmother was still very young. She was only eleven when her father was sent to prison."

"Right now, we can only guess at a lot of this. Matt was—" Meredith laughed suddenly. "I just thought of something else that makes it likely that Matt was the one who washed up on that beach."

"And that would be?" Julia asked.

"What was Matt's full name?"

"Matthew Andrew Van Orden," Spencer said.

Meredith nodded. "And what was your great-great-grandfather's name?"

"Drew Robinson." Spencer gave her a grudging grin. "Andrew Robinson. Matthew Andrew."

"Exactly."

Spencer raked one hand through his dark hair. "That's pretty incredible. I suppose we could rule him out of being in the family plot if we had that body exhumed and DNA tested."

"It's possible, I suppose," Julia said. "But that would take a court order, and we'd have to have some pretty good reasons for doing it unless the family agreed up front."

"Which I doubt they'd do," Meredith added.

"Especially not if we find evidence that they've been involved in illegal activities for the past hundred-plus years and we make that evidence public."

"True. That probably wouldn't endear us to Mrs. Van Orden."

"So what do we do?" Spencer asked.

"We keep investigating." Meredith started writing again. "We still need to find out more about KBMJ, which hasn't been an easy task so far."

"And it would be good to find that letter," Julia put in. "It will either confirm or refute this particular theory."

"Fair enough." Spencer took the documents he had brought with him and the pocket watch and returned them to his backpack. Then he stood up. "Let me know what you find out. I have some other things I'd like to look into."

"Like what?" Julia asked him.

For a moment, Meredith thought he was going to clam up again. "We're on your side, okay?" she said. "You're paying us to help you find out what happened and what's happening. If you have some kind of lead, then you ought to tell us. It might fit in with something we're already investigating. Or maybe we'll get some ideas based on yours. Now's not the time to be secretive."

He smiled sheepishly. "Yeah, I guess you're right. My family thinks I should keep my head down and not stir up trouble, so I've been keeping this to myself for a while now. I'm not used to having anybody in my corner."

Meredith gave his shoulder a pat. "That's what we're here for. Really. Now tell us what you have going on."

"To be honest, it's not much. That guy from Van Orden, Jack, I'm trying to figure out more about him. He wouldn't tell me much of anything when I talked to him that first day, but then he told you to check into KBMJ. I've caught him a couple of times since then when he was leaving the Van Orden Building. Both times he told me to take off. The second time he said there would be trouble if I didn't stay out of it."

"Out of what?" Julia asked. "The investigation?"

"I'm sure that's what he meant, but I'd like to try to talk to him one more time if I can."

Meredith studied him for a moment. "If he will talk to you, see if you can find out why he was willing to tell us about KBMJ and not you."

"Yeah, that's something I'd like to know too. All I can figure is that, since you're the pros, he thinks you can do something about what's been going on and that I'd only get in the way."

"Just be careful, okay? We can't stop you from talking to people, even if we can't let you in on the official investigation."

"We do think it would be a good idea if you stayed out of it though," Julia added, and Meredith nodded.

"Yeah, I know." Spencer swung his backpack onto his shoulder. "I'll let you know if I get any leads, okay?"

"Sure," Meredith said.

Spencer started out of the office door and then turned back. "This theory about Matt being Drew is quite a kick in the head." He smiled. "But it's pretty interesting too. I might just about believe it."

"It seems to fit. We'll see if we can find anything to back it up."

"I'll get back to you if I get ahold of anything worth passing on."

With that, he gave them a wave and disappeared into the hallway.

Meredith heard him tell Carmen thanks and then the opening and shutting of the front door. She stared at Julia. "Wow."

"Tell me about it," Julia said. "But it sure would be nice to have something to confirm our theory."

"The letter again." Meredith sighed. "We can't pin everything on the possibility of finding it. Maybe we'd better see what we can figure out about KBMJ and whether they're involved in anything illegal now."

"Fair enough. I'll be happy to help you research that until five o'clock," Julia said, "but after that, I'm going home." She had a mischievous smile on her face. "Got a hot date."

Meredith chuckled. "Well, I'm not going to stand in the way of that. Beau would never forgive me."

They spent the rest of the day trying to get information on KBMJ, but apart from its bland website, there was very little mention of the company on the internet, and all of those merely parroted the information the company had already put out. If Mr. Jarvi at Van Orden was a figurehead, what was going on behind the scenes? And what exactly did Jack know?

***

Meredith was on her way home when her phone rang. She pulled into a parking lot to answer.

"Hi, Meredith. It's Spencer Robinson."

"Hi, Spencer. How are you?"

"I'm fine." Spencer said, sounding almost breathless. "Listen, Jack Jackson just called me up."

Her heart immediately started to beat faster. "Jack? What's going on?"

"He told me to call you. He said he promised you some information, but he's afraid to call your office or even your private number in case somebody finds out."

"Okay. And?"

"He said he has more information about Van Orden Munitions. He told me there's a warehouse where they store a lot of the stuff they don't want anybody to know about. It's not owned by the company. Actually, he said it's owned by the girlfriend of one of the company lawyers. Financed by Van Orden, of course, but bought in the girlfriend's name so it wouldn't be obviously connected to the company."

"So what's the deal? What are they hiding there?"

Spencer huffed. "He wouldn't tell me. I think he's still worried about Vanessa finding out about him helping us. He said he'd leave the place unlocked for us so he could be somewhere else when we had a look around. That way if Vanessa found out about us being there, he wouldn't be implicated."

"When are we supposed to do this?"

"Tonight. Jack said that area's pretty much deserted by six and he's already been by to unlock the place for us if we want to go."

"I don't know. Those munitions plants are pretty secure. I can't see it being as easy as just leaving a door unlocked for us."

"No, it's not their plant. It's just a warehouse. A big storage unit. Anyway, I'm going. If you're interested, I'd love for you to come."

Meredith considered for a moment. She ought to call Julia, but she and Beau had a romantic evening planned for their anniversary, and she hated to disturb them. Just having a quick look at a warehouse would likely be no big deal. And Spencer was a Marine. He ought to be well able to deal with anything unexpected they might run into.

"If he's putting himself on the line to give us this opportunity," Meredith said, "I guess we should take advantage of it while we can. What time did you have in mind?"

"Right now, if you can," Spencer said. "I want to get some real evidence about what Van Orden has been up to, not just currently but for the past century or more. And I want it to be more than suspicion or gossip. I want to have some hard evidence about what they're doing. Jack says we can find it in this warehouse tonight."

Meredith considered calling Quin to let him know where she was going, but then she decided against it. She didn't want to make him feel obligated to come along. She wasn't going to start off their relationship by being needy. She and Spencer would just go see what was in that warehouse and then, she hoped, tell the police they had proof of what they had suspected all along.

"Okay," she said. "Should we meet somewhere and go together?"

"That's probably a good idea. We're less likely to be noticed if there's just one vehicle."

"Right. Let me come pick you up. I don't drive a bright yellow sports car."

He chuckled. "Got you. Yeah, if you'd pick me up at my hotel, that'd be great. I'll be watching for you."

Meredith went back to the office and left a note on Julia's desk as a little bit of insurance. A few minutes later, she pulled up to the hotel and found Spencer standing out front. She chuckled a little to herself seeing he was all in black, from the combat boots to the T-shirt that hugged every muscle in his arms and chest. At least he didn't have black under his eyes.

He hopped into the car, and she pulled away from the curb.

"Where to?" she asked.

He gave her an address. "Do you know where that is?"

"No. I can ask my phone."

"That's all right. I already looked it up."

He gave her precise directions, and soon they were in a group of warehouses off Highway 21.

"It still looks pretty busy around here," Meredith observed.

"I'm guessing these are some of the big operations. They probably run twenty-four hours a day. The one we want is a little bit farther out."

They drove on, made several turns, and ended up in a place that was, as Jack had told Spencer, deserted. The warehouse was old. It had probably been there since old Thomas Van Orden's time, maybe even earlier. Meredith parked at the side of the building so the car wouldn't be immediately spotted.

"This looks like it was used for cotton back in the day," she said once they had gotten out.

"Yeah." Spencer looked the building up and down. A wan light from the shaded bulb over the door gave everything a yellowish tint. "I bet there's a lot of history here. Let's see what we can see."

As promised, the door was unlocked. It was dim inside, the overhead lights turned low for the night, and Spencer took a small flashlight from the clip on his belt.

"We might not need it," he said, "but I thought I'd bring it just in case."

She looked it over dubiously. "It doesn't look like it would put out much light."

Spencer grinned and, shielding the end of the flashlight between his free hand and his chest, he switched it on. It gave out a brilliant white light.

"LEDs," he said. "There's nothing like 'em."

"I'm convinced," she said, shading her eyes with one hand. "I'm convinced."

He turned the light off, and the warehouse seemed dimmer than before. It wasn't a huge space, but it was still a warehouse. It was still large, and it was packed with crates, crates that stretched far back into the shadows.

"Did Jack give you any clues about what we're supposed to be looking for?" Meredith asked, refusing to whisper even though she wanted to.

"He said we'd know it when we saw it."

Meredith moved forward, looking at the boxes and how they were marked. Mostly they were labeled with only a series of numbers. Sometimes there were letters or a combination of both. Frequently, there was a date. These boxes could be holding anything. She and Spencer moved farther into the warehouse, and pallets of boxes were replaced by huge shipping containers.

Spencer looked one up and down. "One of those would be convenient for getting rid of anything the company didn't want found."

"I guess so," Meredith said with a shiver. "But what are we supposed to find in here? I'm assuming these are all Van Orden munitions being shipped out. It's not illegal for a munitions company to ship munitions."

"Unless, for some reason, what's in these boxes isn't what it seems to be."

"I don't know how we'd know. We'd have to know where they're going and to whom and at what price and what quality they are and—"

"Maybe there's some kind of transaction record in here," Spencer said. "Log books. Names, addresses, I don't know."

"And Jack didn't tell you anything else besides what you told me?"

"No, just that we'd know what he was talking about when we saw it. I—"

They both froze at the sound of a low, feminine laugh. Then there were footsteps from at least three or four pairs of feet.

"Who's there?" Spencer asked, shining his flashlight into the black gap between two of the shipping crates.

Vanessa Van Orden stepped into the light, a cool smile on her full lips and a stylish, nickel-plated pistol in her hand. "Good evening."

Meredith licked her suddenly dry lips when she saw three security guards behind her.

"Jack told you you'd realize what he was talking about when you came across it," Vanessa told them. "Well, here I am."

Chapter Eighteen

"WHAT ARE YOU DOING HERE?" Meredith tried to keep her voice steady in the dimness of the warehouse.

Spencer put himself between her and Vanessa. "This was a setup. You've had Jack leading us on all this time."

Vanessa gave him a slight smile. "He'll do anything I tell him to, and I realized how useful he could be in finding out what's going on with you." She looked Spencer up and down, her expression turning hard. "Who are you? A reporter? Or only someone trying to get a nice payoff to keep quiet? Exactly what have you found out?"

Meredith nodded toward the gun, trying to look as if it didn't bother her. "You don't need that."

"You're trespassing," Vanessa said. "I have every right to keep thieves and vandals out."

"We didn't come to take anything. We were just looking for information."

"Information?" Vanessa asked, clearly unconvinced.

"You might be interested in what I found out about Spencer here," Meredith said. "You know I was helping Lydia Cooper look into that jewel theft back in 1918."

"What does that have to do with him?"

"In looking into that, I found out something that might interest you. A family matter."

Vanessa pursed her lips expectantly.

"You're related."

Vanessa frowned. "What do you mean?"

"I'm your great-great-great-nephew," Spencer told her.

"He didn't come here to find out anything but who his great-great-grandfather was," Meredith said. "As it turns out, strange as it sounds, that was your brother-in-law, Matt Van Orden, who disappeared in 1918."

Vanessa gaped at them both. "What? Matt died in World War I. His ship sank."

"It sank, but Matt survived. He didn't want to go back to the navy, so he changed his name and stayed where he was."

Vanessa stared at her and then laughed abruptly. "I'll give you points for creativity, but that has to be the most ridiculous explanation I've ever heard. And what does it have to do with your being in here?"

"The door was open," Spencer said. "You can see for yourself."

"But that doesn't explain why you were asking so many questions and why you took the bait to come snoop around here. So tell the truth. Are you a blackmailer or a whistleblower?"

Meredith moved into Spencer's view and gave him a subtle warning glance. "We wanted to find out more about Matt," she said to Vanessa. "Jack made it sound like we could find some information here. We haven't touched anything. We didn't break in." She took Spencer's arm and started to back toward the door. "If you say there's nothing to see here, then there's nothing to see and we'll get out of your way."

"You'll get out of my way all right," Vanessa said. "Or I should say, my security staff will put you out of my way." She nodded to the trio of burly men behind her, and they moved up to either side of her. "I'm not buying your story, and it doesn't matter what you've found out at this point. Neither of you will be telling anybody anything."

"It's true about Matt," Spencer said, his dark eyes flashing. "His ship sank, but he got to shore in Ireland, and he still had the jewels he stole from his father. He used them to help the war effort, World War I and World War II. He wanted to do something to make up for what his father had been doing. For what his brother did. For what you're still doing now, buying off politicians, cheating the government, sending military personnel out with substandard equipment."

Meredith's hold on his arm tightened. They wouldn't be bluffing their way out of this now.

Spencer made a sudden move toward the gun, and there were suddenly four guns on them rather than one.

"No!" Meredith attempted to hold him where he was, and he glared at her, his breath coming in frustrated huffs.

"Don't try it," Vanessa said sweetly.

"My business partner knows all about what we've found out so far," Meredith told her evenly. "If we disappear, she'll take it all to the police. You won't be able to cover it up. I sent her a text about where I was going and why. The police will trace this all back to you."

Vanessa's laugh was echoed by her employees.

"They might trace you here, but they won't be able to connect me to any of this. Our warehouses are right in the middle of the busiest part of the district. They run 24/7. These?" She gestured toward the stacks of boxes and containers that surrounded them. "They're computer parts headed overseas. They're owned by someone who doesn't even know we're here. I chose this place because it's out of the way, and you came right to it."

"You're still going to be checked out," Meredith said. "My partner knows—"

Vanessa grabbed Meredith's purse, riffled through it, and took out one of her business cards.

"Get over to their office." She handed the card to one of her men and then thrust the purse back into Meredith's arms. "If there's a note, get rid of it. If there's a file on us, get rid of that too. And if there's anybody in the office, well…" She smiled matter-of-factly.

The man nodded. "Got it."

"I've been very successful for the past twenty years or so," Vanessa said as the man's echoing footsteps faded away. "But really, my husband and his father had this all in motion long before I came along. All I had to do was not mess it up. I've done under-the-table deals with politicians and foreign governments and revolutionary leaders. I'm not about to let an old lady and a kid with a hero complex spoil it all now."

She nodded to the two men still flanking her, and they stepped toward their hostages.

"What about Jack?" Meredith asked, scrambling for something to stall them.

"What about him?" Vanessa asked.

"He knows what's going on here. He can tell the police."

"He's the one who's been warning me about you all along." Vanessa blew out a contemptuous breath. "I didn't realize how much he knew about our operations, but when he found out, he decided he wanted part of the take. It was his idea to get you out here. I'll have to give him a raise."

"We'll have to give him a medal," a voice said from the darkness behind her.

At that, the dim lights turned blindingly bright, and then there was the telltale click of guns being cocked from all around them.

"Stay where you are," the voice said, "and put the weapons on the floor."

The two security men looked at Vanessa and then put their guns down.

"I didn't tell you to do that!" she screamed at them.

"Come on now, Mrs. Van Orden," the voice said. "They're only doing the smart thing. They don't want to die. Do you?"

She stood there a moment longer, her chest heaving and her jaw clenched tight.

"Come on." Spencer held out his hand for her gun. "It's over."

She dropped her head and dropped her gun a little as if she were going to surrender, but then she suddenly lurched forward, raising it again. Spencer grabbed her wrist, twisting it to turn the gun aside, twisting it until, with a low cry, she let it go.

"Get those," he told Meredith, and she quickly scooped up the other two guns while he kept Vanessa and her men covered.

"Good job," the voice said.

From out of the darkness came a police captain and two officers. With them were two men in dark suits. Four more officers came from behind the packing containers behind Meredith and Spencer. Last of all was Jack.

"You set me up," Vanessa spat, seeing him. "You all set me up."

"I couldn't let you do it anymore," Jack said as the police hand-cuffed her and her men. "I knew something was wrong about the company a long time ago, but it wasn't until last year that I started actually doing some looking around of my own."

Vanessa glared at him. "Last year? What about last year? I happen to know you got an eighteen-percent raise and an executive benefits package last year. What did—"

"Last year," Jack said, his voice shaking. "Last year, I buried my son. Remember?"

"So?" she spat.

"They sent him home in a coffin with a flag draped over it."

Vanessa gave a slight shrug. "I had Dinah send a wreath or something. I don't know the details."

"I talked to one of his buddies. He was with my son when he was killed. He's not fighting now, because he doesn't have legs anymore. He told me about the group that set their unit up. Do you know who made the weapons that group had?"

Vanessa's mouth hardened, and she stood there, unmoving.

"They were KBMJ. They were Van Orden made. Just like the assault rifle that blew up in my son's hands that day. Jason's friend told me all that. He said nobody here at home knew, but he wanted somebody to know." Jack's face was white and still, but his eyes were cold flames. "Now I know. Now everybody will know."

"But all this?" Meredith asked. "How did you—?"

"You started asking questions, enough to make her nervous," he told her. "You didn't know much, but I made her think you did. I kept telling her somebody at the company was leaking information to you and that you were going to take it to the government. She started questioning me about what you were doing, and I told her I had a plan for getting rid of you both."

Spencer chuckled.

"And so you set this all up with the police and with...?" Meredith looked at the dark-suited men.

"FBI, ma'am," one of them said. "We helped Mr. Jackson set up this little meeting. When he realized that you were investigating Van Orden, he finally got the courage to let us know what he had suspected for some time, and we thought it was something we ought to check out."

Meredith put one hand up to her hair. "I may have to cover a little more gray next time I go to the salon, but I'm glad you did."

"You can't arrest me," Vanessa said, wrenching around to face the police captain. "I haven't done anything wrong."

"No?" one of the FBI agents asked. "I think the recording we just made might prove otherwise."

"That doesn't prove anything," Vanessa insisted. "I was just trying to get these people to leave me and my company alone. They've been pestering me for days now, and I've had enough."

"It sounded to me like you were planning on killing them both. That along with the information we already have from Jack here ought to be enough to have the federal government go over Van Orden Munitions with a fine-tooth comb."

"I want my lawyer!"

"Sure, sure," the captain said.

He read her and her men their rights and then told his officers to take them out to the squad cars.

"What about the other one?" Meredith asked, still anxious. "The one she sent out to my office. I don't think there's anybody there, but if my partner happened to come in for something—"

"Don't worry," the captain said. "My men took him into custody as soon as he got out the door. He won't be bothering your partner or anybody else."

Meredith exhaled. "Thank God." She looked over at Jack and shook her head. "You could have let me know what was going on."

"Sorry," he said with a sheepish grin. "I thought it would be best if you got Mrs. Van Orden to actually admit to what she'd been doing, at least enough for the police to make an arrest and to have probable cause for investigating the company."

"Actually," one of the FBI agents said, "that one's on us. We didn't want either of you giving anything away before Mrs. Van Orden incriminated herself." He gave Spencer a stern look. "You nearly blew the whole operation."

"Sorry," Spencer said. "I was only trying to keep Meredith from getting killed."

"And you," Meredith said.

"Yeah, well, that too."

He beamed at her, and she couldn't help a smile in return.

"You two are going to have to come to the station and give us statements about what happened here tonight and anything else you know about Mrs. Van Orden and her business dealings," the captain said.

"We'd be happy to," Meredith said.

Spencer nodded. "Absolutely. This has been a much wilder ride than I expected when I started asking questions."

"What was that you were saying about her brother-in-law and a jewel theft and World War I?" the captain asked.

"It's a pretty crazy story," Spencer admitted. "But I think we've got it all figured out now." He turned to Meredith. "We've got to let Mrs. Cooper know about all this too. I guess she'll be pretty happy to tell her mom that James Brandon was innocent all along."

"I think she would have been happier if we had found Matt's letter," Meredith said, "but she'll be happy to know that Van Orden Munitions & Manufacturing won't continue the way it has been all this time."

The captain nodded. "Sounds like there are some pretty important people involved in this, from what Mrs. Van Orden said. All the way up to Washington."

"I hope they find them," Spencer said tightly. "I hope they blow all this sky high. Making money off this kind of thing, especially at the expense of giving people in the service the kind of support and protection they need to do their jobs, and putting all their lives in danger is so wrong I don't even have the words for it."

Meredith put one soothing hand on his arm. "We've got them now. Let's go give the police our statements. We'll meet you there, Captain." She nodded to the FBI agents. "Gentlemen."

One of them nodded back. "Ma'am."

"About that letter," Jack said once the others were gone. "Mrs. Van Orden was worried about what Mrs. Bryleigh said about it, afraid it might look bad for the company, so she sent me out to the home to see if I could find it. I told her I came up empty, but I was lying."

Chapter Nineteen

"Is THIS THE LETTER?" MEREDITH reached out to take the slightly yellowed page Jack held. "Matt's letter?"

Jack handed it to her. "It was in the frame of that family picture."

"Mrs. Bryleigh really did a good job hiding it," Meredith said. "And then forgot where it was."

"But why?" Spencer asked. "Why keep it hidden?"

Jack nodded toward the letter. "You read that. You'll understand."

With Spencer looking over her shoulder, Meredith carefully unfolded the paper. The message inside was written in an easy, masculine hand with decided lines and few flourishes. It was dated May 27, 1979.

Dear Mrs. Bryleigh,

I had every intention of sending this letter to your mother, the daughter of James Brandon, but I understand she has recently passed away. Please accept my sincere condolences. Please accept also my deepest apologies for the hardship I unwittingly brought to your mother, to your grandfather, and to all your family by the actions I took over sixty years ago.

Looking back, I realize that what I did was in many ways rash and badly planned. All I could see at the time was that I was going to war, quite possibly to my death, and I had to seize that opportunity to, at least in some part, make up for the wrongs done by generations of my family. I truly thought that the theft of my father's jewels would either be traced back to me or be forever left a mystery. It was quite a shock when I chanced to read only recently that your grandfather had been convicted of the crime and had died in prison.

I know this may not be of great personal comfort to you, Mrs. Bryleigh, but please believe me when I say that this was not entirely in vain. Those jewels were used to fund operations that were vital in not only the First World War, but the Second and beyond. I realize that it is small compensation to you and your family for the pain I have caused you all, but please know that the training, materials, and missions made possible by the proceeds of my theft have saved many lives.

So many have sacrificed to keep us and our loved ones safe. Thank you for your own sacrifice, unaware as it was. If you are able, please forgive me. I meant only to compensate in some small way for decades of my family's wrongs.

I will ask one other favor of you. I realize my half brother runs the company now and my father passed away some years ago. For the sake of all those who have been wronged by my family and by Van Orden Munitions & Manufacturing, I would like you to take this letter to the proper authorities and let them know what the company has been doing.

They have for decades been contracting with the federal government for munitions and supplies, overcharging for everything, splitting the profits with the politicians who made those contracts possible. They have cut corners by making substandard arms and related items. And those they could not sell under their own name, they passed along to another company. When I knew about it, that company was managed by friends of my father, Robert Kline, Adam Barrett, Frank Millhouse, and Walter Jefferson. It was called Coastline Commercial, but I know they had changed the name several times in the past and may have done so many times since then. It will take a major investigation to untangle all the connecting threads, but if you take this to the authorities, they will see to it that this evil practice is stopped for good.

For your peace of mind and my own, I wanted you to know the truth about your grandfather. Please rest assured that he was innocent of any involvement in the theft of the Van Orden jewels. Please use this letter to stop for all time the wrongdoing of Van Orden Munitions & Manufacturing.

With the most fervent prayer that God will bless you and your family, I am

Sincerely yours,

Matthew Andrew Van Orden

For a long moment, there was only silence.

"Was there an envelope?" Meredith asked finally.

"No," Jack said. "That was all that was there. And it seems like Mrs. Bryleigh never did anything about it."

"Why?" Spencer asked, his lips trembling. "She had all the information. At least she had enough to get someone to start an investigation."

"I don't know," Meredith said. "All we can do is ask her about it. I'll have to make an actual comparison, but this handwriting does look a lot like the sample we have of Matt's. We'll have it verified to be sure."

"I think Drew would still want this letter to be used in evidence," Spencer said. "I mean Matt. Vanessa will have to answer for her part in what Van Orden Munitions has been doing all this time."

"Good," Jack said, his voice low and hard.

"How long have you known?" Meredith asked him. "Since your son's death?"

"I wondered for a while before that, but I told myself not to make any waves. I didn't want to end up under a slab of concrete somewhere. But after Jason—" His voice broke, and then he cleared his throat. "After last year, I started doing a little snooping on my own. I didn't know what to do with the information I found out until he started asking questions." He nodded toward Spencer. "Sorry, son, but when you showed up out of the blue, I didn't know whether or not I could trust you with what I knew. But Magnolia Investigations is a professional organization." He looked at Meredith. "And when I knew you were on the case, I figured if you were the ones who blew the whistle on the company, I wouldn't have to be involved." There was a sudden wryness in his expression. "Chicken, I know, but I figured it was enough anyway. At least it is now."

Meredith smiled at him. "Jason would be proud of you."

Jack gave her a rueful grin and shrugged, and they followed him out of the warehouse.

***

"Happy now?" Meredith asked Spencer as she drove him back to his hotel.

"Yeah. I mean, I hope so."

She glanced over at him, puzzled. "What else do you want to happen?"

"I guess that's all. I found out about my great-great-grandfather, and even if he was a Van Orden, he was a hero, and I'm proud of that."

"But?" Meredith pressed.

"I don't know." Spencer slumped in his seat. "There's no guarantee that what Van Orden's been doing will really be investigated or that they'll be stopped."

"It's a start, Spencer. Don't despise small beginnings. We'll testify about what we know. So will Jack. Maybe we can even put Matt's letter into evidence, to show that this isn't a new thing for Van Orden. One step at a time. And if we save even one life by shutting them down, it's all worth it."

"This is what I wanted most for Christmas."

Aileen sat before the blazing hearth, nestled in Drew's arms. The war had been over for more than a month now, but it was Christmas Eve before he and Bran had finally come home.

"He has potential," Bran had said in the telling of his missions with Drew. "He's raw yet, but he's got the knack for it and nerves of steel."

Drew had chuckled then. "I was terrified the whole time."

"I always am. But you didn't show it, and that's the trick. The captain has big plans for you, lad. The war may be over, but that doesn't mean we don't still need men like you."

"That's what I came here for," Drew said, and then he'd taken Aileen's hand. "Besides one other thing."

He had written to her often while he was gone. One time he had written, When I get back to Ballycastle, when I get home, I want to ask you a question.

That had thrilled her and frightened her all at once, but now, sitting here before the late fire with Da already gone to bed and Bran asleep on the settee, Drew reminded her of the question he wanted to ask.

"A question?" she said, trying to make her lips smile and not tremble. "What is it?"

"Not the one I'd really like to ask," he admitted, his face flushed in the firelight, "but the best one for now."

"Well?"

"I want to go on with what I've been doing," he said. "I have a lot to learn, but I feel I've done some good. Much more than I would have if I were still back where I came from, being no good to anybody."

"I think that's a fine thing," she said, knowing there was pride shining from her eyes. "It's a noble thing to want to do."

"But it's likely to keep me away from here more often than not. For now anyway. I'd like— Well, I hope—"

"Yes?" she breathed.

"Will you wait, Aileen? At least for a little while. The war's over. I hope to get settled into something I can make a living at, and then I can actually have a home." He squeezed her hand. "A wife."

Of their own accord, her lashes fluttered to her cheeks. "I'll wait. As long as you want."

For a moment, everything was still, and then he took one finger and tilted up her chin.

"Look at me," he said softly.

She did as he asked, and his lake-blue eyes were soft and warm.

"I love you, Aileen," he whispered as he touched his lips to hers. "Always."

And I love him, she wrote in her diary once Bran had suddenly awakened and told her to get to bed so he and Drew could lay out their pallets before the fire and get some sleep. I would never have thought such a thing could happen to me, that by mere chance I should find him and that we should end up pledged to each other.

But no, I cannot believe it mere chance. The dear Lord has a way of taking what is meant for evil against us and turning it into great good. All that has happened, it was not how I would have fashioned it, but looking back, I see it could have happened no other way. And whatever lies ahead for us, I know we can trust Him to bring good out of it. Isn't this holy season, more than any other, good proof of that?

Chapter Twenty

THE NEXT DAY, MEREDITH ARRANGED to meet Lydia and her mother out at White Oak Arbor. She and Julia picked up Spencer on the way there.

"I know you don't know them," she told him, "but they'll be interested in your story, and I think they'd love to see the citations your great-great-grandfather got."

"I'm sure they'll be more interested in that letter, but at least they'll have some proof that Drew did what he claimed he did with the jewels."

Lydia and Mrs. Bryleigh were waiting for them in her room.

"Don't you look nice?" Meredith could see that the older woman was made up and had her hair done.

"You were here before," Mrs. Bryleigh said. "I remember. Did you find my letter?"

Meredith smiled.

Lydia's eyes widened. "Did you really? I mean, there really is a letter?"

"We didn't find it," Meredith said. "Someone else did."

"But who? Where was it?"

"I'll explain everything, but I thought you'd like to meet a couple of people first. This is Julia, my partner, Mrs. Bryleigh."

Lydia's mother nodded.

"And this is Spencer Robinson."

Spencer offered his hand to Mrs. Bryleigh. "Hi. I think we have some good news for you."

"Did you bring my letter?"

"Your letter was from Matt Van Orden, right?"

"He wrote to me," she said.

"Well, I just found out that Matt Van Orden was my great-great-grandfather."

"Oh really?" Mrs. Bryleigh patted his hand. "Aren't you sweet?"

"You're kidding me," Lydia gasped. "But—"

"Maybe we should all sit down so they can tell you everything," Julia said. "I heard all of this last night, and I still don't quite know what to think."

They pulled up some chairs so they'd be close to Mrs. Bryleigh, and then Meredith took out Matt Van Orden's letter.

"I think we'll save all the explanations for later. This is what you and your daughter want to see."

Lydia held her mother's hand as Meredith read the letter to them.

"'Please rest assured,'" she read finally, "'that he was innocent of any involvement in the theft of the Van Orden jewels.'"

"Now everyone will know for sure," Mrs. Bryleigh said, a tremor in her voice and her eyes shining. "They can't think I made it up anymore."

"Oh, Mom," Lydia murmured, a tear running down her cheek. "Now we can prove it's true."

"I have a question," Julia said. "Matt wanted all this about Van Orden to be made public. He wanted the company to be investigated. Why didn't that ever happen?"

Mrs. Bryleigh stared at her for a long moment, and Meredith thought she was going to be nothing but confused by the question. Then she shook her head.

"It was Danny."

Julia and Meredith looked at each other and then at Lydia.

"Danny?" Meredith asked.

"Danny Bryleigh was my father," Lydia told her, and then she knelt down at her mother's side. "What was it, Mom? What did Daddy say about the letter?"

Mrs. Bryleigh's lips trembled. "He said it was too dangerous. He said people like that killed little people like us if we said what we knew. He told me to burn the letter and not talk about it anymore. He— He made me afraid of what might happen. To me. To him." She clutched her daughter's hand. "To you."

"So you put it away."

Put it away, Meredith thought, and then forgot where it was.

"I didn't want anything to happen," Mrs. Bryleigh said. "I was scared."

Mother and daughter were both crying now. Meredith wanted to comfort them, but to her surprise, Spencer beat her to it.

"It's okay," he murmured, clasping his hands around theirs. "It's all right."

"One other thing," Meredith said. "Matt mentioned that he found out about James Brandon's death in a recent article. Do you know anything about that?"

"I think I know what it was," Lydia said. "I don't think I know where it is now, but when I was still in my teens, he was mentioned in a piece about people in the early part of the twentieth century who were convicted more on somebody's say-so rather than hard evidence. His part was just a couple of paragraphs. Mom kept the article, but I never thought much about it."

"You might want to see these too." Spencer handed Mrs. Bryleigh his great-great-grandfather's citations. "He did a lot of good with those jewels."

"And if you don't mind," Meredith said, "I'd like to include this letter as part of the evidence against Van Orden Munitions. It's not much, but it does mention the illegal activities that have been going on there for decades now. And it would make public the proof of James Brandon's innocence. Maybe we could even get him officially pardoned."

Mrs. Bryleigh reached out to clasp her hand. "Oh yes. Please. It would mean so much."

"Can you do that?" Spencer asked.

"I can't," Meredith said, "but I think Kevin Patterson can make it happen."

"The representative?" Lydia looked at her mother and then at Meredith and Julia. "Will he be interested in a case like this?"

"We've already contacted his office," Julia said. "Mostly about what's going on with Van Orden, but this is part of that. I think he can rattle enough cages to make something happen."

Spencer beamed at her. "That's great news. Maybe he can actually get something done, and we won't have any more incidents like what happened to Jack's son and his buddy."

"It might take some work from all of us," Meredith said, "but it'll be worth it." She picked up the citations. "Matt went on to do great things even though he didn't have a clue how it would turn out when he first started. But he was willing to do his best to do what's right. That's all we can do too."

***

It took a while for them to tell Lydia and her mother everything that had happened and all they had found out, but by the time they were through, both women were smiling and more than grateful. Lydia said more than once that her mother hadn't looked so at peace in weeks.

"I'm glad Jack found that letter," Spencer said as Meredith pulled up to his hotel to drop him off. "Mrs. Bryleigh won't have to worry anymore."

Julia nodded. "And that's exactly what Lydia wanted."

"I suppose you'll be going back to Atlanta," Meredith said. "You're going to have a lot to tell your family."

"Oh, I told my mom and dad most of it last night." Spencer gave her a sheepish grin. "Well, not about Vanessa Van Orden nearly killing us, but everything else." He opened the car door. "I guess this is only 'so long' for now."

"We'll still have to do some testifying," Meredith told him. "But that might be some time in the future. There's going to have to be a lot of investigation done first, and by people much higher up than we are."

"I'll be ready." He got out of the car and then leaned down a little. "Thank you both for what you've done. I know it's only a start about putting Van Orden out of business, but at least it's something. I'll keep in touch."

He shut the door and then walked up to the hotel. With a quick wave, he went inside.

Before Meredith had done more than pull away from the curb, her phone rang. She answered at once.

"Quin. Oh, it's good to hear from you."

"I just wanted to say hi since we didn't have a chance to talk yesterday. Would you like to have dinner with me tonight so we can get caught up?"

"Dinner?"

Julia grinned but didn't say anything.

Meredith felt her heart beat a little faster. "I'd love that."

"How about I pick you up at seven?"

"That would be fine. I'm heading back to the office right now to tie up some loose ends on the Van Orden case, and by tonight I'm sure I'll be ready for a nice relaxing evening with my steady date."

He chuckled. "Van Orden, eh? Anything interesting going on?"

She gave Julia a wink.

"Are you sitting down?" she asked Quin.

"Yes. Why?"

"Because I have quite a story to tell you."

Dear Reader,

When I start planning out a book in this series, one of the first things I consider is the historical portion of it. I love historical fiction because I get to visit times, people, and places that are so different from what I experience in my everyday life. I'm always eager to figure out how events that happened in the past affect the mysteries Meredith and Julia have to solve in the present day.

For this book, I decided to look at some of the historical events that had to do with Savannah and Georgia roughly a hundred years ago. I came across the sinking of the Troopship *Otranto* off the coast of Scotland in World War I, and I was a little surprised at first that it had appeared in my search results. What did any of that have to do with Savannah or even Georgia? Then I found out that 130 Georgians died when that ship sank, and I started wondering who could have been on board when it did.

From there, I started imagining three young men from Savannah who enlisted together and were heading overseas when tragedy struck. What happened to them, and what had they left behind at home? More than that, what sort of case would Meredith and Julia have that would eventually lead to them finding out more about these men? And how did they tie into the current mystery?

It's always fun for me when all the little pieces fall into place and I have a mystery for our detectives to solve. I hope you enjoy solving it too!

Love,
DeAnna

About the Author

THE AUTHOR OF TWENTY-SEVEN TRADITIONALLY published books and with more to come, DeAnna Julie Dodson has always been an avid reader and a lover of storytelling, whether on the page, the screen, or the stage. This, along with her keen interest in history and her Christian faith, shows in her tales of love, forgiveness, and triumph over adversity. A fifth-generation Texan, she makes her home north of Dallas with three spoiled cats and, when not writing, spends her free time quilting, cross-stitching, and watching NHL hockey. Her first novels were a trilogy of medieval romances (*In Honor Bound, By Love Redeemed,* and *To Grace Surrendered*) for Crossway Books, and she has since written a number of contemporary mysteries for Annie's Fiction and for Guideposts and has more in the works. Also, as Julianna Deering, she writes the Drew Farthering mysteries set in 1930s England. The series debuted from Bethany House with *Rules of Murder* and is followed by *Death by the Book, Murder at the Mikado, Dressed for Death, Murder on the Moor,* and *Death at Thorburn Hall.* She is represented by Wendy Lawton of the Books & Such Literary Agency (booksandsuch.biz).

The Truth Behind the Fiction

HMS *Otranto*

HMS OTRANTO WAS BUILT IN 1909 and served as a passenger ship, traveling chiefly between England and Australia, until it was converted into an armed merchant cruiser when England declared war on Germany on August 4, 1914.

On September 25, 1918, a year and a half after the United States entered the war, the *Otranto* was the flagship for a convoy heading to England from New York carrying American troops. The convoy ran into a heavy storm on October fourth, and by the sixth the storm was a Force 11. The weather was so bad that accurate navigation was impossible, and the officers of the ship couldn't tell whether they were off the west coast of Scotland or the north coast of Ireland. Most of the ships in the convoy thought that the coastline ahead of them was Scotland and turned to the south, but the *Otranto*'s Officer of the Watch mistook it for the Irish coast and turned the ship north.

This put the *Otranto* on a collision course with another of the troopships, HMS *Kashmir*, just to the north of the *Otranto*. Despite evasive action by both ships, the *Kashmir* ran into the *Otranto* off the coast of Islay, the southernmost island of the Hebrides of

Scotland. The collision tore a twenty-by-sixteen-foot hole in the *Otranto* well under the waterline, flooding the boiler rooms and killing the crewmen there. Soon other bulkheads collapsed and flooded more of the ship. Due to an earlier collision with a fishing boat, many of the ship's lifeboats were damaged. This new collision destroyed most of the remaining ones. Many men were washed overboard or crushed between the two ships.

The *Kashmir,* though damaged, was eventually able to move away from the wreck, but the *Otranto* was left powerless and without sufficient lifeboats. Continuing high winds and tossing waves prevented any of the passengers and crew from attempting to swim ashore. Half an hour after the collision, the *Mounsey,* a British destroyer that had been searching for the *Otranto*, arrived on the scene and was able to rescue 266 officers and crewmen and 300 American troops.

Three hours after the wreck, the *Otranto* was washed onto a reef where the huge waves broke the ship in half and tore out its bottom. When the *Mounsey* left, there had been approximately 489 men aboard the *Otranto*. Only 21 of these, 17 of them American, were able to swim ashore. By morning, the ship was completely torn apart, leaving the coast littered with the wreckage and with the bodies of the dead. It is believed that 470 men died due to the collision—12 officers, 84 crewmen, and included 358 Americans, 130 of them from Georgia.

World War I ended little more than a month later.

MAGGIE LU'S DOWNHOME LEMON CAKE

Cake Ingredients:

2½ cups granulated sugar

1½ cups butter, softened

4 eggs

3½ cups all-purpose flour

½ teaspoon salt

½ teaspoon baking soda

1 cup buttermilk

1 Tablespoon lemon juice

Zest of 2 lemons

Directions:

1. Preheat oven to 350 degrees.

2. Grease and flour a tube or Bundt pan. (You can substitute granulated sugar for flour if you'd like a sweet, sparkly, crunchy crust!)

3. Beat sugar and butter together until light and fluffy, about 10 minutes.

4. Add eggs 1 at a time, beating thoroughly after each.

5. Sift together flour, salt, and baking soda.

6. Add ⅓ of flour mixture to butter mixture; mix well. Pour in ½ the buttermilk and beat until combined. Repeat, adding

remaining flour mixture and buttermilk, beating well after each addition, and ending with flour mixture.

7. Stir lemon juice and lemon zest into batter.
8. Pour batter into prepared pan.
9. Reduce oven temperature to 325 degrees and bake until toothpick inserted in center of cake comes out clean, about 60–75 minutes.
10. Cool 10 minutes in pan before removing to serving plate.

Glaze Ingredients: (Maggie Lu says extra glaze never hurt anyone. Feel free to double and save extra to drizzle over individual pieces.)

2 cups powdered sugar	2 Tablespoons butter, softened
¼ cup lemon juice	1 Tablespoon lemon zest

Directions:

1. Beat powdered sugar, lemon juice, butter, and lemon zest together in a bowl until glaze is smooth.
2. Pour about half the glaze over cake; let cool. Or use a pastry brush to apply glaze to entire cake.
3. Pour remaining glaze over cake.

*Read on for a sneak peek of another exciting book
in the Savannah Secrets series!*

A Bone to Pick

BY KATHLEEN Y'BARBO

IT WAS FINALLY FRIDAY AND the end of the first week of August. Monday, August 9, would begin the first of the two weeks that private investigators Meredith Bellefontaine and Julia Foley had agreed to close down Magnolia Investigations and take a vacation. While Meredith's children were whisking her away on a family trip, Julia had planned absolutely nothing.

That suited her just fine, especially given the news she'd just received via her quarterly retirement fund statement. At the insistence of the new account executive who'd taken over when their previous investment advisor retired, she and Beau had made a decision to move their money from lower-earning bonds into a more aggressive portfolio.

That had been four months ago.

Apparently a lot can happen in four months. Julia sighed. And it had.

While they hadn't wanted to live out their final years in luxury, Julia had hoped they could at least maintain their current lifestyle.

From the numbers staring up at her from the page, that lifestyle just might include a massive downsize in living arrangements should she ever think of fully retiring.

"How could this happen?" Julia whispered. "We've worked so hard, and the bottom line is going in the wrong direction."

Meredith stuck her head into Julia's office, her purse slung over her shoulder and a briefcase in her hand. "I thought you'd be gone by now," she said.

Julia glanced up at the clock. "It's not yet three. If I'm taking two weeks off starting on Monday morning, I figure the least I can do is put in a full day's work on the Friday before."

Not that she would be much good for concentrating on work after the bad news she'd received.

"Good for you," Meredith said. "If I didn't have to be fully packed and ready to go by eight o'clock tomorrow morning, I might do the same."

Julia sat back and placed her pen next to the legal pad where she had been making notes. "Eight o'clock? On a Saturday morning? Do you have an early flight?"

"I have no idea," her business partner admitted. "The kids are keeping it all very hush-hush. I was told to pack cowboy boots if I have them. That concerns me a bit."

"I'm sure you'll have a great time, whatever it is you'll be doing." Julia punctuated the statement with a smile that she didn't quite feel.

"Okay, what's wrong?" Meredith crossed the distance from the door to take a seat across from Julia.

"Nothing," Julia said, brightening her expression. "Everything is fine. Now go home and get packed, and I want to hear all about your adventure with your family when you return."

Meredith sat back and sighed. "You still have nothing planned for our rare two weeks of vacation time?"

"Not a thing," Julia told her with a genuine smile this time. "I'll enjoy my time with my husband and read several books, I think. I may even cook a few meals. But I'm going to try very hard to do absolutely nothing."

"Nothing?" One perfectly shaped brow rose. "No organizing?"

"Well, all right. Maybe I do have a project or two in mind."

Meredith chuckled. "Of course you do. I've never met a more organized woman, and yet I guarantee if I asked you right now which part of your house needs work, you'd have a list."

"Bathroom cabinets, master closet, and that sock drawer I keep ignoring," Julia rattled off. "And let's not even talk about the home office."

They shared a laugh. "Seriously though," Meredith said, "do something fun while you've got this time away. You and I both love our job, but life isn't just about work. Take a long weekend with Beau somewhere. Be impulsive, Julia. You might actually like it."

Julia shrugged. "You're right," she said. "And I promise I'll do something fun, okay?"

Meredith studied her a moment and then nodded, apparently satisfied with what she saw. "Okay then." She stood. "I'm off. Pray for me. I'm terrified about what the directive means to bring cowboy boots if I have them."

"It means you're going to have a good time. Now go!"

"I'm going! But promise me you won't stay until five. It's a beautiful day out there. Get your weekend started early."

"If she won't, I will," their assistant Carmen Lopez called from her desk in the foyer.

Julia and Meredith laughed. "Go," Julia repeated. "And give my love to the kids."

"I will. See you in two weeks!"

Meredith scooted out of the office, bidding Carmen goodbye, and then her footsteps receded as she headed toward the back of the grand old home in the historic district where their office was situated. A moment later the back door closed.

Julia looked down at the notes she'd made on her retirement fund statement and sighed. Meredith was right. She had two weeks ahead with absolutely nothing required of her. Staring at the numbers was not going to undo a bad decision and return hard-earned money to their account.

She folded the statement and tucked it into her briefcase, then looked around her office. Was there anything she needed to take with her when she left today?

Carmen's cell phone rang, and she answered. Due to the proximity of Julia's office to Carmen's desk, Julia could hear their assistant's side of phone conversations unless she closed the door. There was no need for that today. No project demanding her attention. So the door remained open, and Carmen's conversation continued to drift toward her.

"Oh no. Not again. If that dog isn't chewing up something, he's running off. But I'll be watching for him."

There was a pause, and then Carmen spoke again. "About Seth. He's super nice, and I'm not saying that because he's also super rich and offering a reward for Bosco. I mean, sure, a rich boyfriend isn't a bad thing for anyone, but he loves you, Amy. I've seen you two together. Stop worrying. Why don't I come by after work, and we can go out looking? No charge. Unless you've got some of those empanadas left from lunch service. I mean, they are my abuela's recipe."

Apparently, Amy had lots to say. Silence fell for quite some time while Julia rose and collected the things she intended to take home.

"Bosco will show up, probably before I get there. As to Seth, trust your heart," Carmen said. "You know a man who loves your dog has a leg up on the competition." She laughed. "No pun intended."

A minute later, more laughter bubbled toward Julia from Carmen's desk. "Well, maybe he needs to buy dog training for Bosco. Then he wouldn't eat such a valuable library card. Now don't worry about Bosco. He'll turn up. In the meantime, I'll pray, okay?"

After a few more minutes of talking, Carmen hung up. Then her chair scraped, and Julia heard her footsteps heading toward the office. She looked up as the young woman stepped inside.

"Has something happened to your friend's dog?" Julia asked.

"I'm sorry if my conversation with Amy disturbed you," Carmen said.

"No, it's fine. I was just getting things ready to go home."

"You know Amy? She owns Amy's Bistro and Bakery."

"That darling place on Oglethorpe Street near the corner of Drayton? Of course I do. Has she lost that little black dog again?"

"Bosco loves his adventures," Carmen said, resting her arms on the back of the chair Meredith had just vacated. "But this time he was with a dog walker. Amy had just given the idea of paying a walker a shot this week. She'd taken Bosco on that historical tour for pets, which is where the dog walker used to work, and—"

"Hold on a second," Julia interrupted. "Woof Walk Historical Tour for Pets?"

"Yes," Carmen said. "It's a walking tour of the historic district geared toward bringing your pets. Since the dog walker Amy chose worked for Woof Walk, she trusted her. But I guess Bosco decided he'd rather walk alone."

Julia shook her head. "I hope he comes home soon."

"So do I." Carmen shrugged. "I'll go help her look once I'm off."

"Why don't you go ahead and close up?" Julia suggested. "I'm about to leave, and we're certainly not going to take on any new cases on a Friday afternoon when neither of the investigators will be here for two weeks."

"That would be great. Thank you, Julia," Carmen said. "I hope you've got something fun planned."

"You sound like Meredith," Julia said, smiling. "Yes, it will be fun for me, I think. Remember, if anything comes up, I'll just be a phone call away. Call me, not Meredith."

"Will do," Carmen said. "But what could happen?"

Julia groaned. "Never ask that on a Friday afternoon, Carmen!"

They closed up the building together and then Julia held the back door open for Carmen to exit first, reaching behind her to turn off the kitchen lights. "Enjoy the quiet the next two weeks," she told Carmen.

"You too," Carmen said before she climbed into her car and drove away.

That evening Julia held on to her thoughts about the unexpected dip in their retirement funds, thinking over how she would tell Beau the bad news. While he had agreed to the change in investment strategy, she'd been the one who'd argued for it.

She went to bed still not sure what to say and spent Saturday mulling over the issue. The next morning Meredith called before Julia and Beau left for church.

"I've been spared," her friend declared.

"Oh?" Julia reached to pour her second cup of coffee. "From what?"

"The family vacation," she said. "It's been postponed due to a raging stomach flu that's making its way through my grandchildren— literally."

"Oh no." Julia took her mug to the kitchen table and sat down. "So you're not doing anything on your vacation either?"

"Not if I can help it," Meredith said with a chuckle. "I'm going to try the Julia Foley vacation plan and just enjoy being home."

Julia smiled. "How long do you think that will last, Meredith?"

"You know me too well," she said. "I do have some ideas of how to spend my unexpected free time, but I haven't settled on anything yet. I know I won't be coming in to the office. I promised Quin I'd take an actual vacation, and I will."

They chatted for a few minutes, but Julia couldn't bring herself to seek her friend's advice on how to speak to Beau about the bad news she'd been keeping to herself. By Monday morning, however, she'd almost figured out the right way to approach him.

Then he announced he'd be spending the day fishing. She was relieved to see him drive away, knowing the hour of her reckoning had been postponed.

The phone rang as Julia stepped back inside. It was the office. Julia checked her watch.

"Good morning, Carmen," she said. "I didn't expect to hear from you before ten o'clock on Monday morning. Is something wrong?"

"Hey boss," Carmen said. "There are a ton of messages, and most of them are from Amy's boyfriend, Seth Davis. I think something happened. He just kept saying he needed someone from the agency to call him back because it's urgent. I thought I'd let you know that before I call him."

"Was the dog found?"

"Bosco?" She paused. "He hasn't turned up as of last night. Amy's beside herself. Likely that's why he's calling. Oh, sorry. The other line is ringing."

They hung up and then a few minutes later, Carmen called back. "Okay," she said without so much as a greeting. "Seth is adamant that we help find Bosco."

"Since when do we look for runaway dogs?" Julia asked.

"I told him that," Carmen said. "Well, I mean I was nice about it, but he's not taking no for an answer. Do you think maybe you could call him and tell him yourself?" She paused. "Or maybe you could make a tiny exception to your no-work-for-two-weeks policy and take this case on?"

"Why would I do that?" Julia asked. "Meredith and I are a team."

Carmen wasted no time answering. "Of course, but you don't have anything planned, and it would help Amy and probably earn us plenty of free food and an immediate pass to the front of the line any time we want to eat lunch at her place. You know that's priceless."

Julia chuckled. "As priceless as line jumping at Amy's might be, I want you to call this Seth fellow back and tell him you've given me his messages. Tell him I'll return his call after I have spoken with my partner and considered whether I'm willing to give up my planned vacation time."

Less than five minutes later, Carmen called back. "Uh, boss, there's been a little unexpected wrinkle and some good news. Which one do you want first?"

"The wrinkle, please," Julia said, dreading whatever it was she was about to hear.

Carmen took a deep breath. "Bosco didn't run away. He was stolen."

A Note from the Editors

WE HOPE YOU ENJOY THE Savannah Secrets series, created by the Books and Inspirational Media Division of Guideposts, a nonprofit organization that touches millions of lives every day through products and services that inspire, encourage, help you grow in your faith, and celebrate God's love in every aspect of your daily life.

Thank you for making a difference with your purchase of this book, which helps fund our many outreach programs to military personnel, prisons, hospitals, nursing homes, and educational institutions. To learn more, visit GuidepostsFoundation.org.

We also maintain many useful and uplifting online resources. Visit Guideposts.org to read true stories of hope and inspiration, access OurPrayer network, sign up for free newsletters, download free e-books, join our Facebook community, and follow our stimulating blogs.

To learn about other Guideposts publications, including the bestselling devotional *Daily Guideposts*, go to ShopGuideposts.org, call (800) 932-2145, or write to Guideposts, PO Box 5815, Harlan, Iowa 51593.

Sign up for the
Guideposts Fiction Newsletter
and stay up-to-date on the books you love!

You'll get sneak peeks of new releases, recommendations from other Guideposts readers, and special offers just for you . . .
and it's FREE!

Just go to Guideposts.org/Newsletters today to sign up.

Guideposts.

Visit Guideposts.org/Shop or call (800) 932-2145

Find more inspiring stories in these best-loved Guideposts fiction series!

Mysteries of Lancaster County

Follow the Classen sisters as they unravel clues and uncover hidden secrets in Mysteries of Lancaster County. As you get to know these women and their friends, you'll see how God brings each of them together for a fresh start in life.

Secrets of Wayfarers Inn

Retired schoolteachers find themselves owners of an old warehouse-turned-inn that is filled with hidden passages, buried secrets, and stunning surprises that will set them on a course to puzzling mysteries from the Underground Railroad.

Tearoom Mysteries Series

Mix one stately Victorian home, a charming lakeside town in Maine, and two adventurous cousins with a passion for tea and hospitality. Add a large scoop of intriguing mystery, and sprinkle generously with faith, family, and friends, and you have the recipe for *Tearoom Mysteries*.

Ordinary Women of the Bible

Richly imagined stories—based on facts from the Bible—have all the plot twists and suspense of a great mystery, while bringing you fascinating insights on what it was like to be a woman living in the ancient world.

To learn more about these books, visit Guideposts.org/Shop